RANDOM HOUSE

LARGE PRINT

The Mistress

DANIELLE STEEL

The Mistress

A Novel

RANDOM HOUSE
LARGE PRINT

Copyright © 2017 by Danielle Steel

All rights reserved.
Published in the United States of America by Random House Large Print in association with Delacorte Press, an imprint of Random House, a division of Penguin Random House LLC, New York.

Cover design: Lynn Andreozzi
Cover images: © Michael Trevillion/Trevillion Images (woman), © Rainer Jahns (Riviera background)
Author photograph: © Brigitte Lacombe

ISBN: 978-1-68331-252-9

Printed in the United States of America

This Large Print edition published in accord with the standards of the N.A.V.H.

To Beatie, Trevor, Todd, Nick, Sam,
    Victoria, Vanessa, Maxx, and Zara,
my beloved and wonderful children,
May your choices be good ones, and
    if they prove not to be,
May you have the wisdom and
    courage to change them,
May you be happy and safe,
    surrounded by people who love
    you and treat you well,
May your paths be easy, and your
    blessings plentiful,
and please always, always know and
    remember how much I love you.

Mommy / DS

The Mistress

Chapter 1

It was dusk on a warm June day, as the enormous motor yacht **Princess Marina** lay at anchor off the coast of Antibes in the Mediterranean, not far from the famous Hôtel du Cap. The five-hundred-foot yacht was in plain sight for all to see, as deckhands of the seventy-five-person crew swabbed down her decks, and washed the saltwater off her as they did every evening. At least a dozen of them were hosing her down. Casual observers could get a sense of just how huge she was when they noticed how tiny the deckhands looked from the distance. You could see lights shining brightly within her, and everyone familiar with that part of the coast knew which boat she was and who owned her, although there were several nearly as large at anchor nearby. The giant superyachts were too large to dock in port, except for ports large enough to handle cruise ships. It was no small thing to dock a boat that size, no matter how large the crew, or how adept they were at maneuvering her.

Her owner, Vladimir Stanislas, had three more motor yachts of comparable size positioned around the world, and a three-hundred-foot sailboat he had bought from an American, which he seldom used. But **Princess Marina,** named for the mother who had died when he was fourteen, was the yacht that he preferred. She was an exquisite floating island of ostentation and luxury that had cost him a fortune to build. He owned one of the most famous villas on the coast as well, in St. Jean Cap-Ferrat. He had bought it from a famous movie star, but he never felt quite as safe on land, and robberies and attacks on important villas were common in the South of France. Offshore, with the crew to protect him, most of them trained in high security and antiterrorist measures, and with an arsenal of guns onboard and a specially designed missile system, he felt secure, and able to change locations rapidly at any time.

Vladimir Stanislas was acknowledged to be one of the richest men in Russia and in the world, with the monopoly of the Russian steel industry accorded him by the government almost twenty years before, due to the remarkable connections he had cultivated with key people since his teens. A great deal of money had changed hands at a crucial time, and more had been made than any-one had thought imaginable or even possible. He had heavy investments in oil now too, and in industries worldwide. The kind of money Vladi-mir had made and had at his disposal was difficult to conceive of. At forty-nine, he was estimated to be worth $40 or $50 billion, on the deals and investments that were known. He was an inti-mate of high-up government officials all the way to the Russian president, and was known to other heads of state as well. And the fabulous yacht that shimmered like a jewel in the twilight was only a small symbol of his connections and the brilliant abilities in business that had served him well.

Vladimir was both admired and feared. What he had accomplished in nineteen years as a major player on the Russian industrial scene had won him the admiration and envy of men in business around the world. And those who knew him well and had made deals with him were aware that there was more to the story. He had a reputation for being ruthless, and never forgiving his ene-mies. There was a gentle side to him as well; his passion for art, his love of all things of beauty, and his knowledge of literature were more recently acquired. He preferred the company of his own kind, the friends he had were Russian, all impor-tant industrialists like him. And the women in his life had always been Russian too. Although he had a beautiful house in London, the villa in the South of France, and a spectacular apartment in Moscow, he associated mostly with his own countrymen. He was a man who always got what he wanted, and he controlled the lion's share of Russia's new wealth.

Despite his importance and influence, he was easy to overlook in a crowd. Preferring to go un-noticed, he was an unassuming person. Simply dressed, he came and went discreetly, as he chose. It was only when you looked into his eyes that you realized who and what he was: a man of infi-nite power. He was a keen observer of everything around him. The jut of his jaw and power of his stance said he would not tolerate being refused anything, yet when he smiled, one suspected a well-hidden and seldom-indulged warmth. He had the high cheekbones and Mongol look of his ancestors, which added something exotic to the mix. Women had been drawn to him since he was a boy, but he never left himself vulnerable, to anyone. He had no vital attachments, and had controlled his world for a long time, and would settle for nothing less.

Tall, rugged, and blond with ice-blue eyes and chiseled features, Vladimir was not so much handsome in the classic sense as interesting, and by contrast, in a rare, relaxed, unguarded moment, he could seem warm, and had the sen-timentality typical of many Russians. Nothing in Vladimir's life was accidental or unplanned, and everything was carefully thought out and part of a larger whole. He had had several mistresses since his rise to power, but unlike his peers and counterparts, he wanted no children with them, and was clear about that with his female companions right from the beginning. He tolerated no encumbrances to tie him down, nor anything that would make him vulnerable. He had no family and few attachments.

Most of his male acquaintances had at least one child with each woman they'd been involved with, usually at the woman's insistence, to secure her financial position in future years. Vladimir refused to fall prey to entreaties of that sort. Children were not part of his plan, and he had made that decision, with no regrets, a long time ago. He was generous enough with his women while he was with them, but he made no promises for the future, nor would they have dared to insist on them, or try to manipulate him. Vladimir was like a coiled snake ready to strike, ever vigilant and potentially merciless if crossed. He could be gentle, but one could sense his innate ruthlessness as well, and that if wronged or provoked, he could be a dangerous man. Few people wanted to test that, and no women in his life had so far. Natasha, his current companion, knew that not having children with him was a condition of Vladimir's being with any woman. He made it clear that there would never be marriage or the status that went with it. And once settled and agreed upon, this was not discussed again, and never would be. Those who had attempted to convince him otherwise, or had tried to trick him, had been dispensed with summarily, with a handsome sum, but nothing compared to what they would have derived from the relationship otherwise. Vladimir was no one's fool, and never compromised, except when it served him well in business. He listened to his head and not his heart in all things. He hadn't gotten where he was by being gullible or foolish or vulnerable to women. He trusted no one. And had learned in his youth to only trust himself. His boyhood lessons had served him well.

Since he had risen to the top, Vladimir had gained strength and amassed wealth at a meteoric rate, and was somewhere out in the stratosphere with nearly unlimited power and a fortune people could only guess at. And he enjoyed the fruits of his accomplishments. He liked owning the many toys he indulged himself with, his homes, his boats, fabulous sports cars, a plane, two helicopters he kept in constant use, moving around the world, the art collection that was his passion. Surrounding himself with beauty was important to him. He loved owning the best of everything.

He had little time for idle pursuits, but didn't hesitate to enjoy himself when he could. Business was always foremost on his mind, and the next deal he was going to make, but he took time out now and then to play. He had few friends, only the important men he did business with, or the politicians he owned. He was never afraid of risk, and had no tolerance for boredom. His mind moved with lightning speed. And he had been with his current woman for seven years. With only the occasional rare exception, which was unusual for men of his ilk, he was faithful to her. He had no time for dalliances and little interest in them. He was satisfied with his companion, and their relationship served him well.

Natasha Leonova was without a doubt the most beautiful woman he had ever known. He had first seen her on a Moscow street, freezing in the Russian winter but young and proud, and he had liked her from the first moment he met her, when she resisted his attempts to help her, wanting to get to know her better. After a year of his relentless advances, she succumbed to him and had been his mistress since she was nineteen, and she was now twenty-six.

Natasha acted as hostess when needed, to the degree he wanted, never putting herself too far forward. She was a spectacular accessory and tribute to him. He required no more of her than that, although she was a bright girl. All he wanted of her were her presence, her beauty, and her availability to him at all times for whatever purpose he needed, without explanation. She knew better than to ask for information he didn't volunteer. She waited for him where he wanted her to be, in whatever city, home, or boat, and he rewarded her handsomely for her presence and fidelity. She had never cheated on him, and would have been long gone if she did. It was an arrangement that suited them both. So much so that she was still there after seven years, far longer than either of them had expected or planned. She had become part of the finely tuned machine that made his life work, and she was important to him because of it. And they both knew the role they played in each other's lives, and asked for nothing more than that. The balance between them had worked perfectly for years.

Natasha had the grace of a dancer as she moved around the spectacular cabin of the yacht that was their home for several months of the year. She liked being on the boat with him, and the freedom it afforded them, being able to change locations at a moment's notice, to go where they wanted, do what they wished. And when he was busy or flew to other cities for meetings, she did as she chose. Sometimes she left the boat for errands or shopping, or stayed onboard. Natasha understood perfectly the parameters of her life with him. She had learned what he expected of her and did it well. And in exchange he loved her flawless beauty and showing her off. She was always on display when they went out, like his Ferrari, or a rare jewel. Unlike other women in her position, Natasha was never difficult or demanding, never petulant. She was an object of envy for other men. She knew instinctively when to be silent and when to talk, when to keep her distance and when to be nearby. She read his moods perfectly, and was flexible and easy to get along with. She demanded nothing of him, so he gave her much, and was lavish with her. And although she appreciated and enjoyed everything he bestowed on her, she would have been satisfied with less, which was unheard of for a woman in her situation.

Natasha made no plans of her own, and knew not to ask questions about the men who visited him and the deals he made. He valued her discretion, her gentle ways, her companionship, and her stunning looks. She was his mistress, and he never promised her more. At times he treated her like a work of art in a museum that he wanted to show off. By virtue of her presence, she confirmed his status to other men, and she was a symbol of his good taste. She knew Vladimir for what he was to her, a kind, generous man when he wanted to be, and a dangerous one when not. And she had seen him switch from one mood to the other in an instant. She liked to believe that he was a good person beneath the hard exterior he was known for, but she never put it to the test. She liked her position in his life, and who he was, and admired him for all he'd accomplished.

Vladimir had rescued her from desperate poverty on the streets of Moscow at nineteen, and she never forgot the hardships of her life before him. She would not let anything interfere with the performance of her duties to him, or ignore what she owed him. She never wanted to go back to the life of destitution she had led before, and took no risks with the life she had now, thanks to him. She was safe and secure under his protection, and she let nothing jeopardize that. She was aware of who and what she was to him at all times. She asked for nothing more and didn't need to. He was exceptional to her in the life they shared, and she was grateful to him for all he'd done for her.

Due to the nature of their life together, she lived in isolation from other women and friends. There was only room for Vladimir in her world, which was what he expected of her. She played by all his rules without regret or complaint, unlike other women in her situation who were in it for what they could get. Natasha wasn't. She was intelligent, and knew her place and his limits. She was totally satisfied, and enjoyed their life together. And she never hungered to be more to him. As his mistress, she had everything she'd ever dreamed of, and more. She never missed having

children, or even friends, or longed to be his wife.
She needed nothing more than what they shared.

Natasha had been dressing when she heard the
helicopter approach. She had just taken a shower
and slipped into a white satin jumpsuit that
molded her exquisite body perfectly. As a little
girl, she had dreamed of being a ballerina, which
hadn't been even remotely possible for her. She
quickly brushed her long, wavy blond hair, put
on a minimum of makeup, clipped on diamond
earrings Vladimir had given her, and stepped
into high-heeled silver sandals. She had a natural
beauty, with no artifice about her, and she needed
to do nothing to enhance it. Vladimir loved that
about her. She reminded him of some of his favorite paintings by Italian masters, and he could
watch her for hours, her long graceful body, her
perfect features, the silky pale blond hair and
huge blue eyes the color of a summer sky. He
took pleasure in looking at her as much as talking to her. He appreciated the fact that she was
intelligent. Vladimir detested vulgar women, and
greedy ones, and stupid ones, and she was none
of those. There was a natural grace about her, and
a quiet dignity.

She hurried up the stairs to one of the two heli-
pads on the upper deck, and stepped out among
the dozen crew members and security men waiting for him, just as the helicopter landed. The
wind whipped her hair, and she smiled, trying to

get a glimpse of him through the windows. And a moment later the pilot cut the engine, the door opened, and he stepped out and nodded at the captain, as one of the bodyguards took his briefcase from him. Vladimir looked at Natasha and smiled. She was precisely who he wanted to come back to, after meetings in London. He had been gone for two days, and was happy to be on the boat where he could relax, although he had an office there where he could work too, and video screens so he could communicate with his London and Moscow offices.

They spent months on the boat at times, and he traveled to meetings when he needed to. The one he had just come from had gone well, and he was pleased. He put an arm around her shoulders as they walked down a flight of stairs to a large handsome bar on the deck below. A stewardess handed them each a glass of champagne from a silver tray, as Vladimir gazed out at the water for a moment and then back at her. She asked him nothing about the meetings. All she knew of his work was what she had heard, seen, or guessed, and she kept it to herself. Her discretion as well as her beauty were important to him. And he was delighted to see her after two days away. As they sat down, neither noticed the bodyguards standing at a slight distance from them. They were part of the landscape for both of them.

"So what did you do today?" he asked in a gentle tone, admiring the way the white jumpsuit fit her like a second skin. Her behavior was never provocative, except in the bedroom, but there was an undeniable sexy quality to her that made men's heads turn and envy him, which pleased him. Just as the boat was an expression of his extreme wealth, Natasha's stunning beauty was a symbol of his virility and appeal as a man. He enjoyed both.

"I swam, had a manicure, and did some shopping in Cannes," she said easily. It was a typical day for her when he wasn't around. When he was, she remained on the boat to be available to him. He didn't like it when she disappeared if he had free time. And he liked swimming with her, having meals with her, and talking to her when he chose to.

Natasha had studied a considerable amount about art on her own, reading books and articles on the Internet, keeping abreast of news in the art world. She would have liked to take some classes at the Tate in London when they were there, or in Paris where they spent time as well, but she was never anywhere for long enough to enroll in courses, and Vladimir always wanted her with him. But in spite of a lack of formal education in a classroom, she had become impressively educated about art in recent years, and he liked discussing his new purchases with her, and the paintings he was planning to acquire. She would

study extensively then about the artists he mentioned, and loved researching unusual facts about
them, which fascinated him as well, and intrigued
him. She had engaged in conversations with art
experts at dinner parties they gave, and Vladimir
was proud of her extensive knowledge.

And since she had no friends to spend time
with, she was used to shopping alone. He let her
buy whatever she wanted and enjoyed giving her
gifts, mostly jewelry he loved picking for her, and
a vast number of alligator Hermès bags, in every
imaginable color, most of them Birkins with diamond clasps, which cost a fortune. He begrudged
her nothing, and loved selecting her clothes at the
haute couture shows, like the Dior jumpsuit she
had on. He liked spoiling her in ways he didn't in-
dulge himself. She was an advertisement for him.
In contrast, he was always simply and conserva-
tively dressed and had returned from London in
jeans, a well-cut blazer and blue shirt, and brown
suede shoes from Hermès. They made a handsome
couple despite the difference in their ages. Occasionally, in a playful mood, he pointed out that he
was old enough to be her father, with twenty-three
years between them, although he didn't look it.

Although she had no life of her own, she wasn't
lonely. He rewarded her richly for monopolizing
her, and she never complained. She was grateful
to him, and he never tired of admiring her. In
seven years, he had never met another woman

he wanted more, or who would have suited him better. He only cheated on her when the men he did business with called in hookers for everyone in another city after an important meeting, and he didn't want to appear uncooperative or un-friendly. The men had usually had a lot to drink by then, and he always slipped away early.

The stars came out as they finished the cham-pagne, and Vladimir said he wanted to go to their cabin to shower and put on something more ca-sual for dinner, although he preferred seeing Na-tasha in the kind of clothes she was wearing. It still excited him to see how beautiful she was, and she followed him to their cabin, and lay down on their bed as he took off his clothes and walked into his dressing room, with the black marble bath-room. Her own dressing room and pink marble bathroom had been designed especially for her.

Vladimir had flipped a switch as they walked into their cabin that turned on a light in the hall, indicating that they didn't want to be disturbed. And Natasha put music on the sound system in their bedroom while she waited for him, and then turned in surprise as she saw him standing naked behind her, fresh from the shower, with wet hair, and smiling at her.

"I missed you in London, Tasha. I don't like traveling without you." She knew it was true, but he hadn't asked her to come with him, which meant he would be busy with meetings late into the night. She had no idea who he had met with or why he'd gone, and didn't ask.

"I missed you too," she said softly, her feet bare as she lay in the white satin jumpsuit, her hair fanned out on the pillow, and he sat down on the bed next to her, slipped the straps of the jumpsuit off her shoulders, and then peeled it down her body, until she wore only a white satin thong that had been made to go with it.

He was murmuring softly to her as he nuzzled her neck, and his body was powerful, as he let himself down slowly on top of her, pulled off the thong, and tossed it aside. He had waited all day to come back to her, and found comfort in the familiar meshing of their bodies. He always reminded her of a lion when he made love to her, and made a roaring sound of victory and release when he came. And afterward, she rested in his arms happily, and sighed as she smiled at him. They never disappointed each other, and found safety and peace in each other's arms in his turbulent world.

They showered together, and she wore a silky white caftan when they went upstairs to the outdoor dining room an hour later. They both looked relaxed as they sat down to dinner. It was after ten o'clock by then, and they both liked eating late, after his business calls had stopped, and his secretaries in London and Moscow had finished work and emailing him. The night was theirs, except when they entertained, which was almost always for business, with men he was doing deals with, or wanted something from.

"Why don't we go to dinner in St. Paul de Vence tomorrow night?" he asked her, as he lit a Cuban cigar, and she breathed the pungent smell that she loved too.

"La Colombe d'Or?" she asked. They had been there many times for the delicious meals in the famous restaurant filled with the artwork of Picasso, Léger, Calder, and all the others who had dined there and paid their bar and restaurant bills with paintings they'd given to the owners in the early years. It was a feast for the eyes, to eat surrounded by the remarkable work of the artists who had congregated there long before they became famous.

"I want to try that place we keep hearing about," he said, relaxing with his cigar, as they looked out over the water and enjoyed the star-filled night together. "Da Lorenzo." It was also a favorite haunt of art lovers, filled with the work of Lorenzo Luca, with only his art on display there. The restaurant had been established by his widow, almost as a shrine to him, in the home where they had lived, with the rooms above the restaurant available for famous art collectors, dealers, and museum curators. It was apparently a total immersion experience in the famous artist's work, and Vladimir had wanted to visit it for years, but reservations for the restaurant were so hard to come by that they always wound up at La Colombe d'Or, which was fun too. "An art dealer in London told me we should call Madame Luca directly and use his name. My secretary tried it, and it worked. We got a reservation for tomorrow. I'm anxious to finally see it." He looked pleased. The owners were notoriously independent about their bookings.

"Me too. I love his work." It was somewhat similar to Picasso's, although it had his own very distinctive style.

"There's very little of it on the market. When he died, he left her most of his work, and she won't sell it. She sells one at auction once in a while, but I'm told she's very stubborn about it. And he wasn't as prolific as Picasso, so there's less of it around. He wasn't successful until very late in his life, and the prices are sky-high now. Her refusal to sell has driven his prices through the roof, almost as high as Picasso's. The last one that sold at Christie's several years ago brought an incredible price."

"So we won't be buying art at dinner," she teased him, and he laughed. Or perhaps they would. Vladimir was unpredictable about where and when he bought art, and relentless in the pursuit of whatever he wanted.

"Apparently, it's like visiting a museum. And she keeps the best work in his studio. I wouldn't mind a tour of that one day. Maybe we can charm

at two, she had never been adopted and remained in the orphanage until she was sixteen. After that came three years of working in factories and living in unheated dormitories, with no prospects. She refused the advances of men wanting to pay to have sex with her. She didn't want to end up like her mother, who records showed had died of alcoholism shortly after she abandoned Natasha.

Vladimir had seen Natasha trudging through the snow in a thin coat when she was eighteen, and had been struck by her beauty. He offered her a ride in his car in the freezing cold and snow, and was stunned when she refused. He had haunted her for months at her state-run dormitory, sent her gifts of warm clothes and food, all of which she'd declined. And then finally, nearly a year after he'd first seen her, sick with a fever, she agreed to go home with him, where he had nursed her himself, while she nearly died of pneumonia. Something about her had reminded him of his mother. He saved her, rescued her from the factory and her abysmal life, although she was hesitant at first.

They never talked about either of their histories, but her worst fear was to be that poor again one day, to have nothing and no one until she died just from being poor. She never ignored the fact that Vladimir had been her savior, and in her opinion continued to be every day. She still had nightmares about the orphanage, the factory, the dormitories, the women she had seen die in her old life. She never said it to anyone, but she would rather have died herself than go back.

In many ways, they were a good match. They had come from similar backgrounds, and had achieved success differently, but they had a deep respect for each other and, although they would never have admitted it, a deep need for each other too.

The past was never far from either of them. The poverty he had grown up with was the fear that had pursued Vladimir all his life, and by now he had outrun it. But he never stopped looking over his shoulder to make sure the specter of it wasn't there. No matter how many billions he had made, it was never quite enough, and he was willing to do anything he had to, to keep the demon of poverty from seizing him again. Natasha's escape had been easier, fortuitous, and more peaceful, but in seven years she had never forgotten where she came from, just how bad it had been, and who had saved her. And no matter how far they had come, or how safe they were, they both knew that their old terrors would always be a part of them. The ghosts that haunted them were still vivid.

Natasha fell asleep waiting for him that night, as she often did. He woke her when he came to bed, and made love to her again. He was the savior who had rescued her from her own private hell, and dangerous as he might be to others, she knew she was safe with him.

Chapter 2

Maylis Luca was still an attractive woman at sixty-three. Her hair, which had gone prematurely white at twenty-five, was a snow-white mane she wore loose down her back in the daytime, or in a braid, or a bun at night, when she worked at the restaurant. She had cornflower-blue eyes, and the gently rounded figure that had made her appealing as an artist's model when she came to St. Paul de Vence from Brittany for a summer at twenty, and stayed. She had fallen in with a group of artists who delighted her and had welcomed her warmly, much to her conservative family's horror. She had abandoned her studies at the university, and stayed in St. Paul de Vence for the winter, and the first moment she laid eyes on him, she had fallen madly in love with Lorenzo Luca.

A year later, at twenty-one, after modeling for

several of the artists the previous winter, she became Lorenzo's mistress. He was sixty at the time,
and he called her his little spring flower. From
then on, she modeled only for him, and many
of his best works were of her. He had no money
then, and Maylis's family was devastated by the
path she'd chosen, and mourned the life and op-
portunities she'd given up. They considered her
lost on the road to perdition, as she starved happily with Lorenzo, living on bread and cheese and
apples and wine in a small room over his studio
with him, spending time with his friends, and
watching Lorenzo for hours while he worked, or
posing for him. She never regretted a moment
of it, and had no illusions about marrying him.
He had been honest with her from the first, and
told her he had married a girl in Italy in his early
twenties. He hadn't seen her in nearly forty years
by then, and they'd had no children. They had
been together for less than a year, but he was still
married to her, and considered it too complicated
and costly to get divorced.

By the time he met Maylis and fell in love with
her, he had had four serious mistresses in the
course of his lifetime, and seven children with
them. He was fond of his children but was can-
did and unashamed that he lived for his work,
and little else. He was a fiercely dedicated artist.
He had privately acknowledged his children but
never legitimized or helped to support them, and

saw no reason to. He had never had money when they were young, and their mothers had never made demands of him, knowing he had nothing to give. All his children were grown by the time he met Maylis, and they visited him from time to time, and considered him more of a friend. None had become artists, nor had his talent, and they had little in common with him. Maylis was always kind to them when they came to visit, and all of them were older than she. Some were married and had children of their own.

Maylis had no urge to have children with him. All she wanted was to be with him, and Lorenzo had no desire for marriage or children either. He treated Maylis like a child much of the time, and she was happy to learn about art from him, but the only work she really cared about was his. He was fascinated with her face and body and sketched her in a thousand poses in the early years of their relationship, and did some very handsome paintings of her.

Lorenzo had been mercurial, alternately wonderful and difficult with her. He had the temperament of an artist, and of the genius she believed he was, and she was happy with him and carefree in her life in St. Paul de Vence, however shocked her family was by the existence she led and the partner she'd chosen, whom they considered unsuitable due to his lifestyle, career, and age. Lorenzo was respected as an enormous talent by his contemporaries, however unknown he was in the world, which he didn't care about. He always managed to scrape up enough money for them to live on somehow, or borrowed from a friend, and Maylis worked as a waitress in a local restaurant a few nights a week when they were desperate for money. Money was never important to either of them, only his art, and the life they shared. He wasn't easy—he was high-spirited, difficult, volatile, and temperamental. They had some fearsome arguments in their early years, which they resolved passionately in the bedroom upstairs. She never doubted that he loved her, as much as she loved him. He was the love of her life, and he said she was the light of his.

As Lorenzo got older, he got more cantankerous, and argued often with his friends, particularly if he thought they were selling out to the commercial world, and sacrificing their talent for money. He was just as happy giving away his work as selling it.

He was hostile and suspicious when a young art dealer came to meet him from Paris. He came to St. Paul de Vence several times before Lorenzo would agree to see him. Gabriel Ferrand had seen some of Lorenzo's work, and recognized genius when he saw it. He begged Lorenzo to let him represent him at his gallery in Paris, and Lorenzo refused. Some of his friends tried to convince him otherwise, since Ferrand had an excellent reputation, but Lorenzo said he had no interest in being represented by some "money-hungry crook of an art dealer in Paris." It took Gabriel three years to convince Lorenzo to let him show one of his paintings in Paris, which Gabriel sold immediately for a very respectable amount of money, though Lorenzo insisted it meant nothing to him.

It was Maylis who finally reasoned with Lorenzo to let Gabriel represent him, which proved increasingly lucrative while Lorenzo continued to call him a crook, much to Gabriel's amusement. He had come to love the inordinately difficult genius he had discovered. Most of Gabriel's communication with Lorenzo went through Maylis, and they became fast friends, conspiring with each other for Lorenzo's benefit. By the time Maylis had been with him for ten years, and Lorenzo turned seventy, he had a very decent amount of money in the bank, which he claimed he didn't want to know about. He insisted that he had no desire to "prostitute" his art, or be corrupted by Gabriel's "venal intentions," and he let Maylis and Gabriel handle his money. He wasn't rich by any means, but he was no longer dirt poor. Nothing changed in their life, so as not to upset Lorenzo, and Maylis continued working as a waitress several times a week, and posing for him. He had declined to have a show of his work at Gabriel's gallery in Paris, so Gabriel sold his work individually, as soon as buyers saw it. And at times, Lorenzo wouldn't send him anything at all. It always depended on his mood, and he enjoyed his love/hate relationship with the young gallerist from Paris, whose only interest was in helping him achieve the recognition he deserved for his enormous talent. Maylis did her best to smooth the rocky road between them, without upsetting Lorenzo unduly. Most of the time, Lorenzo gave his paintings to Maylis, who had a huge collection of his work by then, but refused to sell any of the paintings he had given her, out of sentiment. Between the two of them, Gabriel had a hard time selling much of Lorenzo's work, but he remained faithful to the cause, convinced that Lorenzo would be an artist of enormous stature one day, and he came to St. Paul de Vence to see them often, mostly for the pleasure of admiring Lorenzo's new work, and of talking to Maylis, whom he adored. He thought she was the most remarkable woman he had ever met.

Gabriel had a wife and daughter in Paris, but he lost his wife to cancer after he had known Lorenzo for five years. After that he brought his little girl, Marie-Claude, with him to St. Paul de Vence occasionally, and Maylis would play with her while the two men talked. She felt sorry for her with no mother. She was a sweet, sunny child, and Gabriel obviously loved her deeply and appeared to be a good father. He took her everywhere with him, to visit artists in their studios and when he traveled, and she was a bright little girl.

Lorenzo was no longer interested in children by then, not even his own, and he still didn't want children with Maylis, despite her youth and beauty. He wanted her to himself, and her undivided attention, which she lavished on him. And it came as an unwelcome shock to both of them when Maylis discovered she was pregnant, a dozen years after they'd gotten together. It had never been part of their plan. She was thirty-three years old, he was seventy-two, and more intent on his work than ever. Lorenzo had been angry at her for weeks when they found out, and finally, grudgingly, he agreed to let her go forward with it, but he was anything but pleased at the prospect of a child. And Maylis was worried about it too. She warmed to the idea only slowly as the baby grew within her, and she realized how much it meant to her to have Lorenzo's child. There was no question of their getting married, since he was still married to his wife, who was still alive. Cousins from the town where he'd been born confirmed it to him every few years, not that he cared.

And as Maylis grew with her pregnancy, Lorenzo painted her constantly, suddenly more in love than ever with her changing body, filled with his child. And Gabriel agreed with him that his paintings of Maylis then were some of his best work. Gabriel thought he had never seen her look more beautiful. Maylis was happy pregnant, and their son was born one night, while Lorenzo dined with his friends at the studio. Maylis had cooked them dinner, and the men drank a great deal of wine. She didn't say anything but suspected she'd been in labor since before dinner, and she finally retired upstairs and called the doctor, while they drank. And Lorenzo and his cohorts barely noticed when the doctor arrived and joined Maylis in their bedroom to deliver the baby, who came quickly and easily. And two hours after giving birth, Maylis appeared at the top of the stairs, beaming victoriously and holding their son wrapped in a blanket in her arms. Lorenzo came upstairs unsteadily to kiss her, and from the moment he laid eyes on him, he fell in love with the child.

They named him Théophile, for Maylis's grandfather, Theo as they called him, and he became the joy of his father's life.

Some of Lorenzo's most beautiful work was of Maylis holding Theo as a baby, and nursing him. And he produced spectacular paintings of the boy as he grew up. And of all his children, Theo was the only one to inherit his talent. He began scribbling next to his father from the moment he was old enough to hold a pencil in his chubby hands. It lent new excitement to his father's work, and Lorenzo attempted to teach the boy all he knew.

Lorenzo was eighty-three by the time Theo was ten, and it was already obvious by then that one day the boy would be as talented as his father, although his style was very different, even at an early age. The two would draw and paint for hours side by side, as Maylis watched them with delight. Theo was the love of their life.

By then, Gabriel had convinced Lorenzo to buy a decent house in St. Paul de Vence, although he still painted in the studio, and Theo joined him there every day after school. Maylis nearly had to drag them both home at night, and she worried about Lorenzo, who was still in good health, and worked as hard as ever, but he was slowly getting frail. He had a cough that lasted all winter, and he forgot to eat when she left him food at the studio, if she wasn't there to give it to him, but he was as passionate as ever about his work, and determined to teach Theo everything he knew in whatever time they had on earth together.

Much to Maylis's surprise, Lorenzo got word that winter that his wife had died, and he insisted on marrying her in the church on the hill, with Gabriel as their witness. He said he wanted to do it for Theo's sake. So they married when Theo was ten.

It was Gabriel who urged Lorenzo to take another important leap forward in his work after that. He had continued to have no interest in a show at the gallery in Paris, but Gabriel wanted to sell one of his paintings at an important auction, to establish a real price for his work on the open market. Once again Lorenzo fought him tooth and nail, and the only way Gabriel convinced him was to tell him he had to do it for Theo, that the money he made might be important for Theo's security one day. And as always, when Gabriel pushed him hard enough, Lorenzo reluctantly agreed. It was a decision that ultimately changed all of their lives. The painting was sold by Christie's, in their May auction of important art, for an absolute fortune, more than Lorenzo had made in a lifetime, or had ever wanted to make. And he insisted that the painting wasn't even his best work, which was why he had agreed to give it up.

Even Gabriel was stunned at what the painting brought. He had hoped to build Lorenzo's prices into a more serious range over time. He hadn't expected to get there in one fell swoop. And what happened after that was out of everyone's control. In the next eight years, Lorenzo's paintings, when he agreed to sell them, brought astronomical prices, and were in high demand by collectors and museums. Had he been greedy, he could have amassed a vast fortune. And as it turned out, he made one in spite of himself. His reluctance to sell them, and Maylis's refusal to sell any of the ones he had given to her, drove the prices up even further. And Lorenzo was a very rich man when he died at ninety-one. Theo was eighteen and in his second year at the Beaux-Arts in Paris by then, which his father had urged him to attend.

Lorenzo's death came as a devastating shock to all, most of all to Maylis and Theo, but to Gabriel as well, who had loved the man for more than twenty years, handled all aspects of business for him, and considered him a close friend, despite the insults Lorenzo had heaped on him unrelentingly till the end. It was an affectionate style of banter they had engaged in since the beginning and that they both took pleasure in. Gabriel had built his career into what it was, and he handled everything for Maylis and her son when Lorenzo died. Lorenzo had been in remarkably good health to the end, considering his age, and had worked harder than ever in his last year, as though he instinctively knew he was running out of time. He left Maylis and Theo a considerable fortune, both in art and in the investments Gabriel had made for him. Maylis was incredulous when Gabriel told her the value of the estate. It had never dawned on her what he was worth. All she had ever cared about was the man she had loved passionately for thirty years.

Despite Gabriel's entreaties, which Lorenzo had ignored, he died without leaving a will, and by French law, two-thirds of the estate went to Theo as his only legitimate child, and the remaining third to Maylis as his wife. Overnight, she became a very rich woman, particularly with all the paintings he had given her, which formed an important collection. And the rest of his body of work went to Theo, and two-thirds of everything he had in the bank and that Gabriel had invested on his behalf. All of which left Lorenzo's seven children by his mistresses without a penny from the estate. And after careful discussion with Gabriel, Maylis directed him to cut her financial share from the investments in half, and she gave half of what she had, exclusive of the paintings, to his seven children, who were grateful and amazed. Even Gabriel was amazed by her generous gesture, but she insisted she had enough money, and she knew that several of Luca's children needed it more than she did. Both she and Theo were set for life, and Theo had twice what she did.

Theo continued his studies at the Beaux-Arts for two years after his father died, and then came home to St. Paul de Vence to live and work. He bought a small house of his own, with a sunny studio. Maylis had moved back into Lorenzo's old studio and was living in the room upstairs where her son had been born. And the house that Gabriel had convinced Lorenzo to buy for them was standing empty and uninhabited. Maylis said she couldn't bear to live there without him, in the house where he had died, and felt closer to him in the studio, which Gabriel thought was unhealthy, but he couldn't convince her otherwise.

Two years after Lorenzo's death, Maylis was still

inconsolable and unwilling to move on. Gabriel came to see her every few weeks. She was only fifty-four by then, but all she wanted to do was stand and stare at Lorenzo's paintings, and go through them sorrowfully, remembering when he had painted each of them, particularly those he had painted of her when she was young, and when she was pregnant with Theo. It depressed Theo profoundly to see the condition his mother was in, and he and Gabriel talked about it often over dinner at Theo's house. As a longtime family friend, Gabriel was like a father to him.

Five years after Lorenzo's death, Maylis was no better, and then finally the deepest part of the wound began to heal, and she started to live again. She had a crazy idea that turned out not to be so crazy after all. She had liked working at the restaurant when she was young, and La Colombe d'Or was a big success. She decided to turn the house Lorenzo had bought for them into a restaurant, and she would show his work there. She had sold only one of his paintings since his death, and had refused all other requests to do so, and didn't want to let Gabriel sell them at auction. She didn't need the money, and didn't want to give up a single one. And for the moment, Theo had no reason to sell his either, so the market for Lorenzo Luca's paintings was frozen, but their value escalated every year. The refusal to sell increased their worth exponentially, although that wasn't her goal. But Maylis liked the idea of showing them in their own restaurant, in what had been their home, almost like a museum of his work. And there were six bedrooms she could rent out as hotel rooms, if she ever wanted to, to special people in the art world.

It sounded like an insane idea to Theo when she told him about it, but Gabriel convinced him it would be good for her, and help her get back to an active life again. She was fifty-seven years old and couldn't mourn Lorenzo forever.

The restaurant did for her what Gabriel had hoped it would. It gave Maylis a reason for living. It took a year to make the needed changes in the house, build a commercial kitchen, and create a beautiful garden for people to dine in during the summer. She hired one of the best chefs in Paris, although she hated going to Paris as much as Lorenzo had, and all the chefs she was interviewing came to see her in St. Paul de Vence. She hadn't been to Paris in nearly thirty years, and had never seen Gabriel's gallery. She was happy in St. Paul de Vence, and she let Gabriel stay in one of the rooms in the house on his frequent trips to check on her and advise her about the restaurant, which she called Da Lorenzo, in honor of the only man she had ever loved.

The restaurant was an astonishing success the first year, with reservations booked up to three months in advance. Sophisticated art lovers came from everywhere to see Lorenzo's work and eat a three-star meal, rivaled only by La Colombe d'Or, who were as surprised as everyone else by what Maylis had done. She hired an excellent maître d'hôtel to oversee the dining room and garden and a top-notch sommelier, and with his help they filled their wine cellar with remarkable wines, and they became one of the best restaurants in the South of France, frequented by lovers of art and gastronomy. And Maylis presided over all of it, talking about Lorenzo, and seeing to the clients, as she had with Lorenzo's artist friends long before. She was the keeper of the flame, and a charming hostess in one of the best restaurants in the area. It was a talent no one had suspected she had, and Gabriel often told her how proud he was of her. They had always been good friends, but had grown even closer in the years since Lorenzo's death, as he continued to advise and help her, particularly after she started the restaurant.

It was two years after Maylis opened the restaurant when Gabriel took his courage in his hands, and told her how he had felt about her for years. He was spending more and more time in St. Paul de Vence, staying in one of the bedrooms over the restaurant, for weeks at a time, supposedly to counsel her, when in fact he just wanted to spend time with her, and be near her.

He was able to be absent from Paris, since his daughter, Marie-Claude, was working at the gallery by then, and he was hoping to ease her into running it. She was doing an excellent job, although she complained about his being away so much and leaving all the responsibility to her, but she was enjoying it too, and had introduced some new contemporary artists, who were selling well. Just as her father had, she enjoyed discovering new artists and presenting their work. And she had a good eye for what would sell in the current art market. Gabriel was justifiably proud of her.

On a quiet night, after the closing of the restaurant, sitting at a table in the garden, Gabriel opened his heart to Maylis. He had been in love with her almost since they met, and only his deep respect for his old friend, and his appreciation of the love they shared, had kept him from speaking to her sooner. But with her new lease on life and the success of the restaurant she had created, he finally felt the time was right. It was now or never, although he was terrified of destroying the friendship they had had for nearly thirty years.

Gabriel's confession came as a shock to Maylis, and she discussed it with her son the next day. Theo knew how much his father and mother had loved each other, and what a brilliant artist he was, but he had by no means been the saint Maylis had portrayed him as since his death. And he had often been hard on her as he got older. She had devoted her whole life to him, and forgave him all his flaws. Theo had a far more realistic view of who his father had been, irascible, cantankerous, difficult, egotistical, even tyrannical at times, and possessive of his mother, with a temper that didn't improve with age. Gabriel was a far gentler, more giving man, who had demonstrated deep concern for her and always put her first, unlike his father, and Theo had suspected since his father's death that Gabriel was in love with her, and hoped he was. He had always thought Gabriel was a wonderful person and good for her, and he encouraged her to give Gabriel's feelings for her some very serious thought. He couldn't imagine a better companion for her and didn't want her to end her years alone.

"But what would your father think of my going off with him? Wouldn't that be a betrayal? They were good friends, after all. Even if your father was rough on him at times."

"Rough on him?" Theo had said, laughing at her. "He called him a crook for all the years I can remember. 'My crooked art dealer in Paris.' I don't know another human being who would have put up with him, except you. And Gabriel always stuck by us, and he's still here with you now, Maman. And if he's always been in love with you, it's to his credit that he never let it show while Papa was alive. He was a true friend to both of you. And if you accept him now, it won't be a betrayal, it will be a blessing for you both. You're too young to be alone. And Gabriel is a good

man. I'm happy for you. You deserve it, and so
does he." And Theo knew that Gabriel would be
so much easier than his father had been, and so
much kinder to her. He was the ultimate gentleman, and Theo was glad that he had finally de-
clared himself and he hoped she would consider
it seriously, and she did.

She gave Gabriel her answer a few days later,
and told him she could never love any man as she
had Lorenzo. She had deep affection for Gabriel,
and admitted that she loved him as a friend, and
it might grow into something more with time,
now that he had expressed his feelings for her.
But she warned him that even if they became involved romantically, which she acknowledged as a
possibility, Lorenzo would always remain her first
love, and the love of her life. Gabriel would have
to be willing to be second best, and have a lesser
role in her life, which she didn't think was fair to
him.

But loving her as he did, he was willing to accept that, and quietly hoped that she would open
her heart to him fully one day. He felt sure it
was possible, and was willing to take the risk. He
proceeded slowly thereafter, courting her gently
and wooing her in small romantic ways. He finally invited her for a weekend in Venice with
him, where things took their natural course, and
they had been lovers ever since. They were quiet
about it at first, and never made a big issue of

it. He kept his room over the restaurant and left his things there, but for the past several years, he slept at the studio with her. They went on trips together and enjoyed each other's company, and she told him that she loved him, and meant it, but she still rhapsodized about Lorenzo, and extolled his genius and his mainly imagined virtues, and Gabriel allowed her to keep her illusions without argument.

They had been lovers for almost four years, and Gabriel was satisfied with the relationship, even with its limitations, out of love for her. He never suggested marriage to her, nor asked for more than she was willing to give him of herself, and now and then Theo scolded her that she shouldn't talk about Lorenzo all the time around Gabriel—it always pained Theo for him.

"Why not?" she asked, looking surprised when he said it. "Gabriel loved your father too. He knows he was a great man, and how much he meant to me. He doesn't expect me to forget him, or to stop telling clients about him when they come to the restaurant to see his work. That's why they come here."

"But Gabriel comes here because he loves you," Theo said gently. He always marveled at Gabriel's tolerance of being number two in his mother's life, playing second fiddle to a man who had been dead for twelve years, and had been anything but the saint she described him as. As much as he had loved and admired his father, he thought Gabriel was the better man, and far kinder to his mother than his father in his final years. He had been a great artist, but a very difficult man. He had never been easy to live with, even in his youth, according to people who had known him then. And his talent, burning within him like a white-hot flame, sometimes seared those closest to him and who loved him most.

Gabriel took a great interest in Theo's artwork too. He never offered to represent him, because he thought Theo should have his own gallery and not live in his father's shadow. Theo was a very talented artist, with an entirely different perception than Lorenzo's, but almost of equal talent, once he developed it for a few more years.

At thirty, Theo was well on his way, and extremely serious about his work. And the only thing he ever allowed to distract him were his mother's occasional requests to help her at the restaurant—if something went wrong, they were overbooked, or short-handed, which only happened from time to time. And as much as his mother enjoyed the restaurant, Theo didn't. He hated having to greet the guests, and listening to his mother extol his father's virtues. He had heard more than enough of it for all the years he was growing up, and even more so since his father's death. Listening to it made him want to scream. And he didn't enjoy the public hustle-bustle of the restaurant. Theo was a quieter, more private person than his mother.

Gabriel had given him the names of galleries he thought Theo should pursue, but he modestly insisted he wasn't ready yet, and wanted to work for another year or two before he had a show in Paris. He had exhibited his work at several art fairs but hadn't settled on a gallery. Gabriel insisted that he should—he was a strong supportive force in Theo's life. Despite the oddity of their lopsided relationship, Theo was grateful that Gabriel was in his mother's life too. And like Gabriel, he hoped that they might marry one day, if Maylis felt ready to move forward, which clearly she didn't yet.

Marriage wasn't high on Theo's list of priorities either. He had had several relationships that lasted for a few months or a year, and many for a lot less. He was too dedicated to his work as an artist to put a lot of energy into the women he went out with, and they always complained about it and eventually left. And he was sensitive to gold-digging women who were interested in him because of who his father was, and he tried to avoid that. He had been dating Chloe, his current girlfriend, for six months. She was an artist too, but did commercial work that sold to tourists out of a gallery in St. Tropez. It was a far cry from what Theo did, with his background and degree from the Beaux-Arts, his genetic heritage

and inherited talent, and long-term serious ambi-
tions. All she wanted was to make enough money
to pay the rent, and she'd been complaining a lot
recently that he didn't spend enough time with
her and they never went anywhere. That was
how most of his relationships ended, and his current one seemed to be heading there. Chloe had
reached the familiar phase of complaining all the
time. He was in a particularly intense work phase
at the moment, developing some new techniques
that he was anxious to perfect. He wasn't in love
with Chloe, but they had fun in bed, and she had
a great body. At thirty, she had suddenly started
talking about marriage, which was usually a death
knell for him. He wasn't ready to settle down or
have kids. And she was becoming increasingly
strident about his work. In the battle between
women and his artwork, his work inevitably won.

Maylis was checking the tables in the garden, as
she did every night, making sure that there were
flowers and candles on every table, the linens were
impeccable, and the silver gleaming. She was a
perfectionist in all things, and ran a tight ship.
She had learned a lot about running a restaurant
in the last few years. And there was nothing casual
about Da Lorenzo. The garden restaurant was as
beautiful as the food and wines were fabulous.
One of the waiters came to get her as she made

her rounds. They had a full house, as usual, and would open for dinner in two hours.

"Madame Luca, Jean-Pierre is on the phone." He was her brilliantly efficient maître d', and the fact that he was calling wasn't a good sign, as the waiter handed her the phone.

"Is everything all right?" she asked, still wearing jeans and a white shirt. She was going to dress in an hour. She usually wore a black silk dress, high heels, and a string of pearls, with her long white hair neatly coiffed in a bun. She was still a pretty woman at sixty-three.

"I'm afraid not," Jean-Pierre said, sounding ill. "I had lunch in Antibes today, and I'm sick as a dog. Bad mussels, I think."

"Damn," she said, looking at her watch. She still had time to call Theo, although she knew how much he hated it. But it was a family restaurant, and when she or the maître d' couldn't work, she always called her son, and he never refused her pleas for help.

"I'm too sick to come in." He sounded it over the phone, and Jean-Pierre never called in sick unless he was really ill.

"Don't worry about it, I'll call Theo. I'm sure he has nothing to do." He was always in his studio working. He had very little social life, and painted on most nights.

Jean-Pierre apologized again and hung up, and she called her son a minute later. It rang for quite a while, and then Theo picked up, sounding distracted. He was going to let it ring and then glanced at the phone and saw who it was.

"Hello, Maman. What's up?" He squinted at the canvas as he spoke to her, not sure if he liked what he'd just done. He was very critical of his own work, as his father had been with his.

"Jean-Pierre is sick." She got right to the point. "Can you bail me out?"

Theo groaned. "I'm just working on something, and I hate to stop. And I promised Chloe I'd take her out tonight."

"We can feed her here, if she's willing to eat late." He knew that would mean dinner between eleven P.M. and midnight, after most of the customers left. And he wouldn't have time to sit down with her until then. He would have to supervise the waiters, and spend time with their most important guests, to make sure their dinners were going well. His mother would keep an eye on the really illustrious ones, and see to their needs, but he would have to take care of his share too. The one thing he never admitted was that he was Lorenzo Luca's son. He preferred to be anonymous when he worked for her, and his mother indulged him, although she thought he should be proud of it. But at Theo's request, she never told any of their customers that he was her son. And she was grateful for his help. He was attentive to her, patient with her, and helpful when he could be. He thought it his duty, as an only child, and he liked his mother, despite her quirks. They had always gotten along, although she worried about him being alone and rarely liked the women he went out with.

"What time do you need me to come in?" He didn't sound happy. He respected her success with the restaurant, and admired her for it, but he hated being there himself and, even more, wearing a suit and tie in the heat, and having to be charming to strangers he'd never see again. His mother was far more extroverted and loved it. The restaurant replaced a social life for her, and gave her contact with a wide variety of interesting people.

"You can come at seven-thirty. Our first sitting is at eight," she said. Sometimes they got Americans who wanted to come earlier, but not that night. All the clients on their reservation list were European, except for Vladimir Stanislas, which was a major coup, and she was aware that he had never been there before. She wanted everything to go seamlessly that night, particularly for him. She knew about his art collection, and was hoping he would stop to admire Lorenzo's work, which was obviously why he was coming. He had booked a table for two, through a regular guest of theirs.

"Chloe is going to kill me," he said, wondering what to say to her. All he could do was tell her the truth, that his mother needed him to help out at the restaurant, which she would think was an excuse to avoid taking her out.

"You can make it up to her tomorrow night," his mother said cheerfully.

"Maybe not. I want to work." He was at a tough spot on the painting he was working on, and hated going out two nights in a row before he had solved the problems that were slowing him down. His father had been that way too. Nothing existed in his universe except the canvas he was working on. "Okay, never mind. I'll deal with it. I'll come in." He never let her down.

"Thank you, darling. If you come at seven, you can eat with the waiters. They're having bouillabaisse tonight, with rouille." She knew it was one of his favorites, although he could order anything he wanted, but he never took advantage of the fact that he was the boss's son. Theo preferred to eat what the others did, and wasn't a demanding person, unlike his father.

He called Chloe as soon as he and his mother hung up, and gave her the bad news. She wasn't pleased.

"I'm really sorry." He had promised to take her out for **socca,** which was like pizza made of chickpeas, baked in a special oven, and they both loved it. It was a local dish, and they were serving it in the square that night. She loved playing **boules** with the old men afterward, which was a thrill for them, to have a pretty young woman join their game. Theo enjoyed it too, when he wasn't working, and now he couldn't do anything with her except midnight supper, if she was willing. "I promised to help my mother. She just called me, the maître d' is sick. She said you're welcome to come to dinner, if you don't mind eating late. We can probably grab a table at eleven, if the guests are starting to leave by then." But they both knew that at Da Lorenzo, people often stayed much later. The surroundings were too romantic and the atmosphere too welcoming for anyone to want to leave early, which was part of the restaurant's success, along with fabulous food and great art.

"I was hoping to be in bed by then," Chloe said tartly, "and not alone. I haven't seen you in a week." She sounded angry again, which had become the norm.

"I've been working," he said, thinking he sounded lame. It was always his excuse.

"I don't know why you can't stop at a decent hour. I leave my studio by six every day." But she did second-rate commercial work, although he would never have said that to her. His was of a far different caliber than hers, but he was never rude about her work.

"I work different hours than you do. But anyway, I'm stuck tonight. Do you want to come to the restaurant late?" It was the best he could offer her, and a fabulous meal if she did.

"No, I don't. I don't want to get all dressed up. I was going to wear shorts and a T-shirt. The restaurant is a little too fancy for me. **Socca, boules,** and bed immediately after sounded good to me."

"It sounded good to me too, and a lot more fun than wearing a suit and tie, but I've got to give my mother a hand." That annoyed Chloe too. She had met his mother a couple of times, and found her a little too serious about art, and possessive of her only son. And Chloe wasn't in the mood for a lecture about the great Lorenzo Luca, which bored her to tears. She wanted to go out and have a good time with him. She had thought he was a great guy at first, handsome and sexy and terrific in bed. Now she found him much too serious about his work. "I'll call you when I finish," he said. "Maybe I could come by." She didn't answer at first, and a few minutes later, sounding petulant, she hung up.

Theo went to take a shower then, and an hour later he was wearing a dark suit and white shirt, and a red tie, on his way to the restaurant, in his ancient **deux chevaux.** Chloe didn't like his car either, and couldn't understand why he didn't buy a better one. He was hardly a starving artist, even though he liked looking like one. He was tall and handsome in the dark suit, with his dark hair brushed. He had dark brown eyes like his father, and he had the unconsciously good looks of Italian men. His mother appeared more French. He had an innate style about him that women loved.

Maylis was in the kitchen, talking to the chef, when he got to the restaurant. She went over the menu carefully every day, and she had been tasting some of the **amuse-bouches,** and was telling the chef they were exceptionally good that night. She smiled when she saw her son. He sauntered into the kitchen, looking strikingly attractive, and she thanked him for coming in. And then she hurried off to check something in the garden again, as Theo chatted with the waiters. They all thought he was a nice guy. And then they all took their places. Theo and his mother were ready and waiting when the first guests arrived at eight o'clock. Another night of unforgettable dining at Da Lorenzo had begun.

Vladimir and Natasha left their cabin, made their way downstairs to the lower aft deck, and walked past all the speedboats and toys they had onboard, to where the tender was waiting to take them to shore. It was a high-speed boat Vladimir had had built for three million dollars and particularly enjoyed. It was designed to outrun anyone on the water, and they were at the dock of the Hôtel du Cap within minutes, where one of the crew members of the boat had Vladimir's Ferrari waiting for him at the hotel. He sometimes took a bodyguard in a chase car, but all was peaceful in his world at the moment, and he didn't feel he needed one tonight. He got behind the wheel of the car, and they took off. It would be a short ride to St. Paul de Vence in the fast car.

Natasha put her seatbelt on as Vladimir turned on the radio, and played a CD he knew Natasha loved. He was in a festive mood, and looking forward to dinner and seeing the art at the restaurant. And Natasha was exceptionally pretty in a short pale pink dress she hadn't worn before. It was Chanel haute couture with a demure little lace schoolgirl collar and no back that he had selected for her, with matching sandals in the same color. She looked exquisite, as always.

"I like your new dress." He smiled at her admiringly as they got on the road, and she nodded, pleased that he had noticed, although he'd picked it himself. She had worn her hair down and looked very young. He was wearing a white linen suit, which set off his tan from being on the boat. With the exception of a few hours in his office that morning, they had spent the day relaxing and lying in the sun. And they both had deep tans. "I love it. You look like a little girl, until you turn around." The dress showed off her perfectly tanned back with no bra line. She always sunbathed topless on the boat. And the back of the dress was cut down to her waist. The dress was sexy and innocent all at the same time. "I'm interested to see the art tonight," he said, as they drove along. Their reservation was at eight-thirty, and he wanted to look around before they sat down to dine.

"So am I," she said easily, as they drove with the top down. The night was warm, and she had tied her hair back for the brief ride to St. Paul de Vence. It took them half the normal time to get there in the Ferrari, the way he drove, and an attendant took their car when they arrived at the restaurant, which from the street seemed like an ordinary, rambling house. They stepped into a courtyard through an archway, as the parking attendant roared away in the Ferrari and a woman in a black dress with snow-white hair in a bun walked toward them with a smile. Maylis had recognized Vladimir immediately. As she approached them and introduced herself as Madame Luca, she glanced at Natasha with interest.

"Your table will be ready in five minutes. Would you like to walk around inside the house and see Lorenzo's work first?" she asked as though they were friends, and Vladimir nodded, pleased that they had time for a quick look before dinner.

Natasha followed him into the house, as she let down her hair. The walls were white so as not to distract from the art, and instantly they were surrounded by Lorenzo's work. The paintings were all hung close together because there were so many of them, and the subtleties of his

palette and the masterful quality of his brushstrokes struck them immediately. When Vladimir
stopped to admire a painting of a beautiful young
woman, they both recognized her as the woman
who had greeted them. And beneath the painting was a small bronze plaque that said "Not for
Sale." Vladimir was mesmerized by the painting,
and could barely tear himself away to move on
to the next one. Natasha was impressed by all of
them as she walked from one to the other, and
noticed the same bronze plaque below each one.

"Well, it's clearly not a gallery," he said, looking slightly irritated, after noticing all the "Not
for Sale" signs too. They toured the room, then
walked down a hall lined with his work and
into another room. None of the paintings were
for sale. "She treats it like a museum," Vladimir
commented.

"I read about it online today. This is all her collection, and supposedly she has many, many more
in storage and in his studio," Natasha explained.
She liked being well informed when they went
somewhere, and sharing the information with
him.

"It's ridiculous not to sell any of them," he said
as they walked back into the first room, and Natasha was aware of a young man in a dark blue
suit watching them. He had dark hair and deep
brown eyes, but didn't speak to them. Natasha
could sense that he was watching her intently,

and then he walked back outside. She had been struck by his serious brown eyes. And she noticed him again as they walked into the garden, where Maylis was waiting to escort them to their table. She smiled at them as they sat down, and couldn't help thinking how beautiful Natasha was, and how perfect her features were, and then Maylis turned her attention back to Vladimir.

"Did you find your walk around the house interesting?" she asked pleasantly.

"I noticed that nothing was for sale." Vladimir looked serious when he answered her. And he didn't seem happy about it. She nodded in response.

"That's right. We don't sell his work. This is part of the family collection. My husband was represented by a gallery in Paris. Bovigny Ferrand." Gabriel had had a partner initially, whom he had bought out years before, but kept the name, since it was already well known by then, and he had paid Georges Bovigny handsomely for it.

"They have none of his work to sell either." He had inquired. "I understand that his work never comes on the market anymore," Vladimir said with an intense expression.

"Not since his death twelve years ago," Maylis said politely.

"You're very fortunate to have so much of his work," Vladimir said pointedly to the owner of the restaurant and the artwork.

"Yes, I am," she agreed. "I hope you enjoy your dinner." She smiled warmly at both of them and then withdrew to where she normally stood when guests arrived. She found Theo standing there, staring at Vladimir's table. "We have an important guest here tonight," she said in an under-voice, and Theo appeared not to hear her. He was watching Natasha's every move, as she and Vladimir discussed the menu.

"I never understand why women are with men like him. He's old enough to be her father," Theo said, looking disgusted, although his father had been forty years older than his mother.

"In their case, it's about the money," Maylis said simply.

He was instantly irritated by his mother's comment. "It can't just be about that. She's not a prostitute. She looks like a work of art herself. A woman like that is not in it for the money." He couldn't take his eyes off her, as she talked quietly to Vladimir, and looked every inch a lady. He had even noticed how graceful her hands were as she held the menu, and he saw a thin diamond brace-let sparkling on her wrist in the candlelight.

"It's about power and lifestyle, and everything he can do for her. Don't waste your time fanta-sizing about her. Women like that are a special breed. And when it's over with him, she'll find someone else just like him, although men as rich and powerful as Stanislas are hard to find. He's in a league of his own, the most important one of his kind." Theo didn't answer her. He just continued to watch Natasha, and then as though shaking himself out of his reverie, he went to check on several of the tables, and walked past theirs on the way back. And for the merest fraction of an instant, Natasha met his eyes. She had seen him watching them before.

"Is everything all right?" he asked her politely, and Vladimir answered for her.

"We're ready to order," he said in a tone that was used to command, and Theo nodded but looked unimpressed. There was nothing to indicate that he was one of the owners, or that his mother was. He was just a maître d' making the rounds.

"I'll send your waiter right over." Theo walked away then, sent the waiter to their table, and continued watching Natasha from the distance. It was hard to think of being with a woman like Chloe again after seeing someone like Natasha. Everything about her was delicate and graceful. She moved as though to music only she could hear, in a private ballet of some kind, and she was totally attentive to her man.

Theo heard from the sommelier that Vladimir had ordered their most expensive bottle of wine. And halfway through dinner, Theo saw Vladimir take his cellphone out of his pocket and answer it—it must have been vibrating. And he quickly rose from the table after saying something to Natasha, and walked outside through the archway into the street to continue the conversation. Theo heard him speaking Russian as he walked by.

Natasha finished her dinner and felt uncomfortable sitting alone at the table, and a few minutes later, she got up and walked into the house, to visit the art again. She stopped in front of the same painting Vladimir had admired, and she stood gazing at it for a long time. Theo felt himself pulled inexorably into the house, and smiled at her from across the room.

"Beautiful, isn't it?" he commented to her.

"Is it his wife?" Natasha asked him. He could hear her Russian accent and found it attractive. And she had a soft sexy voice that ran a finger down his spine.

"Yes," Theo said, watching her, "although she wasn't his wife then. They married much later. They'd been together for more than twenty years and had a son before they married." He gave her some family history without admitting it was his own.

"The little boy in the paintings is their son?" Theo nodded, but still had no intention of telling that it was he. He preferred remaining anonymous, which made him feel almost invisible. He had no need to be "seen," he just wanted the pleasure of looking at her, in the same way that she was enjoying the art. She was every bit as beautiful as the paintings of his mother. "She's right not to sell them," Natasha said softly. "It would be too hard to give any of them up." He loved the sound of her voice. She almost purred as she spoke, and looked innocent and shy, as though she didn't speak to strangers very often.

"That's why she doesn't, although she has a lot of them. And he gave many of them away when he was young, to friends or collectors of his work. He was never interested in money, only in the quality of his work. None of the paintings here are for sale," he said quietly. "His widow won't sell them."

"Everything has a price." They both jumped at the sound of the voice behind them, and turned to see Vladimir standing in the doorway, with the same expression of annoyance on his face. He didn't like things he couldn't buy. "Shall we go back to the table?" he asked Natasha, which was more a command than a question. She smiled pleasantly at Theo and walked back outside, as he followed her with his eyes. He saw that they had a cheese course, and ordered dessert, and after that Vladimir lit one of his cigars, as she smiled at him. He had just told her that she was even more beautiful than the art.

Maylis frowned when she saw Theo watching Natasha. She walked to where he was standing quietly. Most of the guests had left, and only a few tables were still occupied with people enjoying the last of the evening, after a splendid meal.

"Don't do that to yourself," Maylis said to him, looking worried. "She's like a painting in a museum. You can't have her." He remembered what Vladimir had said about everything having a price. "Besides, you can't afford her."

"No, I can't," Theo said, as he smiled at his mother. "She's pretty to look at, though."

"From the distance," his mother reminded him. "Women like that are dangerous. They break your heart. She's not like the women you know. For her, this is a job."

"You think she's a hooker?" He looked surprised, and Maylis shook her head.

"Far from it. She's his mistress. It's written all over her. Her dress cost more than one of your paintings. Her bracelet and earrings are worth one of your father's. It's a profession, belonging to a man as rich and powerful as he is."

"I suppose it is. I've seen his boat. It's hard to imagine anyone having that kind of money . . . and a woman like her." There was longing in Theo's voice as he said it, and not about the boat.

"You have to be as rich as he is to have a girl like her, although I have to admit, she looks better than most. It must be a lonely life. He owns her. That's how it works." Thinking about it made him feel sick. His mother talked about her as though she were a slave, or an object he had bought. Everything had a price, or that was how Vladimir saw it. Even the girl with him.

They left a little while later. Vladimir paid in cash and gave the waiter an enormous tip, equal to half the bill, as though money meant nothing to him. And Maylis thanked them with a warm smile for coming. Theo was in the kitchen then, talking to the chef, and trying not to think of the girl who had left with Vladimir. He wondered if his mother was right, and if Vladimir felt he owned her. It was a frightening thing to say about another human being, and as he thought about her, he knew he had to paint her. It was the only way he could get close to her, or see into her soul, to paint her, and make her his.

He was still thinking about her when he left the restaurant, tossed his suit jacket into the backseat of his car, pulled off his tie, and called Chloe. He had a sudden longing to see her, but she didn't sound happy when she answered. It was nearly one in the morning by then, and she had been asleep.

"Do you still want company?" he asked in a voice raw with desire, and she sounded instantly incensed.

"For a booty call? No, I don't. You finish working for your mother and want to get laid on the way home?"

"Don't be stupid, Chloe. You said you wanted to see me. I just finished work."

"Call me tomorrow, and we'll talk about it." And with that, she hung up, and he drove home.

His mother was right—he was crazy to be fascinated by the girl he'd seen at the restaurant that night. She was someone's mistress, it had nothing to do with him. And he wouldn't have known what to do with a woman like her, although she had been so easy to talk to, with her gentle voice, when he followed her inside when she went to look at the art again.

He walked into his house, and tossed the car keys onto the kitchen table, sorry that Chloe hadn't let him come over. He had no idea why, but he had never felt so alone in his life. He went into his studio and pulled out one of the blank canvases he had leaning against a wall, and all he could see as he looked at it was Natasha's face, begging to be painted.

Natasha and Vladimir had reached the dock in Antibes by then, where the tender was waiting to take them back to the boat.

"I have a visitor coming tonight," he said quietly, as the tender sliced through the water at high speed. The sea was flat, and the moon was high, casting light over the water. She didn't ask him who the visitor would be, but she knew it was someone important, if he was coming late at night. "I have to read some papers before our meeting, and I don't want to keep you up. I'll stay in my office until he arrives." She knew from what he said that it was someone who didn't want to be observed meeting with him. They were usually very important men, who had dealings with him. She was used to it. She would hear them arrive on his helicopter, and then leave again before dawn.

Vladimir walked her to their bedroom, put his arms around her, and kissed her with a slow smile.

"Thank you for a lovely evening," she said. She had liked the restaurant and the art, and her time with him, before he went back to work.

"It's a silly place with none of the paintings for sale." She could see that it had bothered him, but they'd had a good time anyway. He kissed her again, and left her in the cabin. He had work to do. And just as she fell asleep, she heard the helicopter land, and knew that Vladimir's visitor had arrived. She was sound asleep by the time the Russian president got out of the helicopter and walked to where Vladimir was standing, waiting for him, and shook his hand, with bodyguards lining the deck. Vladimir and his visitor walked down a flight of stairs to Vladimir's soundproof, bulletproof office. They had work to do that night, and a deal to sign by morning.

Chapter 3

When Natasha woke up in the morning, the bed next to her was empty, and she opened her eyes to see Vladimir smiling at her, wearing city clothes, and carrying his briefcase. He appeared tired but satisfied, and she knew he'd had a long night, with the visitor who had come by helicopter to see him. He had that fierce look in his eyes that he got when a deal had gone well, like an animal that had eaten its prey. He looked sated and victorious.

"Are you going somewhere?" she asked, as she stretched her long, exquisite body, and he sat down beside her.

"To Moscow for a few days" was all he said to her. They had signed the preliminary agreements the night before, for a major mineral deal that would bring him billions. Now they had to sign the final papers to seal the deal. It was worth a trip to Moscow. He had been in competition with two other major players on the Russian scene, and his manipulations and connections had won him the prize. They almost always did. He knew just where to apply pressure, to what degree, and on whom. He knew all his enemies' and competitors' weak spots, and never hesitated to use them. "I'll call you later," Vladimir promised her and leaned over to kiss her, wishing he had time to make love to her, but he needed to get down to business, and his plane was waiting for him at the Nice airport for the flight to Moscow. "Do some shopping while I'm gone. Go to the Hermès in Cannes." And there was a Dior she liked there too. She had been to Chanel a few days before, but there were plenty of shops on the Croisette to keep her busy. It was at times like this that she sometimes wished she had a girlfriend to go with her, but women in her situation had no time for women friends. She was always on call for Vladimir, and his plans could change in an instant. His schedule was as mercurial and unpredictable as he was. Being always there for him was part of their unspoken arrangement.

"Don't worry. I'll find something to do." She put her arms around him, and he felt her breasts rub against his chest, and he leaned away to cup them with his hands.

"I should take you with me, but I'll be busy, and you'd be bored in Moscow. Stay on the boat.

Don't go to the house without me." She knew the risk of random attacks and burglaries, and never went to the house in St. Jean Cap-Ferrat without him. "We'll do something fun when I get back. Maybe St. Tropez or Sardinia." She looked pleased at the idea, and followed him to the door of their bedroom for a last kiss. He slipped his hands into her satin nightgown, and dropped it to the floor at her feet, to reveal her remarkable body in all its splendor. It still thrilled him to know that she was his, like a dazzling piece of art he owned, and he knew that he was envied by all who saw her. They kissed one last time, and then he stepped out of their bedroom, and gently closed the door behind him, as Natasha headed for the bathroom, smiling as she thought about him, and turned on the shower. And as she got into it a moment later, she heard the helicopter take off from the upper deck. She didn't even think about why he was going to Moscow, and didn't need to know. There were questions she never asked herself. All she needed to know was that she belonged to him, and in his own way, to the extent that he was capable, he loved her. It was enough. And she loved him too—he was her savior.

Maylis was going over the restaurant books that morning when Gabriel called her from Paris. She kept a close eye on everything, and always made sure that no one was stealing. Their food bills were high, the produce costs were ridiculous, flown in from all over Europe, and their wine bills were astronomical, but so were the prices they charged, and everything appeared to be in order. She sounded serious when she took Gabriel's call.

"Is something wrong?" He was sensitive to all her moods, and tried to solve all her problems. He had protected her almost like a child since he began representing Lorenzo, and did so even more now that he and Maylis were lovers. He treated her with all the respect due a wife, and the concern of a loving father, although he was only four years older than she was. And at sixty-seven, he looked considerably older than she did. They both had white hair, and hers was no longer premature, but her face was youthful and unlined, and her body was still sensual and appealing, just as it had been when she modeled for Lorenzo.

"No, I was just going over the books. Everything looks fine. When are you coming down from Paris?"

He smiled at the question. "I just left you three days ago. I have to spend some time here, or Marie-Claude will scold me." He spent as much time as possible in St. Paul de Vence, even though he still owned the gallery in Paris. For the past three years, since becoming a couple with Maylis, however unusual their arrangement, he tried to be with her as much as he could. But in her mind, she was still married to a dead man, and treated Gabriel like an illicit lover. She rarely admitted to anyone that she and Gabriel were lovers, but he accepted all her quirks and eccentricities to be with her. And his daughter Marie-Claude had run his gallery for years now. She had just turned forty, was married to a successful lawyer, and had two teenage children, whom she said Gabriel saw too little of, because he was always in St. Paul de Vence with Maylis, and far more involved with her and Theo than with his own family. It upset Marie-Claude, and she had resented it for years, and was very vocal about it with her father.

"Marie-Claude can manage without you. I can't," Maylis said simply, and he smiled, and knew that it was true. Maylis had proven capable with the restaurant, but was much more intimidated handling her own financial affairs, or Lorenzo's, which were considerably more complicated. Gabriel had a great head for finance and loved taking care of her in any way he could, and making her life easier. He had done it for years. His daughter was an excellent businesswoman too, but she didn't like being in constant competition with the Lucas for his attention. She thought his single-minded attachment to them unhealthy, and his efforts unappreciated. She thought Maylis was an incredibly selfish woman who never hesitated to monopolize her father's time, to his detriment, and used him.

"I'll be back soon. I thought I'd spend a week here and see what Marie-Claude has been up to. She signed a flock of new artists." In recent years, he had become barely more than a silent partner in the gallery he had founded. Lorenzo's affairs still took up all his time—the estate was huge, and more intricate than ever to manage. He wanted to make sure that Maylis would be in great financial shape forever, in case anything happened to him, and he also advised Theo and managed his finances for him. Theo was more astute about his affairs than his mother but preferred focusing on his painting. "I had a call this morning that I want to discuss with you, Maylis."

"Oh, please don't tell me they're raising my taxes again, and how you want to manage it. It always gives me a headache." She sounded instantly nervous as she said it. "Can't you just take care of it for me?"

"Not this time. It's not about taxes—you have a decision to make. I got a call from an attorney in London, representing a client. He wishes to remain anonymous but is an important art collector. He wants to buy a painting he saw at the restaurant."

"Don't bother going any further," Maylis said brusquely. "You know I'm not selling. There are 'Not for Sale' signs on every painting in the house."

"He's offering an important price, Maylis. And

I had to at least relay the offer to you. I didn't want to turn him down without your consent."

"You have my consent. Tell him Lorenzo's work is not for sale." She didn't even want to hear the offer.

"They did their homework. And they're offering the same price the last of Lorenzo's paintings sold for at Christie's. That's a very handsome price, and this is just their opening offer." Although the price was high, Gabriel guessed from the lawyer's tone that they would go higher.

"It was seven years ago, and they would go for more now. **If** I were selling, but I'm not. Just tell them no. Do you know who it is?"

"No, I don't. The prospective buyer does not wish us to know."

"Well, it doesn't matter. Tell him nothing is for sale."

Gabriel hesitated for a moment. They had offered an enormous price, although she was right, and if she put a painting of Lorenzo's in a current auction, it would bring even more. But the prospective buyer knew that too. It was a shrewd initial bid. "I think you should discuss this with Theo," Gabriel said quietly. He thought her son should at least know, but he had wanted to call Maylis first, and if the painting in question was on display in the house, it belonged to her. But Theo would give her good advice, and Gabriel was tempted to encourage her to sell it, to establish a new value for Lorenzo's work, which would inevitably be higher than what had been established before. He was prepared to negotiate for more if she agreed to sell, and told her which one the offer was for.

"That painting doesn't belong to Theo. And he doesn't want to sell anything either. We don't need the money, and I'm not giving up any of Lorenzo's paintings." She had a modest lifestyle, and made a handsome living with the restaurant, aside from what Lorenzo left her.

"Just let Theo know. I'd be interested in hearing his opinion," Gabriel said gently. He never pushed her, or forced her to do anything. He advised her.

"All right, I'll tell him," she said grudgingly, and went on to discuss other things of more importance to her, like their margin on great wines at the restaurant. She wanted to know if Gabriel thought they should raise their prices. He advised her on everything, and she relied on him to be there for her. She followed all his suggestions, except about selling her late husband's work, at least from time to time, but before they hung up she promised again to call Theo. She finished what she was doing with the restaurant ledger, and then called her son.

As always, he took forever to answer, which meant he was painting. He sounded totally distracted when he picked up the phone and said,

"Yes?" He could see that the call was from his mother, and he just hoped she wasn't asking him to work at the restaurant again that night, and that Jean-Pierre was in good health and back at his post as maître d'. "I'm painting."

"Obviously. When aren't you? Gabriel told me to call you. I'm sorry to interrupt."

"Is something wrong?"

"No, everything's fine. He had a call from an attorney in London, representing an anonymous private collector, who wants to buy one of my paintings."

"Did you tell him it's not for sale?" Theo couldn't see the point of the call, and he hated losing his train of thought while he worked. For him, painting was an intense business.

"Gabriel knows that. Apparently they're offering our last Christie's price, which is too low now anyway. But Gabriel thought you should know. And he said he could negotiate a higher price if we want to sell, which I don't."

Theo hesitated for a moment before he answered, and frowned.

"That was an inflated price at the time, driven up by a bidding war between two buyers. They paid a lot more than they should have." Still, Maylis and Theo had been pleased with the result at the time. "And this anonymous buyer is willing to match that as an opening bid?" He sounded surprised.

"That's what Gabriel said. I told him to turn it down, but he wanted me to discuss it with you first." Theo could understand why. It was an enormous price for his father's work, and would prove its market value, even more so if the buyer would go higher.

"Maybe we should think about it," Theo said quietly. "And see how much Gabriel can get, and how badly this buyer wants it."

"I'm not going to sell it," she said with steel in her tone. "It's one of the first paintings your father painted of me, when I was still just his model." And suddenly, when she said it, as he thought about it, Theo realized which one. It was the painting Vladimir Stanislas had been fascinated by at the restaurant the night before.

"I think I know who the buyer might be. Stanislas was mesmerized by it last night." And he remembered his irritation that it wasn't for sale, and his comment that everything had a price. "If it's him, you could probably negotiate with him and ask for more. I don't think he's familiar with the word **no,** and if he wants it badly enough, he'll pay any price."

"It's **not for sale,**" Maylis repeated, digging her heels in. "I don't care what he offers."

"It might set a new benchmark for Papa's prices, and set the bar even higher than it is now, after the last time."

"What difference does it make if we don't want to sell any?"

"You might want to one day, and it's always good to take the temperature of the current art market. Gabriel always says that it's good to sell one from time to time. And Papa painted better paintings of you than that one, like the ones of you once you were together." His love for Maylis and for his son had shone through every painting after that. "This might be a good one to sell," Theo said thoughtfully.

"The answer is no." She was incredibly stubborn at times, especially about her late husband's work.

"It's up to you, Maman. But I think I'd negotiate with them and see what you get." It was good advice, and Gabriel would have said the same.

"I told Gabriel to turn the offer down." She confirmed that to him five minutes later, after she and Theo hung up. Gabriel was faintly disappointed that she wasn't willing to listen to him or her son.

"I'll tell them," he said quietly. He knew better than to argue with her about Lorenzo's work. And he called the attorney in London shortly after and declined.

He was looking over images of some of the new work Marie-Claude had taken in, marveling at her eye for contemporary work, when the attorney in London called again, and offered a considerably higher price. Gabriel managed not to sound shocked, although he was. Clearly, the anonymous buyer was willing to pay any price to acquire the work. He was offering fifty percent more than the price set at the Christie's auction. It was an extremely handsome offer. Gabriel promised to relay it to the artist's widow. But when he did, Maylis sounded stubborn. She wouldn't even agree to call Theo this time.

"This is an extraordinarily high price." He tried to reason with her. "I don't think you should turn it down, Maylis. It establishes an astronomical level for Lorenzo's work in the current art market."

"I don't care. It's not for sale."

Gabriel sighed audibly, and called back the attorney in London, feeling like a fool. He knew it was a fabulous price for the work, and he had to explain that Mrs. Luca had no interest in selling her husband's work for now. He wanted to leave the door open for later, but he wasn't sure she would sell any of it in her lifetime, and Theo wasn't hungry for money either. He led a very simple life. They both did.

"My client has authorized me to make a final offer," the attorney said in a clipped British voice, and doubled their initial offer, making it one of the most expensive paintings ever sold, if Maylis was willing to accept the price.

Gabriel was silent for a moment, stunned by

the offer. "I will relay it to my client," he said respectfully, and this time he called Theo directly instead, and told him the amount. When he heard it, Theo whistled.

"Jesus. It must be Stanislas. No one else would pay that."

"I don't know what to say to your mother. I think she should sell it," Gabriel said honestly, not sure how to convince her. She listened to him about most things, but not about selling Lorenzo's work. She was deeply emotionally attached to all of it. And no one could accuse Gabriel of having a financial interest in it, since he had stopped charging her a commission on any potential sale with the last one. He no longer felt right about it, so his advice to her was pure and without self-interest.

"I think so too," Theo agreed with him. "I didn't like the guy when I saw him last night, if it's Stanislas, and I think it is." He'd had a visceral reaction to him. "But it's a hell of a price. She can't turn that down."

"I think she will, no matter what we tell her." Gabriel sounded discouraged.

"The only good news is that he painted it when she was just his model. I doubt she'll agree to sell any of the later ones once she was his mistress, or once they were married. She really shouldn't turn down this offer. I think it's an important milestone for my father's work. It's double what we got for the last one at Christie's. That's a huge jump," Theo said practically.

"I'd remind her of that," Gabriel agreed. "See what you can do."

Theo called her as soon as he and Gabriel hung up, and he told her what he had said to Gabriel, that it was a major price to pay for his father's work, and put him out in the stratosphere in the art world, and she couldn't deprive him of it. He said that he was sure his father would want the painting sold, and he hoped his saying that would sway her. Sometimes it made a difference to invoke Lorenzo's name and his imagined wishes.

"I'll think about it," she said, sounding distressed. Parting with any of his paintings felt like giving up a child to her, and losing a piece of Lorenzo again.

Much to his amazement, she called Theo back an hour later. What he had said had resonated with her, and she wanted to do what Lorenzo himself would have wanted. "If you really think this is an important milestone for him, and what he'd want, I'll do it." She sounded near tears as she said it. Theo knew how hard this was for her, as did Gabriel, which was why he hadn't pushed her, but only tried to encourage her gently. And Theo had said the magic words: "You owe this to Papa. It's what he would have wanted. It's a tribute to his work."

"I think you've made absolutely the right decision, Maman. This really is what Papa would want." And it was a crime to turn down a price like that. They had doubled Lorenzo's prices with a single sale, even without a bidding war at auction. Theo congratulated her on her wise decision, and urged her to call Gabriel immediately before the buyer changed his mind, or she did. And Gabriel was as surprised and impressed as Theo. And after Theo hung up with his mother, he was reminded of Vladimir Stanislas's comment the night before, that everything had a price. He hated for him to be right, but in this case he was. And he wondered if Vladimir believed that about people too, and suspected he did, which was even worse. But if he was the buyer, he had won this time, and so had they. It was a winning situation for all.

Gabriel conveyed their acceptance to the lawyer in London, who said the buyer would be pleased. He called Gabriel back ten minutes later and said that the money would be wired into the gallery's bank account in Paris within the hour. The buyer wanted the painting delivered to a motor yacht called **Princess Marina,** and a tender would be waiting for them at the dock of the Hôtel du Cap-Eden-Roc in Cap d'Antibes at five o'clock that afternoon. It confirmed Theo's initial suspicion that the purchaser was Vladimir. Now that the negotiations had been successfully concluded, he was willing to have his identity known. Gabriel called Theo the moment he hung up and told him who the collector was.

"I knew it," Theo said. "He looked like he wanted to tear it off the wall and leave with it under his arm last night. I hate to let him have it, but at that price, how could we refuse?"

"I'm glad you didn't, and what you said to your mother is true. This is a major milestone for your father's work. It will set the floor, not the ceiling, for the next sale. This is a very, very important price, for the next time you or your mother decide to sell one of his paintings, and it doubles the value of his estate. That is no small thing." Theo suddenly realized the impact of it. The value of his entire fortune, and his mother's, had doubled with a single sale. He didn't like the man who had bought it, and he had a bad feeling about him, but he had done them all a service. "He wants the painting delivered to his boat at five o'clock this afternoon. I'm sorry to bother you, but could you get it there? I think it would be too emotional for your mother to do it." And it was a large piece in a heavy frame and too cumbersome for her to carry.

"Of course," Theo said quickly, wondering if he would see Natasha, or only Vladimir. For that kind of money, undoubtedly he would want to receive the painting himself.

"They'll have a tender waiting for you at the dock of the Eden Roc, at Hôtel du Cap. All you have to do is go onboard the yacht, and hand it to Stanislas. And you're done. They said they'd have the money in the gallery account in an hour. I'll wire it into your mother's. But once we have the funds, you can deliver it." Wire transfers usually took longer, but not for Vladimir.

"I'll be at the dock at the hotel at five. I'll help my mother unbolt it from the wall this afternoon." All the paintings were heavily secured to prevent theft and to satisfy their insurance company, since the house was a public place because of the restaurant. The ones in his father's studio were less secure, but no one went there except his mother, since she lived there, and they had installed an alarm there years before. They were never cavalier about his father's work.

"I'll confirm to you as soon as we get the funds in the account, but I don't think there will be a problem. Stanislas must be made of money," Gabriel said, still amazed at the price he had paid for Lorenzo's work. But clearly when he wanted something, Vladimir was willing to go to any lengths to get it.

"It looks that way," Theo said, sounding a little grim. Even the incredible sale didn't make him like the man any better. Everything about him was distasteful to Theo. He was all about possessing what he wanted, people, industries, and things. Theo wondered how the beautiful young woman felt, being one of his possessions. He hated the thought of it, she had such gentle eyes in her lovely face, and he had liked talking to her. He would like to catch a glimpse of her on the boat when he delivered the painting, but doubted he would. And he would be treated like a delivery boy, and dismissed the moment the painting left his hands. He expected it. They had no way of knowing he was Lorenzo's son, and he didn't want them to. It was none of their business, and would have been out of character for Theo to introduce himself that way. He never did.

Theo was on the dock just below the Eden Roc at the Hôtel du Cap, promptly at five. The painting had been carefully wrapped in art paper, then in a soft fabric, and after that in bubble wrap and a heavy plastic wrapping to protect it on the trip to the boat. Theo was holding it as the tender approached. The sailors from **Princess Marina** saw him immediately, carefully took the painting from him, helped him jump aboard, covered the wrapped painting with a tarp, and then they took off at high speed across the water toward the yacht. He was asked to wait in a holding area, with the painting. Then the purser came to meet him with a security guard, and led him into an elevator. They treated him respectfully, but his mission was simple and clear: to hand over the painting to a designated person, whose identity he didn't know. And at that price, it would only be Stanislas himself, who wanted the pleasure of

receiving what he now owned and had paid a fortune for.

Theo stepped out on a deck high up in the boat
and saw an enormous bar, and a woman seated on
a couch in shorts and a T-shirt. Her long blond
hair was piled on top of her head, informally,
and Vladimir was nowhere to be seen, as Natasha
stood up and walked toward him on bare feet.

"Thank you for bringing the painting." She
smiled easily at him, and recognized him from
the restaurant the night before, even without his
suit. He was wearing shorts and a T-shirt too, and
had left his shoes downstairs in a basket when he
came aboard the boat. "Vladimir said someone
would deliver it. It was nice of you to come." He
noticed her Russian accent again, but her French
was excellent. She had no idea what Vladimir had
paid for it, and how normal it was that someone would carry it to the boat. She assumed Theo
was the maître d' at the restaurant, acting as messenger and delivery boy now. She took the painting from him officially, handed it to the security
guard, and told him to lock it in Mr. Stanislas's
office, per Vladimir's instructions. He had sent
an email advising them of delivery instructions.
She was polite to Theo, and turned to him with a
warm smile. "I guess Vladimir was right when he
said that everything has a price," she said with a
shy glance at Theo. "He usually is."

"Not everything. But in this case, selling it was

the right thing to do for all concerned," Theo said seriously. Vladimir hadn't bested them, or taken advantage of them, he had offered a fantastic price and a very good deal, and Theo was cognizant of it, whether he liked the man or not.

"He's very pleased," she said quietly. "And the painting is beautiful." She remembered it perfectly from the night before, and had known which one Vladimir wanted.

"Where will you hang it?" Theo asked her, wondering if they would take it to Russia, London, or somewhere else. He liked knowing where his father's paintings went, the rare times they were sold. The one purchased at Christie's seven years before had gone to an important collector in Brazil.

"Probably on the boat," she answered. "All our favorite art is here. The apartment in Moscow is very modern and stark. We have some Jackson Pollocks there, and Calders. And Old Masters in London. We don't have much in the house in St. Jean Cap-Ferrat yet, and we seldom use it. We keep the art we love best on the boat, so we see it more often." And it was more secure there under constant surveillance.

And then she thought of something, and guessed it might be nice for him. "Would you like a tour of the boat, as long as you're here?" If it meant leaving her presence, and roaming the huge yacht with a deckhand or even an officer, he didn't want to. He would rather talk to her for a few more minutes, especially since Vladimir was obviously not there, or he would have received the painting himself. He was about to decline the offer, when she suggested taking him around herself. She looked like a young girl as she led him inside the boat, and down the grand staircase. Theo followed her in fascination. She was far more intriguing than the boat, and completely unaware of how taken with her he was.

He couldn't keep his eyes off her as she took him through the engine room, the galley, the food-freezing units, the spa, the enormous gym fully equipped with every kind of machine, and the ballet studio with an exercise barre. There was a hair salon, a racquetball court, outdoor and indoor swimming pools, a huge hot tub, a bar in some form on every floor, a dining room that would seat forty people, and an outdoor dining room just as large that they used every day. There were leather floors and walls that had been installed by Hermès, incredible wood paneling, gorgeous furniture, and mind-boggling art. He counted six Picassos on their tour, and now his father's work would be part of their permanent collection, and Theo was proud of that.

Theo noticed at least a dozen staterooms, and living quarters for the seventy-five crew members she said lived and worked onboard. Four full-time chefs, and twenty sous-chefs. He was startled to see an entire cold room where a full-time florist worked, making arrangements for every room on the boat. They had their own fire department, a huge room for all the security guards, a gigantic laundry and dry cleaning facility, a luggage room for all their bags, and another where all the uniforms for the crew were kept and dispensed, with three attendants. There were different uniforms for every job and rank.

She showed him a movie theater that could accommodate fifty, with large comfortable chairs that swiveled, and several locked rooms she didn't explain to him. He wondered if weaponry was involved since one was next to the security guards' position. It seemed obvious to him that a man as rich and powerful as Vladimir would have arms on the boat to protect him. And they ended up at the wheelhouse, where the captain and several officers were talking amiably in front of radar screens and state-of-the-art computers and electronic equipment. The captain was British, as were most of the officers, but Theo had noticed that there were many Russian crew members too, and all the security guards were Russian. There were deckhands from Russia, the Philippines, Australia, and New Zealand. The kitchen staff was all Italian. And he heard a veritable United Nations of languages spoken, from French to Chinese, as they walked through, though mostly Russian.

Natasha greeted all of them as though she knew

them, and they were polite and respectful to her. She clearly had an important position. She wasn't just some bimbo or pretty face brought on to entertain Vladimir. He was the lord and master here, but she was the lady of the house, and it was obvious that they liked her, with her gentle ways. She didn't show off as she took him around, or put on airs. She was simple and casual, and acted like an ordinary person. When they got back to the outdoor bar where the tour had started, she offered him champagne. He accepted but didn't know what to say. He had never seen anything like it, and it had taken them nearly an hour to tour the gigantic boat. It was as intricate and complete as a cruise ship, but so much more beautiful. And every single thing in it was of the finest quality, from the art to the fabrics, the furniture, and the priceless objects scattered around as part of the décor. Vladimir had an eye for beauty in all things. And Natasha was proof of that as well. Theo couldn't help wondering what it was like to live in his exalted world and be part of such a dazzling machine.

"It really is incredible, and even bigger than it looks from onshore," he said admiringly as he accepted the glass of champagne she handed him.

"Yes, it is," she agreed. "Do you like boats?" she asked, curious about him too, and he laughed as he answered.

"I do, but I've never been on one this big." It

was an entirely self-contained world, almost like a city. And she hadn't taken him to their suite, or Vladimir's office, which were never part of any tour, but she had shown him everything else. And he noticed that the security guards had disappeared once the painting had been delivered. They hadn't brought any guards to the restaurant either, which surprised him. He imagined that for a man as rich as Vladimir, security must be a constant issue, but he didn't comment on it. "Thank you for the tour," he said as they sat down on the couch, and looked at the coastline quietly for a minute. He liked being there with her. She seemed like a sweet person, and when he looked into her eyes, they were wide open and clear, and she looked intrigued by him too.

Neither of them spoke for a long moment, as he felt himself being inexorably drawn to her, and for an insane moment, he wondered what would happen if he kissed her. He would probably be grabbed by a dozen bodyguards and thrown overboard, or maybe killed, he mused to himself, and then laughed at the insane fantasy. She smiled at him as though she could read his thoughts, and what attracted him to her most was that while she was sensual and beautiful, there was nothing vulgar or overtly sexy about her. She was the most delicate woman he had ever seen, and she seemed innocent somehow, as though she wasn't really part of any of this, and yet she was, and lived with the man who had created it and could afford to pay for it, and four other boats, and several houses that were just as legendary. He wanted to ask her what it was like to live like this, but didn't dare. They finished their champagne quietly, and then she stood up. She seemed more relaxed than she had the night before, and was clearly at home on the enormous boat, with an army of crew members around her to meet her every need.

She walked him to the lower deck, and smiled at him as he got into the tender. The sailors onboard were already gunning the engines, ready to take off, as he wondered if he would ever see her again, and doubted that he would. Even if she came to the restaurant, he wouldn't be there—he would be at home painting in his studio. And then she thought of something right before he left.

"I forgot to ask your name." She looked like a child as she smiled at him. They had spent nearly two hours together without introduction.

"Theo."

"Natasha," she said, sounding very Russian. "Goodbye, Theo. Thank you." He didn't know it, but she was thanking him for two hours as a normal person, talking about ordinary things, even as they toured Vladimir's boat. She never got to spend time with people like him, and had given up the opportunity to ever do that when she became Vladimir's mistress. She lived in the lofty isolation of his universe now, and renounced mundane pursuits like coffee or drinks or even lunch with a friend, or laughing about silly, unimportant things. She lived in the shadows of Vladimir's life, far from the nightmare of her youth but also far from an everyday life. She was like a precious jewel being kept in a safe and was rarely out in public.

She waved as the tender pulled away, and ran back upstairs on light feet. She stood at the rail, and watched the tender speed back to the dock at the hotel, and he turned to look at her, and saw her like a speck at the rail, her hair flying in the breeze, as they took distance from the yacht and approached the shore. And then at last she walked away from the rail, and he couldn't see her anymore. All he had left was the memory of two hours in her company, a memory he was sure he would cherish forever.

On the drive back to his studio, after assuring Gabriel and his mother that the painting had been delivered, he decided to stop and visit Chloe. Part of him didn't want to see anyone after spending two hours with Natasha. He didn't want anything to spoil it, or intrude on his mental vision of her. And another part of him wanted to reenter reality and get both feet on terra firma again. His mother had been somewhat right—women like Natasha were fatally attractive and totally unattainable. He needed to touch a real woman now. One who wasn't out of his reach. And Chloe seemed like a simple solution.

He pulled up in front of her house, and walked into her studio. She was drinking a glass of wine, and had just finished work for the day. She was completing some commercial canvases that she had promised to a bath shop in St. Tropez. She turned in surprise when he walked in.

"What are you doing here?" she asked, not sounding entirely welcoming. She was still annoyed by his call the night before.

"I just delivered a painting of my father's to one of the big Russian yachts."

"I thought your mother didn't sell them," she said, waving him to a chair, but she made no move to kiss him.

"She usually doesn't, but made an exception for this one." Chloe could guess easily that the Russian must have paid a fortune for it, or his mother wouldn't have sold it. It irritated Chloe at times how uninterested he was in material comforts. But he didn't need to be—his father had left him a huge fortune. She had been struggling for years, trying to make ends meet, and she was tired of it. She was ready to settle down, stop working, and have someone pay her bills. And his lack of interest in commitment had been aggravating her and made her irritable with him. She hadn't been satisfied with the relationship they'd had for several months.

"I'm always impressed by the women who hang out with those Russians. They must be real pros in bed, for the men to spend money on them the way they do. Couture clothes, incredible jewels, furs, art. I see a lot of that stuff come up at auction, when I go to Drouot in Paris. Those girls really know how to work a guy and make their bodies pay off." He felt sick as he listened to her, and thought of Natasha, who was a far cry from what she was describing. He couldn't see her in that light and didn't want to.

"I think there's a big difference between the hookers they hire, and the women they live with, their mistresses," Theo said in quiet defense of them.

"Not really," Chloe said confidently. "Maybe the mistresses just do it better. They're the elite. But they sure know how to make a guy pay his dues." Her views on relationships made his skin crawl, as he looked at her, feeling as though he were seeing a stranger, someone he didn't want to meet.

"Is that what it's all about? 'Making a guy pay his dues'? Forgive me, maybe I'm an idealist, but does love fit anywhere into that picture?" His parents had adored each other, and their love affair had started when his father was dirt poor. He liked that model a lot better than the one she was describing, and obviously looking for. She had gotten more direct about it recently.

"Probably not for those girls. And let's face it, marriage is probably just a better version of the same idea. You give up your life for a guy, service him forever until you can't stand each other's bodies anymore, and he takes care of you. What's wrong with that? At least I'm honest about it. And so are those Russian girls, and the guys they're with know what they're buying. You play, you pay, and if a girl knows how to operate the machinery, she gets a lot more. Take a good look at those Russian girls. They know what they're doing." He felt as though she were insulting Natasha when she said it, and there was something so pure about her. Vladimir might be supporting her, and surely was, but she looked like a woman with a heart and soul. Chloe made all relationships between men and women sound like prostitution. He stood up after he had listened to her for as long as he could stand to. He had dropped by to take her to dinner, and hopefully go to bed with her, but it was suddenly the last thing he wanted, and all he wanted to do was run out the door.

"You've got a very materialistic view of marriage," he said, looking down at her, sitting on the couch, holding her glass of wine. She had a nice body, and knew how to use it, and now he realized why. She was using it as a bargaining tool, hoping he would marry her and pay her bills. She had never made it quite this clear before.

"My father didn't leave me a lot of money like yours did," she said bluntly. "I can't hide in my ivory tower, perfecting my brushstrokes. I have to be more practical than you do. And if playing my body like a harp makes you want to marry me, and support me, what's so wrong with that?" She had no idea how she sounded, and didn't care.

"Because playing your body like a harp isn't enough," he said honestly.

"You thought so last night when you tried to come by to get laid when you left your mother's restaurant." He couldn't remember her being as openly venal as this before, but the months they had spent together hadn't been fruitful for her. He wasn't in love with her, he didn't want to marry her and never would. And she was angry that things hadn't turned out as she had hoped since the beginning, when she found out who his father was. She thought she had hit a gold mine when she met him, and instead he wanted to live as if he were a starving artist, and become an important painter like his father, and she wasn't getting any younger. And she was turning out to be precisely the kind of woman he went to great lengths to avoid.

"I still have this crazy idea that I want to fall in love with someone before I spend the rest of my life with them, or pay their bills, as you put it. I didn't realize the bills were such an essential part of the deal on the way in. I'd like to think that a woman could fall in love with me, before she falls for my wallet."

"It's all part of the same picture," Chloe said cynically.

"So why don't you go after one of the big Russians? There are plenty of them around here." He sounded angry as he said it.

"They only go for their own. Have you ever seen one of those major Russian guys with a French mistress? Or even a French date? They only date Russian girls. They stick to what they know." He had never thought about it before, but she was right. The Russian men he had seen at his mother's restaurant always had Russian girls with them. And Natasha proved the rule. "Those girls must know something we don't."

"Maybe you could take lessons from them," he said, disappointed. He hadn't fallen in love with her, but he had liked her for a while. Now he couldn't stand what he was hearing. She had never been this honest with him before.

"Maybe I need some practice," she said, smiling at him. He had disappointed her too, and hadn't spent enough time with her or made a commitment, but she was willing to overlook it, for a night at least. "Want to go to bed?" She took all the romance and seduction out of it. And he had gone to see her with that intention, but suddenly it was the last thing he wanted.

"Actually, I don't. I think you just summed it up pretty well. You're looking for a guy to pay your bills, long term, in exchange for sex and your other talents. And I'm not looking for marriage, but I still have these childlike illusions about being in love with the woman I'm with, if I'm going to stick around long term. I think we've exhausted the possibilities here, and we both need to move on." She was startled when he said it, as he stood at the door and turned to look at her. "Good luck, Chloe, I'm sure you'll find the guy you're looking for."

"I thought you might be it for a while," she said softly, and then shrugged.

"I'm not." He looked relieved as he took one step out the door.

"I know. I figured that out for myself," she said coldly.

"Russian lessons, maybe?" he said in a slightly cynical tone. She had all the makings of a gold digger and had finally tipped her hand. He hadn't seen it before. She had played a better game at first.

She didn't answer, and he walked out, and all she saw as she watched him go was the gold mine he represented, slipping through her fingers, again. She wasn't sure why, but it always went wrong.

She threw her empty wineglass at the wall, and started to cry when it broke.

And all Theo wanted to do was go home. She made him feel unclean somehow, as though it were all about a trade of sex for money. There had to be something more meaningful than that. He thought of Natasha then, and she was exactly what Chloe was talking about and aspired to, but Natasha wasn't crass or cheap and didn't seem like a gold digger, even though she was a kept woman. She seemed like a nice girl, and talking to her had been so easy and light and fun.

He walked into his studio the minute he got home, and stood there looking lost for a moment. He knew what he had to do, and felt compelled to, although he knew he shouldn't. He couldn't stop himself—it was a force more powerful than he was. He picked up the blank canvas he had pulled out the night before, and set it on his easel. He knew the only way to get her out of his mind was to paint her. He didn't even lay the groundwork with a sketch before he started painting her in oil. He didn't need to. She was seared into his memory, and he could see her face as though she were standing before him. He could see her laugh when he said something to her, and her wistful smile as the tender pulled away from the boat, taking him away from her. He could hear the way she pronounced her name when she said it. Natasha . . . Natasha . . . the sway of her hips, when he followed her down the stairs, the way her hair flew in the wind, when she stood watching him from the rail . . . she filled every inch of his mind and electrified his body as he started painting her, and within a short time he could see her emerge from the mists on the canvas . . . Natasha . . . she had bewitched him body and soul . . . he felt possessed as he continued painting her in a frenzy until dawn. He didn't know or care what time it was, just so he could be near her. Her eyes were already looking deep into his by then.

Chapter 4

Vladimir landed back on the boat three days after Theo had delivered the painting. He asked to see it moments after he came onboard and sent one of his security guards to get it from his office. He unwrapped it carefully, and slowly unveiled it, as Natasha watched. He hadn't asked who had delivered it, which was immaterial and didn't even occur to him, so she had nothing to explain. She never had guests onboard, so the time she had spent with Theo was unusual, but there had been no harm in it. It was just a tiny slice of a "normal" life she had never had and never would, and had willingly given up to be with Vladimir. It was fun just tasting it for an instant, talking to someone close to her own age, who wanted nothing from her. She had so little contact with anyone beyond Vladimir's world. In lieu of friends, she had Vladimir. And she had no regrets about it. But it had been nice talking to Theo about art and life, and showing him the boat, like two kids exploring each other's homes, although she had a sense that Vladimir wouldn't like it. He saw no need for her to talk to anyone but him. She wondered where and how Theo lived—probably in a small apartment somewhere, or a room, with his job at the restaurant. She didn't know people like him. Theo was the first man she had actually talked to in years, other than Vladimir, or without his being present and watching her closely. And she could only have conversations with Vladimir when he was in the mood and on the subjects he chose. Her conversation with Theo had felt so open and free, although she knew nothing about him.

The painting was even more beautiful than Vladimir and Natasha remembered, and he was delighted with the purchase, particularly since Lorenzo Luca's work was so rare. It had been a major coup to acquire it, and knowing him so well, Natasha wasn't surprised he had. He could convince anyone of anything once he decided that he wanted something. He never relented until he had the desired object in hand, and now he did. Not unlike the determined way he had pursued her, and won her in the end. It was his way.

They had dinner on deck that night, and she could tell that he was pleased with his time away. He was in a festive mood, and they chose a spot for the new painting in their bedroom, and moved a Picasso into the hall. And then they went back on deck. He had told her that they were moving the boat that night. He had told the captain to go to St. Tropez.

"You can shop for a day. I thought we'd go to Sardinia after that. We haven't been for a while. There's a mistral coming at the end of the week. We can outrun it before it hits and stay there." There was a spot in Porto Cervo just outside the port where he liked to anchor. They were too big to go in, which was the case everywhere they went. And he knew she liked to stop in Porto-fino on the way. They were all familiar places to both of them. They went to Croatia, Turkey, and Greece at times too, and Capri. Venice was one of her favorite spots and big enough for them to anchor comfortably, with a perfect view of the churches and the square. She was excited to go to St. Tropez and Sardinia, and she didn't mind if the crossing to Sardinia was rough. She was a good sailor, and had been in storms with him before. She never got seasick, and sometimes had better sea legs than the crew.

They set sail around two A.M., once she and Vladimir were in bed and asleep after they made love. And when they woke up in the morning, they were anchored outside the port of St. Tropez. She went shopping that morning, with two deckhands with her to carry her purchases, and she met Vladimir for lunch at Le Club 55, which she always enjoyed. She had bought some bathing suits at Eres, and a white summer bag at Hermès, and had fun wandering in and out of the shops.

The streets were already crowded. It was the weekend, and even though it was early June, the season had begun. In July and August, the crowds would make it unbearable, but for now it was still easy to get around. And Vladimir wandered through the town with her after lunch, and then they went back to the boat, and pulled out, so they could swim. They started toward Sardinia at dusk. They were going to stop in Portofino in the morning, for more shopping, and then head south to Corsica, and Sardinia after that. It was a route they both knew well.

As Natasha lay on the deck after she swam, and they picked up speed, she watched the wake behind them and looked at Vladimir, asleep in the sun. She was grateful for her life with him. It was like life in a bubble, alone with him, on his terms. She felt safe there with him. She knew that there were risks involved with his work, which was why he had bodyguards, but he kept all that well away from her. She was like an innocent child, in his shadow, which was the impression Theo had had of her as well. There was nothing conniving about her, or manipulative. She just existed like a bright flower to cheer Vladimir when he wanted to talk to her, or make love to her, or take her somewhere to show her off.

The only thing she really missed was the opportunity to learn more, and she would have loved to go to a school, or take classes at a museum to study art. But there was no time for her to do so, given how he lived. Vladimir traveled a lot, and took her with him at the drop of a hat. He would tell her to pack, and they would leave to go to one of his homes, or to the boat. And he always objected whenever she mentioned taking classes, and told her she already knew all she needed to know for him. He saw no reason for her to learn more, other than by reading books or going on the Internet, which she already did. He had no degrees and had barely gone to school, and thought education superfluous, particularly for her. Her job was to entertain him in all the ways she already did so well. She was like a geisha of sorts, without the restrictive old-fashioned traditions, but the concept was the same. And in some ways, she was proud that she had kept him happy for so long, still interested him, and satisfied him. And as far as Vladimir was concerned, all she needed to do was please him. And she didn't need to go to school for that.

Vladimir made a comment to her at dinner, once they were under way to Sardinia. The boat was so large that it was steady even while moving at full speed, and it had stabilizers. It was pleasant dining outside in the gentle breeze, as two stewardesses and the chief steward served their dinner.

"Why did you give the delivery boy a tour of the boat when he brought the painting?" He looked at her steadily, his eyes boring into hers, and her heart skipped a beat. She felt suddenly guilty, although she had done nothing wrong. But she had enjoyed Theo's company, and he had been onboard talking to her for two hours. She wondered if Vladimir knew that too, or that she had offered him champagne. There were no secrets from Vladimir. But her beautiful face was a portrait of innocence when she answered.

"It wasn't a delivery boy. It was the maître d' from the restaurant who brought it. He was fascinated by the boat, so I took him around before he left."

"Were you afraid to tell me?" His eyes dug deeper into hers, but she didn't react, although her heart was beating faster. He had made his point. He knew everything she did, and everything that went on. He had the ultimate control.

"Of course not. I didn't think it was important. I was just being polite. I think he was hoping to see you." Natasha always knew what to say to put him at ease, and she looked uninterested in the subject, although she had enjoyed the two hours she'd spent with Theo, which didn't show in her face now.

"You should have sent him with the purser, if he wanted a tour of the boat," Vladimir corrected her gently.

"I think he was onshore. I had nothing else to do, and I was excited about the painting." She smiled at him, and he leaned over and kissed her hard on the mouth. He said nothing more about it, he had said all he needed to, and the kiss reminded her that he owned her. Natasha got the message loud and clear. She always did, and lived accordingly. Her two hours with Theo had been a momentary slip she wouldn't do again. She knew better than to upset Vladimir.

Theo had been working on the painting of Natasha for days, barely taking time to eat or sleep. He was driven and felt compelled to stay with it until he captured her, which proved to be harder than he thought. There was something elusive about her that he kept wrestling with, and finally realized it was something in her expression, or her eyes. There was too much about her he didn't know, and yet she had hooked him to his very soul. And there was no one he dared confess it to, for fear that they would think he was crazy to be obsessed by another man's mistress, and even worse that it was Vladimir's. There was no way he could compete with that, and he was sure Natasha wouldn't want him to. She seemed content where she was.

He was sitting in his kitchen, lost in thought and eating a stale sandwich. It was the first meal he had eaten in two days, and he looked crazed, his cheeks covered in beard stubble, his hair a tangled mass, his eyes vague as he thought about the painting. He didn't even hear his friend Marc walk in. They had gone to the Beaux-Arts together, and known each other since they were boys. Marc was a sculptor, and had only recently moved back from Italy. He worked in marble, and had gone to work in a quarry to better understand the stone. He was a talented artist and barely made enough to live. He worked for a company that made tombstones when he needed money to pay his rent or eat.

"Oh my God, what happened to you? You look like you've been shipwrecked. Are you sick?" Marc had flaming red hair and freckles all over his face. He was tall and thin, and still looked about sixteen years old, although he was thirty-one, a year older than Theo. He had a fatal weakness for needy women and was always giving them the little money he had, and was constantly broke, but didn't seem to care.

"I think I am sick," Theo said in response to his question. "Or maybe I just lost my mind." Marc sat down at the kitchen table across from him, took a bite of the other half of the sandwich, and made a face.

"Where did they find that? In an archaeological dig? It must date back to King Tut. Do you have anything decent to eat here?" Theo shook his head with a grin.

"I haven't stopped to eat."

"No wonder you're nuts. Are you out of money? Do you need a loan?" Although he needed it more than most, Marc was his only friend who never borrowed money from him. He made enough to just squeak by, and their friendship was based on the bonds of childhood, not on who Theo was, which made him a trusted friend. "What are you working on that has you looking like that?"

"A portrait of a woman. I can't get her out of my head."

"A new romance?" The fiery redhead was intrigued. "What happened to Chloe?"

"We broke up. She wants a guy to pay her bills, which is her interpretation of romance. It seems so depressing to me. She wants to trade her body for a guy to pay her rent." Marc looked thoughtful for a minute, pondering what Theo had said.

"She has a hell of a great body. How high is her rent?"

"Never mind. You need a woman with a heart, not a human calculator to have sex with. She's not a lot of fun, and she complains all the time." He hadn't missed her for a minute since he walked out of her house. And he'd been working on the portrait of Natasha ever since.

"So who's the hot new romance?" He looked more intrigued.

"I don't have one. She's my fantasy life dragging me through hell."

"No wonder you look like shit. A figment of your imagination?"

"Sort of. She exists, but belongs to someone else. She's a Russian guy's mistress I saw at my mother's restaurant. Beautiful girl. She's in slavery to the man she lives with, who's twice her age and keeps her locked up on his yacht."

"A rich Russian guy?" Marc asked with interest. He met all his women in local bars. Theo's fantasy woman sounded far more exotic, and way out of his reach.

"A very rich Russian guy. Possibly the richest, or one of them. He owns Russia or something like that. He's got seventy-five crew on his boat." Marc whistled at the image Theo had created.

"Are you sleeping with her? A guy who owns Russia might kill you for something like that." Theo laughed at the thought.

"I'm sure he would. I've seen her twice in my life, and may never lay eyes on her again. All I know is her name."

"And you're in love with her?"

"I don't know what I am. I'm obsessed. I'm trying to paint her, and I can't get it right."

"Why do you need to? Just make it up."

"I'll probably never see her again, except in the portrait I paint. I feel driven to paint her. I can't get her out of my head."

"This sounds very bad. Is she obsessed with you too?"

"Of course not. She's perfectly happy with her Russian. Why wouldn't she be? She's Russian too, by the way."

"You're screwed. It doesn't sound like you have a chance. You could always kidnap her, or stow away on the boat." They both laughed at that. "What got you so wound up about her?"

"I don't know. Maybe the fact that she's completely unattainable. She's so damn nice, and she looks like a prisoner when she's with him. He owns her, like an object he uses to show off."

"Does she look miserable with him?"

"No, she doesn't," Theo said honestly. "I guess I'm just crazy to be thinking about her. She's completely inaccessible."

"This doesn't sound like a good situation. Can I look at the painting?"

"It's a mess, and the eyes are all wrong, I've been working on them for two days." Marc wandered into the studio, and glanced at the painting on the easel, and then stopped and stared at it for a long time. "See what I mean?" Theo had followed him in, and Marc turned to stare at him.

"This is your best painting ever. Something about it just reaches into my guts and turns my heart upside down. She's the most beautiful woman I've ever seen." The portrait was unfinished, but the most important elements were already there. The woman in the painting had a soul, and Marc could see it too. "Are you sure there's no way to get to her? Maybe she's obsessed with you too."

"Why would she be? She doesn't know who I am, or even that I'm an artist. She knows nothing about me. She thinks I'm a headwaiter at my mother's restaurant, or some kind of delivery boy. I dropped off a painting to her. We talked for two hours, and I left."

"One of your paintings?" Marc asked with interest.

"No, my father's. My mother sold it to the woman's boyfriend. I dropped it off. He wasn't there, so we had a chance to talk for a while and tour the boat."

"I can't even imagine the price you got for it. I can't believe your mother sold one. He must have paid a fortune."

"He did," Theo confirmed.

"Well, I don't care if you see her again or not. You have to finish the piece—it's a major tour de force. I really think it's your best work yet. Go on suffering with it, it's worth it."

"Thank you." Theo looked warmly at his friend.

"Do you want to go get something to eat?"

Theo shook his head. "I think I'll get back to work. You've encouraged me not to give up."

Marc left a little while later, and came back in half an hour with some bread and cheese and a couple of peaches and an apple, so he'd have something to eat. It was the kind of friend that Marc was, and they were always critical of each other's work, and painfully honest, so for him to say it was the best piece Theo had ever done meant a lot. Theo went back to work on the portrait, and painted straight through the night. He fell asleep as the sun came up, lying on the floor of his studio, gazing up at what he'd done. He was smiling. He had finally gotten the eyes right, and she was smiling down at him from the portrait. It was the face he remembered so perfectly, smiling at him, as the tender pulled away.

The mistral, a fierce northerly Mediterranean wind that usually blew for three days, hit **Princess Marina** as they came down the coast of Corsica and went through the straits of Bonifacio. And even the huge boat was pitching and rolling in the heavy seas. Natasha always said she liked it when the sea was rough, and felt like a baby being rocked in a cradle when she woke to the rocking, although many of the crew members were sick. It calmed when they got close to Porto Cervo and threw anchor as near the port as they dared, but Natasha knew from experience it would blow for several days, which didn't bother her. She still wanted to ride into port in the tender and have a look around. She liked shopping there, there were several art galleries, some jewelers, all the important Italian designer brands, and a furrier where she had found coats she liked before.

"Are you sure you want to go in?" Vladimir asked her when she was getting ready. The sea was rough, the tender would bounce all over on the short trip into port, and she'd get soaked. She was fearless about bad weather and heavy seas, and she knew she was in no danger in their tender and didn't care if she got wet. The deckhands always admired her for what a good sailor she was.

"I'll be fine," she reassured Vladimir, and there were three of their sailors in the boat when she got in. Vladimir didn't go with her. He had work to do. And he didn't enjoy shopping as much as she did, except for major purchases like jewelry or haute couture, but she could manage the ordinary shops alone. He didn't need to be with her to buy a new pair of sandals, or a handbag at Prada, and she had a credit card that was designated to her on one of his accounts. He never cared how much she spent, and she was reasonable when she shopped on her own. Vladimir spent far more money on her than she ever did on herself.

The tender bobbed around like a cork in the water as Natasha hopped out onto the quai, and a crew member followed her in case she needed help carrying shopping bags on the way back. She made her way through several stores and was trying on a bright pink fur coat at the furrier where she'd been before, when the first officer from the boat appeared with three of their security guards at his side.

"Mr. Stanislas would like you back on the boat," the first officer said seriously, and Natasha looked surprised.

"Now? Is something wrong? Is he ill? I haven't finished shopping yet." And she didn't want to go back. She was having fun. She had nothing to do on the boat, and they couldn't go out swimming in the high winds and rough seas.

"He appears to be fine," the officer said stiffly. He had had his orders directly from Vladimir, and didn't want to have to explain to him that Natasha had refused to come back, but she didn't see why she had to rush. They weren't going anywhere in the mistral.

"Tell him I'll be back in an hour," she said with a smile. She was still wearing the pink fur coat, and wanted to take a serious look at it again.

"I believe Mr. Stanislas wants you to come back **now,**" he said with emphasis and worried eyes.

"I won't be long." She smiled at him and took another look at herself with the coat. She was concerned it was too bright and Vladimir might not like it, but it was fun and she could see herself wearing it with jeans or over a black dress. She took it off and tried another more traditional one while he conferred with the three bodyguards outside. She could see that they were radioing the boat. And a moment later, he walked into the shop again, carrying his cellphone, and told her Mr. Stanislas was on the phone. She took it from him with a smile, and joked with Vladimir when she heard him at the other end.

"I promise I won't spend all your money. I just want a little longer to look around. The shops are so nice here, better than St. Tropez."

"Get back here **now.** When I give you an order, you are to obey my commands." He had never spoken to her that way before, and she was stunned.

"What's happening? Why are you upset?"

"I don't owe you explanations. Get back to the tender immediately, or I'll have them carry you out of the store." With a shocked look, she thanked the woman for showing her the fur coats, and left the shop. She noticed that the guards were walking unusually close to her, and the first officer was directly in front of her. Clearly something was happening, but she had no idea what.

She got into the tender at the quai a few minutes later, and there were four security guards waiting for her. The boat was heavier in the water, and lower. She was soaking wet when she walked up the swaying ladder to reach the deck. There were security men lined up along the rail, and five of them followed her inside. It looked like their full complement was out, and there were four more with Vladimir when she found him in his office.

He was on the phone and hung up as soon as she walked in, dripping water on a priceless Persian carpet. He nodded, and the security guards left the room.

"What's going on?" she asked as she tried to kiss him, and he brushed her off. He seemed distracted and upset.

He hesitated for a moment and then looked at her. There was something rock hard in his eyes, and a fury she had seen there only once or twice, but never directed at her. And she could see now that he wasn't angry at her, but at someone else.

"I'm not going to tell you a lot about it. But I made a very large deal in Moscow in the last week. It has to do with a segment of the mineral industry, and very important territory was awarded to me by the president of Russia. There were three contenders for the land I was allowed to buy. Myself, and two others. I was awarded the land and the mineral rights fairly, and paid a very large sum of money for it. The two men who were in competition with me were murdered this morning, along with their female companions, and one with his oldest son who was in the business with him. And there was an assassination attempt on the president half an hour ago. Whoever is unhappy about this deal means business. We believe we know who it is. It looks like random acts of terrorism, but I think it's more specific than that. You're in danger, Natasha, because of me." He said it clearly and simply and didn't beat around the bush. He had never explained as much about his business as he just had. "We have a protective system here on the boat, and all the weapons and guards we need to keep us safe, but I don't want you outdoors at the moment, anywhere on deck, or going ashore. And as soon as the wind dies down, we'll pull up anchor and go somewhere else. But right now, I want you to do exactly as I say. I don't want you to get killed." She didn't like the sound of the situation, and she looked frightened as she listened. She had never seen him look so intense. "Do you understand?"

"Yes, I do," she said softly. She had never before felt at risk. Whatever business he engaged in, it had nothing to do with her. This time, it did. If the female companions of the other two men had been assassinated, they would be gunning for her too. For the very first time, she knew that her life was in danger because of him.

"I want you out of sight for the next few days. We're moving to an inside cabin, so there will be no portholes where they can see you. But the electronic devices our enemies use are so sophisticated that they can find you just about anywhere. Hopefully, the Russian intelligence services will find them soon." His eyes were icier than she had ever seen them, and she could tell that he meant business. She wondered if he was frightened too. But he looked angry more than afraid.

For the next few days, they remained confined in an inside cabin, and moved around the boat very little. There were two bodyguards with them inside the room, several lining the halls, and a full commando team on deck. The helicopters were being protected, and she overheard that their missile system had been armed, and all the guards were carrying machine guns. She felt as though they had been transported to a war zone, and it was terrifying knowing that she was a target too.

She was very quiet as she sat in the cabin reading, and glanced over at Vladimir occasionally. He was in constant contact with Russian intelligence and antiterrorist details, and finally after three days, he got a call at four in the morning. Vladimir said very little, and listened, and then spoke in Russian. His questions and responses were curt, but Natasha understood what it meant.

"How many? . . . Do you think that's all of them? . . . The answer to that is simple . . . kill them. **Now.** Don't wait." He listened again for several minutes, agreed with whoever he was talking to, and hung up. Natasha didn't dare ask him any questions, and in the dim light of their night lamp, Vladimir looked murderous as he lay in bed and thought about it. And then Natasha fell asleep. In the morning, the wind had finally died down, and she could feel that they were moving.

"Where are we going?" she asked Vladimir when he came back into the room. He had gotten up while she was asleep, and had been awake for hours. He looked more peaceful than he had the night before. But Natasha couldn't get the conversation she'd heard out of her head. He had given the order to have someone killed, probably the people who were after them, but it was upsetting nonetheless. She had never seen this side of him before.

"Back to Corsica, to stay out of the way for a little while, until everything calms down. The problem is over," he said quietly, "as of an hour ago, but it's always good to be sure. And after this we might go to Croatia, Turkey, or Greece. But we might not have to." He smiled at her then and seemed more like the man she knew, not the frightening stranger she had seen in the past few days. "No shopping for a while. I want you to stay on the boat." She nodded and went to put on white jeans and a T-shirt and one of the uniform windbreakers the female crew wore on the boat, with the insignia of **Princess Marina.** It had been a terrifying few days, while Natasha prayed that neither of them would be killed. It brought home to her just how high the stakes were in his new deal, and she wondered if a threat like this was likely to happen again, but she didn't dare ask him. She didn't want to upset him further.

Everything calmed down during the five days they spent in Corsica. Several of the crew members took her fishing, and she went swimming several times a day. Vladimir let her go sunbathing while he stayed in his office, in constant contact with intelligence services and the president of Russia, but a week after it had started, the problem was over.

Vladimir took her to Portofino, where they went shopping, and he took her to dinner onshore at a simple pasta restaurant in the port that she loved. They kept six bodyguards with them just in case, and she knew that they were armed. And then they went back to the boat. They had moved back into their cabin, and everything appeared normal except that their security guards were still carrying machine guns on the boat— just to be sure, Vladimir explained to her. "We're not in danger now." And she knew by then from what she'd overheard that five people in Russia had been killed in retaliation.

They floated around Portofino for a few days, and all the reports Vladimir got were good, and then they motored back to the South of France. It had been a frightening time. Ten people in all had been killed, the five victims and their five attackers. She was just grateful that she and Vladimir weren't among them. But she knew as they reached Antibes that she would never feel totally safe again.

Chapter 5

When Gabriel came back to the South of France, he had a surprise for Maylis. He had planned a little trip for them to one of their favorite cities. He wanted to take her to Florence for a week, before the restaurant got too busy during the summer and it got too hot in Italy. June seemed like the perfect month to travel. The only problem for her was that she needed Theo to agree to take her place at Da Lorenzo, and he seemed to be working very hard these days. She had hardly seen him.

She called Theo as soon as Gabriel told her about the trip, and left it up to him.

"I'm so sorry to do that to you, I know you hate standing in for me. But I'd feel bad telling Gabriel that I can't take the trip. Our trips together mean so much to him."

"They should mean a lot to you too," Theo

scolded her, and for once he didn't complain about working at the restaurant for a week. He was secretly hoping that Vladimir and Natasha would come in again. He said nothing about it to his mother, but he accepted willingly. His only caveat was that he was showing two of his paintings with a New York gallery, at the Masterpiece London art fair in late June. They wanted to include his work in their exhibit, although they didn't represent him, but they might want to in the future. And he wanted to be there to see how they hung his work and the rest of the fair, and make sure his work was well displayed. It was a new gallery for him. He hadn't signed a contract with them, but he was pleased to show his work with them.

"I promise we'll be back in time," Maylis said when he gave her the dates, and she was very grateful that he was willing to cover for her. And so was Gabriel when she told him the good news. She had bought him a beautiful gold watch at Cartier, to thank him for the painting sale he had negotiated, since he no longer took a commission, and he loved it. He loved everything that Maylis gave him, and as unaware as she sometimes was, singing Lorenzo's praises, she was nonetheless very generous with him. And Gabriel never complained when she talked about her late husband, since he had loved him too.

Gabriel went to visit Theo at his studio, and

immediately saw the portrait of Natasha on the easel. It was nearly finished, although Theo insisted he still had to add some final touches. It was a remarkable piece of work, and Gabriel concurred with Marc that it was one of his best.

"I think you're ready for a show in Paris," Gabriel said seriously. "In September, I want you to go and see the galleries I recommended to you. There's no reason to wait." Theo wasn't sure but said he'd think about it. He wanted to see how his work did at the London art fair first. "You should exhibit at the Biennale in Venice next year," Gabriel encouraged him, as he had done for his father so many years before. "You can't hide your light under a bushel forever. The world needs more artists like you, Theo. Don't deprive them of your work." It was a lovely thing to say, and he was such a nice man, brilliantly knowledgeable about the art world, and a far kinder person than Theo's father had ever been. Theo often reminded his mother how lucky they were to have him in their lives, and she agreed. Although it didn't stop her from extolling her late husband's virtues, many of which he'd never had, or her memory had exaggerated to an unreasonable degree. Lorenzo had been a great artist, but never a great man. Theo remembered it more clearly than she did, and Gabriel never said a word in criticism of him. He let Maylis have her fantasies about Lorenzo. He was happy with her, and other than always making him feel like second best, she was good to him too.

They left on their trip to Florence in high spirits, and Theo took over her place at the restaurant, greeting guests as they came in, and escorting them to their tables before turning them over to the maître d'. And each night he checked the reservation book, hoping to see Vladimir's name, but the week sped by, and he and Natasha never came in. He wondered if they were on the boat or someplace else, and had no way to know. And he feared that he'd been right, when he last saw her, that he'd never see her again. The portrait was almost finished, and the eyes were perfect now, and had the gentle expression he remembered so well. And her mouth was exactly as it looked, as though she was about to speak. Marc said that just from her portrait, he was falling in love with her too. Theo hadn't admitted to being in love with her, but acknowledged that he was obsessed, which he insisted was different, and even more uncomfortable than love would have been. But he spoke of his obsession to no one else, only his old friend. He wouldn't have dared admit it to his mother or she would have told him he was insane, and repeated her earlier warnings about not falling in love with the mistresses of fabulously rich Russian men.

Theo was happy to be relieved of duty at the restaurant when his mother and Gabriel returned.

And he worked on the portrait for a few more days before he left for London. There were several art fairs on at the same time, and he was staying at a small boutique hotel filled with artists and art dealers, and every conversation he heard around him, at the hotel, or on the street, or at the art fair, was about some aspect of art. And he was very pleased when he met the owners of the gallery in New York, whom he'd only corresponded with before, by email. They had hung both of his paintings prominently in their booth, and although he didn't like it, in his biography they had mentioned that he was the son of Lorenzo Luca. He hated riding on his father's coattails, but they were in the business of selling art, and it was a positive point for him, and one they wanted to capitalize on as best they could. But whoever's son he was, his work spoke for itself.

He was standing just outside their booth on the night of the opening, when he saw a man walk by who seemed familiar, and Theo realized instantly who it was. It was Vladimir, and Natasha was walking just behind him in a micromini black leather skirt, with a gray sweater that looked like it had been torn, and black high heels that showed off her legs. She looked spectacular, with her hair in a knot, and blond tendrils framing her face. She recognized Theo immediately and was surprised to see him there. Vladimir had already walked past without recognizing him.

"What are you doing here?" she asked, suddenly confused, as Vladimir turned around to look for her, and had no idea who she was talking to. "Are you an artist or just enjoying the fair?" As Theo answered, he could feel himself stumbling over his words.

"I have some work at the fair." He didn't indicate the two paintings that were in plain sight behind him.

"How interesting," Natasha said, looking excited about it, as Vladimir beckoned to her. There was a painting he wanted her to see several booths away. "It's good to see you," she said, hurrying away. Theo's heart started to pound as he watched her. He couldn't believe it, but every time he met her, she turned his world upside down. He was incapable of not reacting to her. It was as though they were joined by an electrical current that shot through him every time.

He caught a glimpse of her later, far down the same row. She didn't notice him, and they were leaving, with Vladimir carrying a painting he had bought. Theo was relieved that they hadn't shown an interest in him, picked up his bio, and discovered who his father was, which would have been embarrassing, since he'd been more or less masquerading as a headwaiter at the restaurant, and never admitted he was Lorenzo's son. Even when he talked to her for two hours on the boat, he hadn't told her. But at least she knew he was an artist now. The other thing she didn't know was that he had been working on a portrait of her night and day since they met, which would have been mortifying. She would have thought he was a lunatic or a pervert of some kind, a stalker. There was no way to explain his fascination with her, or the time he spent thinking about her and wishing he knew her, or the way he felt now, as though someone had ripped his heart out of his chest. He knew he had to get over her, but he had no idea how. Maybe time. Or he could make a career of painting portraits of her. The whole idea of it was ridiculous, and he was still thinking about her and how she had looked in the leather skirt, as he walked back to his hotel that night.

He was walking through the lobby with his head down, when he crashed into a young woman and almost knocked her over. She was coming out of the elevator, wearing military boots and a short red skirt, with dyed pink hair and a million-dollar smile. She was a pretty girl, although with what she was wearing, she looked a little like a clown, and he noticed that she had a diamond stud in her nose.

"Well, hello, you! Aren't you a sight for sore eyes? Going somewhere—like my room?" she said, eyeing him with a broad smile. He laughed at how bold she was. She was embarrassing but fun, and people around them smiled. "Would you like to go to a party with me?" she asked without hesitation—she was anything but shy. "Italians, Spaniards, a whole bunch of people from Berlin. Where are you from?" She had an aristocratic British accent, but said she lived in New York, since her family was unbearable.

"St. Paul de Vence," he answered, more than a little startled by her, "in the South of France."

"I know where it is, for heaven's sake. What planet do you think I'm from?" It was a good question, given how she looked. "I'm Emma, by the way." And suddenly he realized who she was. Lady Emma Beauchamp Montague. Her father was a viscount. She owned one of the most avant-garde galleries in Chelsea, in New York. He had read about her, but never met her before.

"Theo." He shook her hand, and she swept him along, and the next thing he knew, he was on the sidewalk, climbing into a cab with her, while she gave the driver a fashionable address, and turned to chat with Theo again. She talked a million miles an hour, and was very funny, and had him laughing uncontrollably by the time they got out of the cab. He had no idea what he was doing there, and found himself in a palatial house with taxidermy everywhere, including a stuffed lion you practically had to crawl over in the powder room. There were several hundred people, many of whom spoke German, and every European nationality seemed to be represented, along with

a large contingent of Americans, and she knew
them all. She spent the evening introducing Theo
to everyone, and kept him close at hand, until she
whispered to him after two hours and asked if he
wanted to go back to the hotel and smoke a joint
with her. He'd been ready to leave anyway, and
the invitation to go back to her room with her
definitely had some appeal.

They shared a cab again, and she was chatting
animatedly as they walked through the lobby, and
he followed her to her room. She opened the door,
and before she could get the joint out to offer it
to him, she crushed her mouth on his, expertly
undid his belt buckle, and unzipped his pants,
and was on her knees ministering to him ener-
getically with excellent results, and the next thing
he knew, they were on the bed, having passionate sex, and everything but Emma was forgotten.
He had somehow managed to get a condom on
before making love to her, and for the next hour
they had sex in every position imaginable until
they both lay spent in a tangle of their clothes,
and she grinned at him like a mischievous elf in
his arms. She was the most amazing girl he had
ever met.

"Two rules," she said before he could even catch
his breath, as he lay next to her, "I never fall in
love, and we don't have to see each other again if
we don't want to. No obligations, no tawdry ro-

mance, no broken hearts. We just have fun whenever we see each other. And you're awfully good
in bed," she said as he laughed at her.

"Do you pick up strange men in hotel lobbies
all the time?" He had never met anyone like her,
or so unabashedly sexual.

"Are you strange? What fun! You actually
seemed quite normal a little while ago," she teased
him.

"I am," he assured her, although he wasn't sure
the same was true of her.

"And I only pick men up when they're as un-
bearably handsome as you are. Why haven't I ever
met you before? Do you come to New York?"

"I haven't been in a long time, and this is my
first art fair." He named the gallery he was showing with, from New York.

"Oh dear, serious stuff. You must be very good.
I have a booth down the way from you. You'll
have to come and see it. And I want to see your
work too." She seemed interested in him.

"It's very classical. You might not like it," he
said modestly, and she rolled her eyes.

"Please don't be insecure, it's so boring." He
spent the night with her, and went to see her
booth the next day. She showed wild edgy work
by famous conceptual artists at high prices, and
although she admitted his work wasn't her cup
of tea, she was very impressed by it, and she rec-

ognized that he had an enormous talent and told him so.

"You'll be very famous one day," she predicted seriously, glanced at his bio, and saw the last name. "Ah . . . that explains it. But you're better than he is, you know. Your technique is very strong." And then she laughed as she said it, and whispered to him, "In other areas too. Excellent style."

They went to a party together again that night, and made love in her room afterward, and she flew back to New York the next day. It didn't seem likely that he'd see her again, but there had been no pretense, no promises, and no attachment. It was just good fun, and the best thing that could have happened to distract him from Natasha, whom he hadn't seen again at the fair, but for those few days with Emma he didn't care. She sent him a text message from the cab on the way to the airport, as he was checking out of the hotel. "Thanx for the great fux, Em." He laughed when he saw it. The art fair had been interesting, and even more exciting, both his paintings had sold, at respectable prices. He had a lot to be pleased about when he went home. And when he got back, he walked into his studio, and there she was again, with those gentle eyes, the lips that seemed about to speak to him, and the soft halo of blond hair. She looked just the way he'd seen her in London, and he turned the easel around so he didn't have to see her. He needed a break from the intensity of his obsession, and Emma had been just what the doctor ordered. He had had a great time with her.

He told Gabriel and his mother about the art fair the next day, when he had lunch with them, and left out the escapade with Emma Beauchamp Montague. He told them that both his paintings had sold, and they were pleased for him. And the following day Gabriel invited him to come and see a gallery with him in Cannes. It was one of the few serious galleries in the South of France. And he had promised to look at an artist for their gallery that his daughter was interested in representing.

"I should work," Theo said, feeling guilty about taking an afternoon off to go with him, but he didn't want to go back to work on the portrait of Natasha either. It was too unnerving having just seen her again.

"It'll do you good to get some air," Gabriel told him, and he enjoyed his company, so they drove in the old Morgan Gabriel kept in St. Paul de Vence to use when he was there. He was much more stylish than Lorenzo had ever been. They talked about the art fair again on the way, and were both disappointed by the work of the artist Marie-Claude had sent him to see. His work was too commercial, and better for the tourists than a serious gallery in Paris. But the girl who ran the gallery was a pretty blonde. Theo noticed her and smiled at her, and then they stopped at her desk to chat for a minute. He picked up her card and thought about calling her sometime, and then decided to take a page from Emma's book, and spoke to her casually.

"I don't suppose you'd have dinner with me sometime?" he asked far more cautiously than Emma would have, and she smiled at the question.

"Are you a gallerist or an artist?"

"That gentleman is a gallerist," he said, pointing to Gabriel. "I'm an artist."

"That would be a no, then," she said pleasantly, and he looked at her in amusement. He hadn't expected that response.

"You have something against artists?"

"Yes, I have a fatal attraction to them. I was even married to one. And in my experience, they're all crazy and addicted to drama. I've given up drama. I'm divorced, I have a five-year-old daughter, and I want to enjoy a peaceful life. That means no artists."

"What nationality was your husband?"

"Italian," she said, grinning at him. She liked Theo, and he seemed like a nice guy, but she wasn't going to fall for another artist, particularly a handsome one.

"That explains it, then," Theo said, relieved. "Italian artists are all crazy and love drama." He thought of his father as he said it, and could understand her attitude. "French artists are totally normal and really great guys."

"Not from what I've seen," she said breezily. She was not about to be swayed by his arguments or his charm, which he seemed to have a lot of. "No artists. Maybe we can be friends sometime, but no dinner dates. I'd rather be a nun."

"How depressing," he said, looking insulted, as Gabriel laughed at him. "I'll call you sometime," he said as he followed Gabriel out and back to the car.

"Nice try," Gabriel teased him. "She sounded like she meant it."

"She's got a great figure and terrific legs," Theo said, looking playful. Emma had put him in good spirits after two days of wild sex and lots of laughter.

"I should tell your mother to stop worrying. She worries about your being alone."

"I wasn't alone in London. I met a crazy British girl who owns a gallery in New York. She's a wild woman." Gabriel laughed at what he said as they both got back in the car, and Gabriel drove them home to St. Paul de Vence. He dropped Theo off at his house, and Theo waved as he walked in and lay down on the couch for a few minutes, thinking about Emma, the girl he had just met at the gallery—the name on her card was Inez—and Natasha. They were three such different women, and in an odd way, he couldn't have any of them.

Emma refused to be tied down and wanted no attachments, Inez was allergic to artists, and Natasha belonged to someone else. He was beginning to wonder what was wrong with him and if he was becoming attracted to unattainable women. But the most elusive of all was Natasha, who had stolen his heart without even knowing it, and was kept in an ivory tower by another man. Life was just too strange. And as he came to that conclusion, he fell asleep.

Chapter 6

The summer in St. Paul de Vence was easy
and peaceful. Gabriel spent two months there instead of one, and enjoyed being at the restaurant
at night. They met such interesting people there.
And he loved being with her. He sat at a corner
table, and she joined him whenever she had time.
And despite her devotion to Lorenzo, Gabriel
knew she loved him. And they got along better
than she ever had with Lorenzo. She didn't need
to admit it to him. Gabriel had seen it, and loved
what they shared, although Lorenzo was the ghost
between them.

Gabriel liked visiting Theo at his studio from
time to time, just to see what he was doing. He
took a fatherly pride in his work, even though he
was just a friend, but he had always been a father-
figure to him. In July, Theo finished the portrait
of Natasha, and stopped at just the right point. If

he had done more, he would have spoiled it; less, it would have seemed unfinished. He had that instinctive sense of great artists to know when a work was complete and move on. He kept the painting in the studio, and looked at it and smiled from time to time. It was like having her with him.

They had a busy summer at the restaurant. And Vladimir and Natasha did not come in again. He had asked his mother, and she said they hadn't.

"Are you still thinking about that girl?" she asked, frowning at him.

"Not really." He wasn't lying. He was slowly getting over her. Oddly, doing the painting had helped exorcise his demons. He was working on another subject, and Gabriel had convinced him to contact at least one of the galleries he had recommended.

"You need a show in Paris, to be taken seriously," Gabriel said sternly, and Theo believed him and felt almost ready. He was planning to go to Paris and meet with one or several of them and see what they had to offer. His two sales at the London art fair had given him more confidence in his work.

And he had tried calling Inez at the gallery in Cannes again. She was always charming on the phone, but refused to have dinner with him. He finally walked into the gallery one day, right before lunchtime, and invited her to have lunch with him. She was so startled, she accepted.

They had a great conversation over lunch, about her job at the gallery, her little girl, and the years she had lived in Rome with her husband. She said he was a sculptor and seldom visited his daughter. Inez was the child's sole support, which was a big responsibility for her. And her ex had just had twins with his new girlfriend, both boys, so his daughter in the South of France was no longer of interest to him.

"We just don't need another crazy artist breaking our hearts. We're doing fine as it is," she said seriously.

"Do I look crazy to you?" Theo asked her honestly, trying to look sane and wholesome, but he was anyway, other than his brief moment of insanity over Natasha, but that was over. He was ready to date real women, and wanted to go out with Inez, if she would.

"They never look crazy at first," Inez said knowledgeably. "They always seem sane in the beginning. And then, as soon as you settle down and figure you've got a good one, they start the drama, other women, past loves who return from the grave and need their help and come to stay with you, women they had babies with and forgot to mention."

"I have no babies that I know of, no past loves to come back to haunt me, no ex-girlfriends in need that I would allow to stay with me. I have some old girlfriends I've stayed friends with," except for Chloe, who had sent him several vicious, bitter emails, which he didn't mention. "My life has been fairly sane. My father, on the other hand, was pretty crazy, and very talented. He was Italian, and in his seventies when I was born, and he married my mother ten years later, when his wife died."

"That's what I mean," Inez said, grinning at him, as they ordered coffee after lunch. She was a very pretty young woman.

"He was incredibly talented, and my mother adored him. He was a fairly cranky old guy by the time I came along, but I know he loved me, and he taught me how to be an artist. He died when he was ninety-one, so I was lucky to have him till I was eighteen."

"Was he well known?" she asked innocently, and he hesitated before he answered, but she looked as though he could trust her. He could tell she was a nice woman, and not some gold digger after money.

"Lorenzo Luca." Her eyes widened as he said it.

"Good lord, he's one of the most important artists of the past century."

"Some people think so. I love his work, but my style is very different. I don't think I'll ever achieve the heights he did, although I work hard at it. He was really a genius, which is probably what made him so hard to get along with." Theo didn't tell her that his father had seven other children, which he was sure would have made her nervous. "My mother was forty years younger than he was. She runs a restaurant in St. Paul de Vence now, and is the keeper of the sacred flame. She owns a huge number of his paintings and rarely sells any." Except to very, very rich Russians, which he didn't add either.

"Did she ever remarry? She must have been fairly young when he died."

"She was fifty-two—they spent more than thirty years together. It's hard to get over that, I guess. And he was a big persona. She didn't remarry, but she has a loving relationship with his art dealer, the man I came in with the day I met you." She nodded, remembering.

"He seems like a nice man."

"He is. He's been like a father to me. Does any of this qualify me for dinner?" He smiled at her as he paid the check, and she thanked him.

"Not really. You're still an artist. But I'm happy to know you." She beamed at him, and he laughed good-naturedly.

"You're tough. I promise, I'm not a crazy artist."

"Probably not, but I'm not up for the long shots anymore. It's too risky, and I have my daughter to think of." He nodded. She had a point. And he wasn't interested in marriage at this point, or in raising other people's children. It seemed complicated and like too much responsibility to him, and he didn't want to screw up someone else's kid. So maybe she was right. He didn't suggest dinner again before he left her at the gallery and drove back to St. Paul de Vence. He liked her, but his life didn't hang on whether he had dinner with her. Still, he had enjoyed lunch.

The rest of the summer passed too quickly. And before Gabriel went back to Paris on September 1, he gave Theo the list of galleries again, and two days later Theo forced himself to sit down and call them. Several of them hadn't opened yet after the summer, but there was one he was particularly interested in, and Gabriel had promised to call them to recommend him. The man who owned it was Jean Pasquier, and he took Theo's call immediately. The gallery was on the rue Bonaparte in the sixth arrondissement on the Left Bank, and he said he was always interested in new artists.

Theo sent him images of his work digitally, and Pasquier called him the next day, and said he'd like to meet with him if he came to Paris, and to bring one or two of his paintings with him, so he could see his brushwork, which was a reasonable request. It was something you couldn't see on a computer. Theo agreed to visit him the following week and bring samples of his work. He had liked him on the phone so much that Theo decided not to call the others until he'd seen him, which Gabriel seconded as a good decision, and he promised to take him to dinner when he came to Paris.

Maylis was already complaining about Gabriel's being in Paris, only days after he left, but she never went with him. She waited for Gabriel to come and see her in the South. He said he'd be back in a few weeks.

And as promised, Theo went to see Jean Pasquier and liked the man and the gallery space, almost as much as Pasquier liked the work that Theo had brought with him. He thought the brushwork was masterful, and the subjects very appealing. And much to Theo's amazement, he offered him a one-man show in January. He had an opening in his schedule, due to an artist just informing him that he wouldn't be ready for his show, and Jean was delighted to fill the slot with Theo.

Theo called Gabriel as soon as he left the gallery to tell him, and thank him for the introduction, and Gabriel took him to dinner that night to celebrate. Selling two paintings at the art fair in London had been good for Theo, but being represented by a Paris gallery and having a show there was an important step in his career. And he had stayed in touch with the New York gallery, and might show with them later. He wasn't ready to pursue that yet.

"You're finally going to have a show in Paris." Gabriel beamed at him. They were having dinner in a small bistro in Gabriel's neighborhood on the Left Bank. Sitting on the terrace looking out at the lights of the spectacular city, Theo thought his mother was foolish never to go there. She was still locked into all the old habits she had had with Lorenzo. Gabriel would have broadened her life so much, if she let him. He said as much to him. "You know how she is," Gabriel said warmly. "I'm happy she travels with me. She'll go to cities in Italy, but never Paris."

"She's a stubborn woman," Theo said less kindly about his mother. "Do you think I'm ready for a show?" He was worried about it now that he had made the commitment.

"Of course. You have enough work in your studio for two shows." He smiled at him. And the work was solid.

"Will you help me pick the right ones to send him?" Theo asked him.

"I can advise you, if you like. But Jean will want to choose them with you." He didn't want to usurp the role of Theo's new dealer, and Gabriel was pleased for him.

The next day Theo flew back to the South of France, and as soon as he got home, he went through his studio and started putting aside the paintings he wanted in the show in January. He looked long and hard at the portrait of Natasha as he made the initial selection. He wasn't sure if he wanted it in the show or not. The portrait was so private, and he didn't want to sell it. He wanted to keep it and remember her forever, as a tribute to his brief obsession. He wasn't haunted by her anymore, and two and a half months after he had last seen her, he was feeling sane again. Dreaming of an unattainable woman was no longer appealing—even the girl who had refused to have dinner with him in Cannes. He put her out of his mind too. And all he wanted to think about now was his upcoming show.

Vladimir and Natasha had left the boat and gone back to London in late August, after drifting from port to port all summer. His security concerns had finally relaxed again, and he no longer surrounded Natasha with a ring of bodyguards every time she went out. The people who had caused the problem were gone, and he never discussed it with Natasha again. And she stopped worrying about it when she saw that he was no longer worried either. It had been a strange interlude but it was over.

They had dinner at Harry's Bar one night, and he told her he had a surprise for her.

"I'm going to build another boat," he said happily, "even bigger than **Marina.** And I'm going to name the next one after you." He looked proud as he said it, and she was touched. She knew how important his boats were to him, and how much he loved them. And it was a huge compliment that he wanted to name one after her.

"How long will it take?" she asked with interest. He looked excited about it.

"If everything goes smoothly, three or four years. Maybe longer. I'm going to have to go to Italy a lot, for meetings with the builders, to work on the plans and watch the construction, and to make changes as the work progresses. And there's the whole interior to design too. And all the materials to be selected. You remember what it was like when I built **Princess Marina.**" He had just been finishing her when he brought Natasha into his life, and her launch had been an extraordinary event, and the president's wife had christened her. It was exciting to think of his doing it again. It had been five years since **Princess Marina** was launched.

They toasted the new boat with champagne, and then he looked at Natasha. "That's only half of the surprise. I don't want you to be bored when I go to Italy to oversee the boat, so I want you to have a project of your own. I want you to find an apartment in Paris, somewhere around four or five hundred square meters. You can decorate it however you want. And we'll have a place to stay when we go to Paris." He knew she liked it there, and she went to the haute couture and ready-to-wear shows four times a year, and they always stayed at the George V. Now they would have a home of their own. Her eyes lit up when he said it, and he was pleased.

"Are you serious? You'd let me do that?" She looked like a child at Christmas.

"Of course. The Paris apartment will be your boat, and it will be finished a lot faster. You can start looking right away. I'm going to Italy for the first meetings next week." They were both thrilled, and she could hardly wait to call a realtor and start seeing apartments in Paris. Five hundred square meters was a big apartment, and there would be lots for her to do. "You can look for a house if you prefer it, but I think it will be easier and more comfortable in an apartment." And she agreed. Houses were so much more work. They had a big staff in London that they had to take care of, and the house needed constant repairs. She didn't want to have to oversee it. She was more interested in the decorating, and he was giving her carte blanche to do whatever she wanted.

"When are you going to Italy for the meetings?" she asked, as she put her arms around him and kissed him. He was happy that she was pleased.

"Next Tuesday. I'll be there till the end of the week."

"I'll start calling real estate agents tomorrow."

She called a realtor she knew in London to get names of Paris real estate agents, and by the following afternoon she had started to call them. Two days later she had six apartments to see, and had appointments for the following week. Two of the apartments were in the sixteenth arrondissement, and one was in the eighth, which didn't sound as interesting. There was another on the Left Bank, on the quais, overlooking the Seine, and there were two on Avenue Montaigne, which sounded perfect.

"Do you want to see them with me?" she asked him that night over dinner, and he shook his head with a broad smile. "This is your project. Your 'boat.' I'll see the one you want me to buy. You have to do the legwork before that."

"I can't wait," she said, ecstatic, and insisted on showing him the photographs on the Internet anyway. He agreed with her—he thought the two on Avenue Montaigne looked like the most interesting and luxurious so far.

"Don't rush into it," he advised her. "Find one that you really love. It will be fun to spend some time in Paris."

Vladimir had the plane take her to Paris on Monday, so it would be back in London for him when he flew to Italy on Tuesday. And his secretary had booked their usual suite for her at the George V. She ordered room service that night, as she always did when she was there without him. And she was excited to get started with the realtor the next day. They were planning to see an apartment on Avenue Foch first, on the sunny side of the street, the realtor had told her. And there was another one farther up, but she said it might be dark.

When Natasha met her at the first address at ten o'clock the next morning, the apartment was disappointing. It was sunny but in poor condition, large and rambling, and needed a lot of work, although as the realtor pointed out, the ceilings were high, and the tall windows were lovely. But it was too old-fashioned and Natasha didn't love it, and she liked the next one even less. And the apartment overlooking the Seine on the Left Bank was much too small, although it was lovely. But they were used to more space, and in spite of the view and balcony, it felt cramped.

She met with a different realtor after lunch, and the apartment in the eighth arrondissement was not right for them at all, and Vladimir would have hated it. They had told her about a listing at the Palais Royal too, which was considered highly desirable, but it was tiny, with one very small bedroom, a small bathroom, and **no** closets. And she was seeing the two apartments on Avenue Montaigne last, with a different realtor. It was a wide avenue where all the best shops were, Dior, Chanel, Prada, and a dozen others, and both apartments had supposedly been recently redone. One was a modern penthouse, and the other was a duplex in an older building. She was beginning to get discouraged before her last appointment. Nothing she had seen was even close to what they wanted, or to what she thought Vladimir would like, although he had told her to pick the one she wanted, but she wanted him to love it too, since he was paying for it.

When she met with the last realtor, the penthouse was pretty but very cold. Everything was either black granite or white marble, and she couldn't imagine feeling cozy there. It was more of a showplace than a home. And she wanted something that felt warm.

And when they got to the last apartment, the moment the realtor opened the door, she knew she was home. It had been redone and restored, but nothing interfered with its original beauty. It had modern systems embedded invisibly throughout, for music and computers, even air conditioning, which was unusual in Paris, and it had beautiful boiseries and moldings, high ceilings, lovely French windows, and spectacular antique parquet floors. It looked like a smaller version of Versailles, and all she would have to do was find furniture for it, and have curtains made for every room. It had four bedrooms upstairs, a dressing room for each of them, a study for Vladimir, and a small sitting room off their bedroom. And downstairs a huge double living room, a large dining room, a modern kitchen, and a cozy den. And each room had a fireplace, even the bathrooms, which had been redone too. It was exactly the size he had wanted. At five hundred square meters, it felt more like a house than an apartment. And the apartment was beautiful. It came with four maids' rooms on the top floor of the building, where they could put their bodyguards, when they brought them, which they didn't always do. And she could have a maid sleep there, to take care of the apartment. It had everything she wanted. It was her dream apartment, and she nearly fainted when she heard the price. It had been standing empty for a year while it had been redone, and it now had a very high price. And she wondered what Vladimir would say when she told him. She had never bought an apartment before, although she knew he was planning to spend half a billion dollars on his new boat, which sounded unimaginable to her, and was even more than **Princess Marina** had cost.

She told the realtor she would call her, and went back to the hotel in a daze. She didn't know what to say to Vladimir, if she should even tell him what they were asking for the apartment, or look for something else. She felt guilty having him spend that much money on a "project" for her, although he would live there too. But it would certainly be cheaper if they continued to stay at the hotel. He didn't usually care how much he spent, but she felt a responsibility to him, since it wasn't her money.

She waited to hear from him after his meetings, and was having room service for dinner when he called. She never went to restaurants without him. She didn't like eating alone, and although he had never said so, she had the feeling that he wouldn't like her going to restaurants on her own. She lived in a bubble he provided, where she felt secure.

"So how did it go today?" he asked her, after he told her his boat meetings had gone well.

"It was interesting. The first five apartments were very disappointing. Some of them were old and needed a lot of work. The penthouse on Avenue Montaigne was ice cold, everything was marble." She hesitated for a beat then, and he knew her well.

"And the sixth?"

"Was unbelievably expensive. I don't know if we should spend that much for an apartment." She felt awkward talking to him about it.

"Did you love it?" he asked, sounding almost fatherly.

"Yes," she admitted, feeling breathless. "It was gorgeous." And feeling her stomach turn over, she told him the price. He laughed when she said it.

"My darling, that won't pay for the dining room furniture they're going to make for the new boat." He was planning to spare nothing for his new yacht, which was going to be more of a ship than a boat, and the most luxurious vessel on the water. And he had told the interior designer he had hired that he wanted to order a sable bedspread for their bedroom. "Do you love that apartment?" he asked again.

"I really do. I was just afraid it was too expensive. I don't want you to think I'm taking advantage. I could be happy with something a lot smaller."

"Well, I wouldn't." She told him all about it then, and the many high-tech features it had, which he liked. And they didn't need to do any work. Everything had been done. "I want you to buy it. It sounds perfect, and I trust your judgment and your taste. I'll call them tomorrow." He wanted a quick closing, and was planning to pay for it in cash, which was how he did everything. He could have the money wired into the owner's account immediately. He didn't want to wait months for a slow closing. "Do they have any technical reports on it, to prove that all the work was done?"

"The realtor says they do." She couldn't believe how simple he made it all seem, despite the expense.

"I'll take care of all the details. You can start planning how you want to decorate it. Unless you want a decorator." He had used one for the house in London, but Natasha thought it would be more fun to do it herself, since this was her "project," and Vladimir was willing to let her.

"I don't know what to say to you. It's so beautiful, Vladimir, I love it. When can you come to see it?"

"I'll meet you in Paris on Friday. I have to go to Moscow the next day, for a week or two. You could stay in Paris if you want to, and get started on the decorating." Natasha was thrilled at how much fun this was going to be. He had had all his homes before she joined him. This was the first home she was going to decorate for them.

She lay awake that night, thinking about it, and all the things she had to do. She finally fell asleep at four A.M., and the one thing she knew was that she was the luckiest woman in the world, and Vladimir was the most generous man. For all the risks that she took being with him, like the scare in Sardinia in June, and the isolated life she lived, they seemed like small sacrifices in the face of his generosity to her, and the golden life he shared with her. She had nothing to complain about, for all the comfort and security he gave her, she knew she had been blessed the day she met him. Her life with him seemed perfect to her. Compared to the orphanage and the factories, and the terrible people she had known who had been unkind to her, and the mother who had abandoned her, being with Vladimir was an incredible gift. She was grateful for it every day. And now they had a beautiful apartment in Paris. She was a very, very lucky girl. Of that, she was absolutely sure.

Chapter 7

As he had promised her he would, Vladimir flew from Italy to Paris on Friday afternoon, and arrived just in time to see the apartment before nightfall and the realtor left for the weekend. He had already had the money wired to an account in Switzerland earlier in the week. The owner did not want to be paid in France, and had moved to Switzerland the year before. They were giving up the apartment so they no longer had a residence in France, and had become tax refugees. They were anxious to sell, and couldn't believe their good fortune when Vladimir offered to pay them all cash immediately. And he was able to get a better price from them by doing so. And the realtor was pleased too. The deal was done and sealed, and Vladimir had told Natasha that the apartment was theirs the day before. It was the fastest transaction the realtor had ever done, although she had done business with Russians be-fore, and knew how quickly it could move with the right ones. They had plenty of cash available and were easy to do business with. They made up their minds, knew what they wanted, and were very straightforward.

She met them at the building, and Natasha held her breath when Vladimir walked in. She was suddenly panicked—what if he hated it, didn't like the wood paneling, the windows, or the antique floors? He looked serious as he ex-amined everything and walked around, and then after they'd been through the last room, he put his arms around her with a broad smile.

"It's perfect, Natasha. You found us a spectacu-lar apartment. We're going to love being here." She almost cried, she was so thrilled that he was pleased. She showed him all the little details then, and it was fully two hours before they left and went to the hotel. She was going to be spending a lot of time there while she shopped for the apart-ment, and even the George V was starting to feel like home.

He made love to her almost as soon as they walked into their suite, and they took a bath to-gether and dressed for dinner. He was taking her to La Tour d'Argent, one of the fanciest restau-rants in Paris, to celebrate their new home. And she couldn't stop thanking him all through the meal.

"I wish I didn't have to leave you tomorrow," he said over dinner. He had ordered caviar and champagne for both of them, and a shot of vodka for him. "But you'll be busy here." She knew she would, but she missed him when he was gone for that long. He had a lot to do in Russia now, with his new involvement in the mineral business. And she had overheard him talking about buying more oilfields, and they were drilling in the Baltic Sea. His empire was still expanding by leaps and bounds. It was hard to imagine that it could get any bigger, but it had in the last six months, and he was still fighting to acquire more. While other economies were failing, Vladimir was making bigger and bigger deals every day. He was insatiable in what he wanted to run and own.

They went back to the hotel after dinner, and she lay in his arms again, as he slowly began making love to her. He had missed her all week, and hated it when she wasn't nearby, but he rarely took her to Moscow with him. He had too much to do there, she was only a distraction, and he knew that it wasn't a happy place for her. She had too many bad memories there, and preferred waiting for him in London or on the boat, and now she would have the Paris apartment as another home. It was perfect for her, and she tried to meet his every fantasy and need as he made love to her, to show him how grateful she was for all he did for her. Their relationship was a trade-off of sorts, she gave him all she had to give of herself in exchange for all the material bounty he bestowed on her.

Her life with him made her think of her mother at times, and she wondered if she was anything like her. Her mother had traded her body, and sex, for money, as a prostitute. And Natasha couldn't help asking herself if that was what she was doing, giving Vladimir her body and her freedom, her life and dedication to him, in exchange for the golden existence she led with him, and the gifts he showered on her. Or was this more like marriage, where a woman cares for a man, gives him her body, and has his babies, while he provides for her? Was it respectable or shameful? Sometimes she couldn't decide and wasn't sure. He was always kind and generous with her. There were no babies involved, and he didn't want any, but she gave him every other part of her, and all she could give.

He lay spent and sated in her arms after they made love. He had roared as he always did, and was sometimes rough with her, but she knew that sometimes it was what he needed, as a release from the pressures he lived with every day. She was the escape he used to free himself from the tension he dealt with, some of which she never even knew about. But she welcomed him into her body whenever he chose. And it didn't seem wrong to her, given all he did for her.

He was up at six the next morning, and she

ordered breakfast for them. He left the hotel at seven and looked at her longingly for a moment. Her beauty never ceased to amaze him, and she had only gotten lovelier and more delicate looking in the past seven years.

"Start shopping for the apartment," he said with a smile as he kissed her. She was standing naked in his arms, with the scent of their lovemaking on her, and he wished he could stay. But they had to be in the air on their way to Moscow by eight, and it would take him half an hour to get to Le Bourget.

"I'll miss you," she said softly, as she kissed him.

"I'll miss you too. I'll call you when we land." And then he was gone. He rarely said he loved her, but she knew he did, just as she loved him, or believed she did. It was love as she knew it.

She started looking for things for the apartment that morning, at antique stores she had walked by often, and now she had a mission, and a job to do. She had never had as much fun in her life, and one of the antique dealers gave her the name of a woman who made fabulous curtains. For the next two weeks, she never stopped. She bought paintings, furniture, fabrics, two beautiful rugs for the living room, and one for their bedroom. She bought an antique canopied bed that had been enlarged. She bought everything they needed for the kitchen, and hired a Russian maid. And when they went back to London, she wanted to do more shopping there. Vladimir called her for reports daily, and before meeting her in London, he went back to Italy, to check progress on the plans for the boat.

It was a busy fall for both of them, and in December, Natasha oversaw the installation of everything she had bought, while Vladimir was in Moscow with the president again. By the time he met her in Paris the week before Christmas, the apartment looked as though they had lived there for years. And when he came to see it, Vladimir loved everything she had chosen, and was impressed by what a good job she had done. They decided to spend Christmas there, and flew to the Caribbean the day after, where **Princess Marina** was waiting for them. She had made the crossing in November, and he was planning to keep her there until April or May, and then bring her back to the South of France in late May or early June. It felt good to be on the boat and relax in familiar surroundings. They were returning to Paris in late January for the haute couture shows, where he loved picking clothes for her twice a year, in January and July. They had a month to relax and spend on the boat until then, while Vladimir worked from his high-tech office on the yacht.

He flew back to Paris with her two days before the couture shows, and it was wonderful having the apartment to stay in. It was beginning to feel like home.

There were only two haute couture houses left of the illustrious old ones, Dior and Chanel, and a third more recent one, Elie Saab, that created custom-made evening gowns, and a small group of new, young designers, whose work had never been considered haute couture by those knowledgeable in fashion. But the two big shows were fun to go to, and the clothes and the settings were spectacular.

The first show they were going to was Dior Haute Couture, which was held in a tent they had built specially, behind the Invalides on the Left Bank. It was a spectacular affair, heated and theatrically lit, all lined in mirrors, with a garden theme that looked like a movie set and had been inspired by the gardens of Versailles. Millions were spent on the décor for each couture show, as well as the ready-to-wear shows, which were almost as theatrical and also occurred twice a year. The ready-to-wear shows were big business and happened in four cities, and were put on to show retailers worldwide what was coming in the next season so they could place their orders, and attracted a host of celebrities and fashionistas as well. The haute couture shows were a different breed, and only in Paris. They were the last survivors of a dying art, and their clients had dwindled over the years to a precious few.

With clothes that cost anywhere from fifty to five hundred thousand dollars—entirely handmade, every single stitch, each one made to order, and never duplicated in the same city, social circle, or event—there were almost no haute couture buyers in the modern world. In years gone by, there were flocks of wealthy society women, many of them on best-dressed lists, who came from around the world to order their wardrobes twice a year. But as the big design houses closed one by one, and the price of couture clothes rose into the stratosphere, there were only a few young women now, the mistresses of very, very rich men, who bought them. The styles no longer suited older women who could afford them, and the young girls they were primarily designed for could never have bought them on their own.

The shows were done more now for their publicity value as a spectacle, and the few girls who were lucky enough to be able to order the clothes were being dressed by the much older men who supported them and wanted to show them off as trophies and symbols of their vast fortunes, power, virility, and business prowess. None of it was what haute couture had been meant for, to dress extremely sophisticated, fashionable, well-dressed women. For the most part, haute couture had become a parody of itself, and only a handful of very wealthy Arab princesses, and the young mistresses, long term or otherwise, of Russian businessmen, were able to order the clothes. And in many cases, what one saw on the runway was never made or sold, it was simply an example of a kind of exquisite craftsmanship that had once been the summit of French fashion, and was now being worn by sexy young girls who had no appreciation for the rarity and quality of what they wearing.

The January show was for summer clothes, and winter clothes were shown in July, in order to place advance orders, to allow time for the handmade and often intricate garments to be created. So when Vladimir and Natasha arrived in Paris to go to the couture shows, she was going to pick her wardrobe for the following summer. And Vladimir always liked to be with her for the show, and he would make careful note of what he wanted her to wear, as the girls came down the runway. They were always the most expensive outfits and gowns. Like his cars and boats, how Natasha looked and what she wore were the outward signs of his immense wealth, just like the jewelry he gave her. Natasha wore jeans and simple clothes around the house, but Vladimir always preferred to see her dressed extravagantly, or at least expensively, when she went out, and even at home, where only he saw her. "Blue jeans are for peasants," he would say, although he wore them. But he wanted all heads to turn when Natasha walked in anywhere, and any one of her outfits cost the price of a luxury car, or a small apartment.

She didn't like disagreeing with him on any subject, or to seem ungrateful, but she always tried to point him toward the simpler clothes when they went to the haute couture shows, particularly for summer, when they spent so much time on the boat, but he brushed aside what she said. Sometimes he liked to see her in an evening gown at dinner, even when they were alone at home. He would no sooner have bought inexpensive clothes for her, or plain ones, than he would have acquired insignificant art. He wanted what he paid for, to show the world without question how far he had come. And although Natasha loved going to the shows and seeing the fashions on the runway, she always dreaded what he would select for her. He allowed her a few of her own choices, but for the most part, he chose what he wanted her to wear, and she didn't argue with him about it. She never liked making him angry. She had done so only a few times, and the look in his eyes and the harsh tone of his voice when he reprimanded her were enough to keep her in line. Whenever someone crossed him, countered his opinion, or disobeyed, it didn't go well. If one did as he commanded and expected, he was a kind, gentle man. But there was a volcano just below the surface. Natasha had seen it directed at others, and did everything she could to avoid having it directed at her. And she certainly wasn't going to risk his anger over what she wore. She was grateful for his generosity, and how could she complain about what he gave her? He spent millions on her clothes every year, and everything he bought looked beautiful on her.

For the stage setting of Dior's haute couture show for the coming summer, there were banks of flowers everywhere, the heavy scent of tube roses and lily of the valley in the air. The clothes were diaphanous and sexy, the skirts were short, almost everything was see-through, bare breasts were frequent in the show. The heels were so high they were almost unwearable. Many of the clothes were backless for summer. They were all clothes she could wear well, although she longed for a few simpler things, and picked out two plain cotton dresses that were flawlessly cut, and less exciting than what Vladimir chose for her that showed off her body but could only be worn in showier circumstances than daily life. There were lots of paillettes and tiny sequins, each one hand-sewn on nude-colored net. There were leggings and bodysuits, entirely sewn with tiny beads in flower-shaped patterns, that cost two hundred thousand dollars, due to all the embroidery and beadwork, and Vladimir ordered three of them for her, and a fourth one in shimmering pink. He told her that you don't dress a spectacularly beautiful woman in rags, which plainer clothes were to him, even if haute couture. In winter, he dressed her in furs, preferably sable, or mink, chinchilla, and ermine dyed exotic colors with fabulous hats

to match, alligator leggings, hip boots in leathers
and skins, with heavy embroidery on remarkable
coats. He bought her clothes to be noticed in,
not simply to wear for fashion and comfort, and
she wondered secretly sometimes what it would
be like to wear ordinary clothes, other than on
the boat. She hadn't done so since she left Moscow with him as a young girl, and then immediately felt guilty and ungrateful for her thoughts.
She knew how fortunate she was to have a man
who bought her haute couture.

He ordered seven outfits for her from the Dior
show, and six more at Chanel, and three summer
evening gowns from Elie Saab, all with plunging
necklines and slits up the side, to her hips. She
wore all the clothes well, and the women who ran
each couture house loved dressing her, and made
a great fuss over both of them. Vladimir made his
choices quickly after he saw Natasha in the dresses
he had made note of, and he rarely changed his
mind. He knew how he wanted her to look. And
Natasha thanked him profusely when they left
each house. They went back to the apartment afterward, curled up in front of the fire in their bedroom, and made love. He was delighted with the
clothes he'd bought her, and couldn't wait to see
her in them the following summer. There would
be three fittings for each dress before they were
delivered, to make sure that they fit her perfectly.
There could not be a wrinkle or a misplaced hand

stitch in a couture gown. It had to be flawless, like the woman who wore it.

The Chanel show was even more spectacular than the one at Dior. It was held in the Grand Palais every season, an impressive glass building. Chanel had once placed an iceberg in the center of it for a winter ready-to-wear show. It had been flown in from Sweden and returned the next day. This time Chanel had created a tropical beach for their summer couture show, with tons of sand brought in, and a boardwalk for the fifty models to saunter down, wearing the clothes. Natasha loved the feeling of the show and the clothes, which were a little less showy and naked than those at Dior, which Vladimir preferred.

There was no question that whichever house dressed her, she was going to be breathtaking in everything Vladimir ordered for her. He consulted her about the outfits he liked, but in the end, he made the final selections, and treated her opinions like those of a child. It was always a little bit humiliating for her when he made it clear that she had no decision-making power, but the managers of haute couture were used to it. Vladimir was no different from the other men they dealt with, all men of power, and in Vladimir's case more than most. Men like him did not simply sit back and let others make their decisions on any subject, even about fashion, or how they dressed their women. And Natasha served a purpose with what she wore. It was her job to make others envy him for the woman on his arm, which she did. Just as the shows were a publicity statement of sorts for the houses that put them on as a spectacle, she did the same for him. She was a beacon for all the world to see. She belonged to Vladimir Stanislas, no different than his boat, which was the most noticeable, spectacular, and enviable on the water. And the new one he was planning would be even more so.

He talked to her about the plans and showed her some of them, when they had dinner at the apartment that night. It was snowing, and they had canceled dinner reservations at Alain Ducasse at the Plaza and decided to stay home. It was bitter cold outside. He did some work, and Natasha read a new book about Impressionist art that she had bought and was fascinated by.

She had bought a number of decorating books too, to get ideas for the apartment, and it was looking magnificent. The curtains had been installed while they were away on the boat, and Vladimir loved them. In spite of his more important pursuits in business, he had an eye for beauty, and always noticed what she did in the apartment, and commented when he liked it. He was very pleased with what she'd accomplished, and she was happy spending more time in Paris, since the apartment was warmer and more inviting than his very showy London house, which had been done by a famous decorator before he met Natasha. It had been photographed by every important decorating magazine when he'd had it done, but Natasha never loved it. The Paris apartment felt more like home, and so did the boat. She hoped the new one would be as nice—his plans for it sounded very grand. But her preferences were always simpler and less grandiose than his. He had tried to "educate" her into being bolder in her taste.

Vladimir spent the weekend with her in Paris after the haute couture shows, before he returned to Moscow. His new mineral holdings, and running them, had proven to be more time-consuming than he expected, and he told her it was too cold for her in Moscow, and he would be too busy, and had to do some traveling within Russia to unpleasant areas. He wanted her to stay in Paris, and then they would go to Courchevel in mid-February in three weeks. It had become the favorite ski resort of all Russians, and he had rented a fully staffed house for them for a week. He was an avid skier when he had time, and had hired ski teachers for her every winter for the past seven years, and she was a decent skier, though not of his caliber. But they had a good time skiing together, and she was looking forward to it.

The apartment seemed empty when he left. It snowed in Paris that week, and she spent most of the time in bed reading, or sitting by the fire in the cozy den, and combing antique shops for treasures when she went out. She always found something new that she loved for the apartment—that week a pair of Louis XV bronze chenets for the fireplace, to hold the logs. They had leaves and cherubs on them, and she put them in their bedroom.

She went to several galleries as well, looking for art for the apartment, and always received a stack of invitations for openings. One had caught her eye for that Thursday night, on the Left Bank. It was a gallery where she had bought a small but pretty painting two months before. And if it wasn't snowing, she promised herself she'd go to the opening on Thursday night. She sometimes preferred going before the opening, if they let her, to snap up whatever she wanted before others had a chance to do so, but she had no time that day. She had workmen coming to add new shelves in the kitchen, and she wanted to oversee the work herself.

It was an hour after the opening had started when she got into the Bentley Vladimir hired for her in Paris, with a driver. She never drove herself in Paris, and was afraid to, with the complicated traffic and one-way streets, although she some-times drove in the South of France. Vladimir kept a Bentley sports car for her on the boat. But in Paris, she preferred to use a driver. Vladimir had one of his own when he was in town, and used a

Rolls. Her Bentley was subtler and less showy as they drove across the Pont Alexandre III to the Left Bank, and into the sixth arrondissement, where the gallery was.

It was small but well laid out, and filled with people drinking wine and talking when she got there. There were the usual arty types, and some serious people from the art world. It was an eclectic-looking group of young and old, as she walked around, looking at the work. It was handsome, serious work, with an odd combination of brushwork that resembled the Old Masters and the lighter colors and subjects of the Impressionists. The artist having the show definitely had his own style, and she hadn't paid attention to the name on the card. All she had noticed was that she liked the work. She picked up a sheet of the artist's biography at the desk as she walked past it, and continued to look around, and as she reached the back of the gallery, she stopped dead and found herself staring at her own face in a haunting painting that had captured her flawlessly. It was a portrait of her, and she was shocked.

And as Natasha stood there staring at herself, instinctively Theo looked up and saw her from across the gallery, and nearly felt his heart stop. He had never expected her to be there and see it.

"What's up? Something wrong? You look like you've just been shot." Inez was with him. He had decided to try one more time, and invited her to dinner just before Christmas. They had been dating for a month, and she was still leery of him, but it was going well. So far he had proven to her that he wasn't crazy, despite being an artist, and he even liked her little girl, Camille. Theo wasn't in love with Inez, not yet at least, but he was enjoying her company. She was an intelligent woman, responsible and sensible, and well able to take care of herself and her child. She wasn't looking to be "saved" or supported. She wasn't interested in marriage, and she'd rather be on her own than with the wrong man. So far he liked everything about her, and she had come to Paris with him for the opening, while a friend baby-sat for her child. They were staying at a small hotel on the Left Bank, near the gallery, and their relationship was still very new. She had seen him go deathly pale when he spotted Natasha at the back of the gallery, staring at her portrait. She stood like a statue gazing at it.

"No, nothing, I'm fine," he said, smiling at Inez, and slipped quietly away from the group they were in, and threaded his way to where Natasha was standing. She was wearing a heavy fur coat, jeans, and high heels, since Vladimir wasn't in town, and she looked as heartbreakingly beautiful as ever, as she turned to him with her soft halo of blond curls, and her hair loose down her back like a young girl.

"You painted that?" she asked him, with enormous eyes, as though accusing him of stripping her naked in a public place and leaving her there, exposed. He couldn't deny it, and the painting was so haunting, so intense, and so obviously personal, that it somehow suggested he knew her intimately and even loved her.

"I . . . yes . . . I did . . . after I saw you last summer. You have a face that begs to be painted," he said, which sounded like a poor excuse, even to him. The painting was so deep that it was obvious to both of them that it was more than that to him.

Her eyes bored into his with all the soulfulness of many Russians; they had a penchant for tragedy and sorrow, which came out in their literature, music, and art. "I had no idea you were such a talented artist," she said softly.

"Thank you for being kind." He smiled at her, embarrassed that she had caught him with the visible sign of his obsession with her. He had gotten over it, but the portrait was ample evidence of how taken with her he had been. She was not just a random subject or a model, or an interesting face to paint. She was a woman he had been falling in love with at the time, even if he had come to his senses since. But everything he had felt for her was in the painting, he had given it his all, which was why Gabriel and Marc thought it was his best work. Gabriel was at the opening that night, but Marc couldn't afford to come to Paris at the moment, and had refused money from Theo to get there. He was planning to come up sometime during the course of the show, but couldn't make it to the opening. "It was wonderful painting you," Theo said, not knowing what else to say to her, to excuse himself for intruding on her and exposing her, "although I had a hard time with your eyes." He felt like an idiot standing there, talking to her inanely, and just looking at her he could feel a vise around his heart, and his stomach start to slide. She did something to him every time he saw her. He had seen her only three times in his life before that night, and on his easel in his studio every day and night for months. The painting of her had become his passion, and the culmination of his work and technique at the time.

"I'd like to buy it," she said quietly. "And the eyes are perfect," she said, and he knew it too. He had sensed it when he finally got it right, and he could see now, looking at her, that he had. He had captured her expression perfectly.

He had looked around when he first saw her, and seen that she was alone, Vladimir wasn't there, so he couldn't insist on buying it at any price. He was tempted to tell her it wasn't for sale but didn't. "I'm sorry. It's already sold." There was no red dot on the wall next to it, to indicate that it had been purchased, and she looked at him quizzically. "We just sold it. They didn't put the red dot up yet." She looked shocked and disappointed as he said it. She didn't want a portrait as intimate as that going to a stranger and hanging in their home. And neither did he.

"Have they paid for it yet? I don't want someone else to have it. I'll pay you more." She had learned some of Vladimir's habits, which usually worked. Few merchants were loyal to their customers, if someone else offered them a better price. And seeing the disappointment and sorrow on her face, Theo realized that he should have offered it to her before this, but he had wanted to keep the painting for himself. He just hadn't been able to resist putting it in the show, and Jean had wanted it at the gallery when he saw it, at least for the opening, to demonstrate Theo's skill.

"They paid for it just a little while ago. I'm truly sorry," Theo said apologetically, looking down at her, wishing he could put his arms around her. She was tall, but he was taller, and despite her height, she looked vulnerable and frail. She was the kind of woman you wanted to protect, and be sure no one would hurt. He had never felt that way about anyone before. "Are you in Paris for a visit?" he asked, trying to get her off the subject of the portrait, which made him seem like a jerk for not having offered it to her privately before the show.

"No." She smiled at him wistfully, sad to have lost the portrait. "I have an apartment here now.

We do. On Avenue Montaigne. It's been fun deco-rating it, and I'm still looking for art." She glanced back at her own likeness. "This would have been perfect. But I'll look at your other work."

"Maybe I could come and see the spaces you have, and the light, and we could pick something together," he said hopefully, not sure why he'd said it. Given the art collection he had, Vladimir didn't need his advice. He wondered where he was. "Where are you located?"

"Number fifteen. I'll contact you through the gallery," she said simply. "I'm here for another two weeks. Will you be here for a while?"

"Another day or two before I go back down South, but I can make time." He would have flown to her side at the merest invitation, but he doubted that she'd call him.

"It's a wonderful show," she complimented him, and she had noticed a number of red dots, indicating that several pieces had sold. She smiled at him then. "Thank you for painting me. It's a great compliment," she said graciously, forgiving him for selling her portrait to a stranger without ever offering it to her. He almost told her the truth then, that he didn't want to part with it. Giving it up would be like losing her, even though he had never had her, and knew he never would.

She walked around the show for a few min-utes then, and when he looked for her again a few minutes later, she had left. And he had gone back to stand with Inez and the others, and tried to seem casual about it when he reappeared after talking to Natasha. Inez gave him a chilly, suspicious look, and spoke to him in a cold tone the moment they were alone.

"I'm not blind, you know. I saw you with the woman in the portrait. You told me you didn't know her." Her eyes were questioning and hard.

"I don't know her, not really," he said almost honestly, but not quite. He wished he knew her, but didn't. "I've seen her three times in my life, four including tonight. At my mother's restaurant with her boyfriend last summer, when I delivered a painting to her, for two minutes at a London art fair, and now. And I didn't invite her tonight. I don't know why she came. She must be on their client list. She had a face I wanted to paint, that's all."

"The portrait is a perfect likeness of her. I recognized her immediately." And then she shocked him with her next question. "Are you in love with her?"

"Of course not. She's a total stranger."

"Artists don't paint women they don't know, unless they're obsessed with them in some way, or they're studio models." And the portrait had that quality of obsession to it, which Inez had sensed. It was a love letter to a woman he longed to know better, and could only guess at. Inez was right. But he'd been obsessed with her six months before. He thought he was over it, until he felt as though someone had ripped his heart out of his chest again the minute he laid eyes on her that night. It was starting all over again, just as it had before. She had magic powers of some kind that he couldn't seem to resist.

"I'm not obsessed," he said, as much to convince himself as Inez, who looked unhappy. And having seen Natasha in the flesh, if he was in love with her, she knew the competition was stiff.

"Why is it that I smell drama in the air?" she said, looking at him intently. "I told you, I don't do drama. If that's what this is, I'll run before you know what hit you."

"You have nothing to worry about," he said, putting an arm around her shoulders, but he felt like a liar and a cheat. He had robbed Natasha of her face to paint her portrait, and now he was lying to Inez about a woman he had been obsessed with and didn't know. He felt like a madman as he left her a few minutes later, went to Jean Pasquier's desk, took out a red dot, and put it on the wall next to Natasha's portrait. At least he could do that much for her, so no one bought it that night.

The rest of the opening went well, and both Theo and Jean Pasquier were pleased. Gabriel congratulated him before he left. And he and Theo agreed that it was a shame that his mother hadn't come. She was busy doing some remodeling and repairs at the restaurant, and claimed she couldn't leave. But they both knew she hated coming to Paris, and preferred her safe, familiar little world in St. Paul de Vence. Theo understood that about her and didn't take it personally.

"I'll tell her what a success the show was," Gabriel promised when he left. And Theo went back to the hotel with Inez after the last guests were gone. He was meeting with Pasquier the next morning to go over sales and a list of clients to send images to who had expressed interest in his work that night.

Theo and Inez were quiet on the walk back to the hotel, each of them lost in thought. And when they got to their room, Inez questioned him again.

"Why is it that I don't believe you when you say you're not in love with that girl?" She was sitting on the bed and staring at him, as though she would find the answer in his eyes and not his words.

"She belongs to the richest man in Russia." He said it as though she were an object, a piece of furniture, or a slave, and hated the way it sounded and what it meant, because in a way it was true. Vladimir considered her a possession and treated her as one.

"And if she didn't 'belong' to him," she pursued it, "would you want her?"

"It's a ridiculous question," he said as he paced

the room, uncomfortable in his own skin. "It's like asking if I want to own the Eiffel Tower or the **Mona Lisa.** They're not for sale."

"Everything has a price, if you're willing to pay it," Inez said coldly, echoing Vladimir's words precisely, which almost made him shudder. He didn't want that to be true. And in Natasha's case it wasn't, and his mother was right, he couldn't afford her. "And you're not exactly a pauper," Inez reminded him, "even if you like to pretend you are. You may not have as much as her Russian boyfriend. But she would hardly starve with you." Inez didn't care what Theo had, but it was no secret in the art world who his father was and what he had left him.

"Women like that are different," Theo said, looking tortured as he sat down in a chair. "And I'm not looking to buy someone at auction, in a bidding war. It's not an issue with her. She's his mistress, she has a fabulous life, materially anyway, and she seems to be happy with him. I wouldn't know what to do with a woman like that anyway. End of story."

"Maybe not," Inez said knowingly. "Maybe only the beginning."

"If that were true, it would have happened seven months ago when I met her. It didn't. I painted a portrait of her because she has a pretty face. That's all." But neither of them felt reassured when they went to bed that night. Inez didn't believe him.

And Theo knew it was happening again. He was haunted by Natasha again as he lay in bed with Inez.

Every time he got near Natasha, she got under his skin, and he could no longer think straight. He felt confused and disoriented, and he couldn't sleep for a long time. And he and Inez lay on opposite sides of the bed, already disappointed by what was happening. There was a space between them big enough for the girl who was bewitching him. Natasha might as well have been in the bed with them. They could both feel her powerful presence in the room.

And on Avenue Montaigne, Natasha was lying on her bed, thinking about him too. There was something so intense about him, although she couldn't figure out what it was, and she liked talking to him. She took the sheet of paper out of her bag, to look at his biography, curious about where he had studied art, and at first his last name didn't strike her, and then she read the third paragraph, which mentioned whose son he was, and that he had trained at his father's side as a boy. She was shocked to realize that he was Theo Luca but had never said anything at the restaurant, or when he dropped his father's painting off at the boat. He was humble and modest, and acted like an employee and a messenger and nothing more.

She read the biography again several times . . . grew up in St. Paul de Vence . . . born in his father's studio . . . and trained at his father's knee from the age of five . . . École des Beaux-Arts in Paris . . . second-largest collector in the world of his father's work . . . talented artist in his own right . . . his first gallery show . . . and she was in it. He had obviously worked hard on her portrait, and she couldn't understand why. Why had he painted her and how had he seen so much in her eyes? He had seen all the pain of her childhood . . . the terrors of the orphanage . . . the heartbreak of her mother abandoning her . . . he had seen it all. It was all in the painting he had done of her, and it was as though she could feel him inside her now, embedded in her soul. He had slipped into her unnoticed, and she could feel that he was still there, silent, waiting, knowing her, and she didn't know whether to run from him or not. But he had no place in her life. She belonged to Vladimir. And she could sense that Theo Luca was a danger to her. Just being near him put her whole life at risk.

Chapter 8

When Theo and Inez got up the next morning, neither of them mentioned Natasha again. They had exhausted the subject the night before. They had a breakfast of café au lait and croissants at a café nearby, and he told her he'd be free by lunchtime and would call her. And then he went to the gallery for his meeting with Jean Pasquier, to discuss how the show had gone, any reviews they'd had, and the sales of the night before. He had sold six paintings, which Jean said was excellent, and had a very favorable review in **Le Figaro,** which reminded Theo of what he wanted to tell him, since the art critic had been particularly impressed by Natasha's portrait.

"By the way, I'm taking the portrait out of the show," Theo said quietly. "I shouldn't have put it in without the subject's permission."

"She was here last night," Jean commented. "I

saw her. You captured her perfectly. Was she upset by it?"

"Shocked, I think. I felt like a jerk not having told her about it."

"You're an artist. You can paint whoever and whatever you want." Theo didn't tell him that Natasha had offered to buy it. He didn't want her to, and he suspected the gallerist would have. He was in business after all. But they both agreed that for a first show, it had gone very, very well.

"I'll take the portrait with me today, and back down South tomorrow," Theo said, trying to sound casual about it.

"I can ship it to you if you prefer," Jean offered, but Theo shook his head.

"I'll carry it. I don't want it to get lost." It was a reasonable explanation, and artists were notoriously paranoid about their work.

They talked about the show for about an hour, and Theo thanked him for doing such a good job and hanging it so well, and giving him such a great opportunity for his first gallery show. And then he left, carrying Natasha's portrait, walked to Boulevard St. Germain, and hailed a cab. He gave the driver the address he remembered on Avenue Montaigne. He knew he couldn't just ring her doorbell and show up, but there would be a concierge, and hopefully he could call her from downstairs and hand it to her. He wondered if Vladimir would be there.

The building was as fancy as he expected it to be in that neighborhood and particularly on that street, and it was small, with a single apartment on each floor, and some occupying two floors, like theirs. There were only six stories in the building. And there was actually a security guard outside as well as a concierge. And there was an intercom to each apartment. He buzzed where it was marked VS, knowing it was them, and a Russian maid answered. He asked for Natasha, and the woman went to get her, then he heard Natasha's voice at the other end.

"Hi. It's Theo. I came to drop something off." She hesitated for a long moment while he waited, and then he heard her voice again.

"You can come up. Fourth floor." She buzzed him in, and he went through a glass door, and got into a mirrored elevator big enough for four people, which was large for Paris. The elevator stopped, and he got out. She was standing in the doorway, in blue jeans and ballerina shoes, with a heavy black sweater and her long blond hair loose and tousled, reaching almost to her waist. He handed her the wrapped painting where she stood, and she looked surprised.

"I want you to have it. I was going to keep it because everyone says it's my best work so far, but it belongs to you."

"Did the buyer change their mind?" She looked confused, and he shook his head.

"There was no buyer. I wanted to give it to you. I knew it when I saw you last night, but I didn't want to tell you with all those people around."

"I want to buy it," she said fairly, as they stood on the landing with the painting between them, and he shook his head again.

"It's a gift. It has no price, and it's not for sale. It's yours."

"I can't just take it from you like that." She was visibly embarrassed but pleased and very touched. She looked incredibly young when he talked to her. He had noticed it before. He didn't know how old she was, but she seemed like barely more than a girl, especially with what she wore. She appeared older only when she was all dressed up.

"Why not?" He smiled at her. "I took your face to paint it, now you can take the result."

"It's a wonderful portrait. Do you want to help me pick a place to hang it?" she asked cautiously as she stood in the doorway, and he nodded. She stepped aside so he could come in, and he carried the painting for her. He had chosen an antique frame and it was heavy.

He followed her into the apartment, and he immediately noticed the antique boiseries and floors, the art she had hung in the entry, which was mostly her choices, and not as important as most of Vladimir's, but warmer and more appealing. He walked into the living room after her, which looked like a little sitting room in Versailles,

but wasn't overdone, with delicate silks and dam-
asks. They wandered into the little sitting room,
the dining room, and then she took him up the
stairs to their bedroom, since she was thinking of
hanging it there. She had a seventeenth-century
painting of a young girl over the fireplace, and
they both had the same thought at the same time.
The portrait would be perfect there. He carefully
lifted down the one she had hanging, and put the
one of her on the same hook, and it was absolutely perfect. They both smiled as they looked at
it, and she seemed thrilled.

"I love it, don't you?" She clapped her hands
like a child, and he laughed, watching her. She
was more like a young girl than a woman, despite
what she'd seen and the life she led with Vladimir.

"Yes, I love it," he said, smiling at her, pleased
that he had made the gesture and given it to her.
And what he'd said was true. It belonged with her.
He wanted her to have it.

They agreed on a place to put the other painting, on the opposite wall in her bedroom, and he
asked her for a hammer and nail. She went to get
them, and he hung it for her, and then she looked
at him with a question.

"Why didn't you tell me you were Lorenzo
Luca's son? Especially when Vladimir bought the
painting?" She had been about to say "we," but
she was conscious that she didn't own it. Vladimir
did, he had bought it, and unlike Theo's portrait

of her, it was not a gift. She had no ownership in the art he purchased.

"It seemed irrelevant. What difference would it make? I don't usually tell people. It's distracting. I don't like to trade on his name."

"You don't need to," she said softly. "Your work is very good. I've been trying to study art history on my own. I'd like to take classes one day at the Sorbonne, but we don't stay in one place long enough for me to do that, and he doesn't want me to," she explained. "Maybe now that we have the apartment here, I can take some classes, or hire a tutor."

"You already seem very knowledgeable to me." He had gleaned it from the discussion they'd had on the boat, when he delivered his father's painting. "You probably know more now than some of the professors you'd have classes with," he said honestly, and she was flattered. She had learned a lot on the Internet and from what she read in her books and magazines.

They both stood back then and admired the portrait again and where they had hung it. They had found the perfect place, and they both looked pleased. He was trying not to think that they were standing in the bedroom she shared with Vladimir, and the bed was only a few feet from them. It gave him a shiver to think it.

He had an idea then. "Are you busy? Would you like to go to lunch?" It was a spur-of-the-moment inspiration, and he didn't know if Vladimir was at work or away and didn't ask. She seemed to be free and on her own. She hesitated for a long moment when he asked her. She never went out to lunch, except with Vladimir. She had never been to lunch with another man in all the years she'd been with him, but there was no reason not to. The invitation wasn't inappropriate, and it sounded like fun to her. Having lunch with him was so out of her normal universe and activities, and she knew Vladimir wouldn't like it, but he didn't have to know. And she didn't want to just take the painting and send Theo away. That seemed wrong too. She felt slightly dazed as she responded, after weighing it all in her head.

"Yes. Why not? I don't usually go out to lunch. But there's an easy restaurant down the street. We have dinner there sometimes, and lunch on Sundays." He knew it too, it was L'Avenue, a casual, friendly, popular restaurant full of models and movie people and people who worked in fashion, ordinary people, and sometimes celebrities, and they had tables on the terrace so Vladimir could smoke his cigars. It was a fashionable Parisian hangout, and only two blocks away. "I'll get my coat," she said, and came back with an enormous Russian sable Vladimir had bought her at Dior. It was a rich dark brown in contrast to her light hair, and she had put on tall dark brown suede boots, and was carrying a brown alligator

Birkin and brown alligator gloves from Hermès. He smiled when he saw her.

"Are you sure you don't mind being seen with me?" He had dressed to go to the gallery, and hang out in the sixth and seventh arrondissements, where the galleries were. He was wearing jeans, a heavy sweater, and a windbreaker that had seen better days, and brown suede boots too. He looked considerably less formal than she did, although he had had a good haircut and looked neat. And she wasn't entirely unaware of his good looks, although she didn't flirt with him. She didn't know how to behave. Having lunch with young men close to her own age, who might even become friends, was entirely out of the realm of the possible for her. It was part of her unspoken agreement with Vladimir. She was entirely his in every way, body, mind, and soul. That left no room for anyone else in her life, which was how he wanted it, and she knew that too. She told herself, as they walked to the restaurant, that this was a one-time exception she would make, and it would do no harm. And this time, with no boat crew to report to him, Vladimir would never know.

Once at the restaurant, they sat down at a table, and she felt awkward with him for a few minutes. He had turned off his phone so no one would bother him, and he gazed at her intensely, as though trying to understand her, and drink her in, but she felt as though he already knew her.

They made casual conversation until they ordered, a salad for her and a veal chop for him. The
food was good there, and the restaurant was busy.
She felt like a child at Christmas, looking around
her. She lived in Vladimir's shadow, and never
spoke to his friends, and they never spoke to her.
The Russian businessmen she saw him with only
spoke to each other. Even when they had women
with them, they never addressed them. The only
thing that interested all of them was work, and
the deals they were making. Women were for dec-
oration, and entertainment later. And Vladimir
was no different. It was what she was used to.

They chatted inanely for a few more minutes,
and then Theo couldn't stand it any longer. He
had lived with her in his studio for months and
felt as though he knew her. It made him braver
about asking her what he didn't know.

"I don't know how to say this nicely," he began
cautiously, "and I know it's none of my business,
but I feel as though I know you after painting you,
and there is always something familiar about you
every time we meet, as though we have a connection. I think I want to understand you better . . .
Why are you with him? Do you love him? It can't
just be the money. I don't even know you, but
that doesn't seem like you." He had great faith
in her, even though they were essentially strangers, but there was a certain purity about her. She
just didn't seem like the sort of girl who would

sell herself for what she could get. The expensive clothes she was wearing and her surroundings seemed to mean nothing to her. And surely not enough to sell her soul.

"He saved me," she said simply, looking deep into Theo's eyes, and he could tell that she was being honest with him. "I would have died in Moscow. I'd be dead by now probably if he hadn't rescued me. I was starving and sick, and freezing cold." She hesitated for a moment before opening up to him. But she felt an odd connection between them too. "I grew up in a state orphanage. My mother abandoned me when I was two, and died two years later. She was a prostitute. I didn't have a father. When I left the orphanage, I went to work in a factory. I didn't have enough money to buy food or warm clothes or medicine . . . women died in my dormitory every month, from illness or despair . . . Vladimir saw me and tried to take me away from all that, and I wouldn't let him. I turned him away for a year, and then I got pneumonia and I couldn't do it alone anymore. I was very sick. He took me to his apartment and nursed me himself, and when I got better, I didn't want to go back . . . I couldn't . . . he was too good to me . . . I didn't want to leave . . . he takes care of me, and where would I go if I left him? I can't go back. He's kind to me and he takes care of me, and I take care of him too. I have nothing to give him except myself. I am grateful for what

he did for me then, and what he does now . . .
it's a special life," she said quietly, well aware that
it might shock him. She felt as though she owed
Theo an explanation. But it seemed like a fair exchange most of the time, and people like Theo,
and most people, had no idea what that kind of
poverty and hardship was like, how hopeless it
made life seem, and there was no way out. "He
understood. He grew up poor too, very poor. He
still has nightmares about it. We both do. You can
never go back to that. I don't care about what he
gives me, although it's nice, but what matters is
that he protects me and keeps me safe."

"Safe from what?" Theo probed deeper into her
eyes and heart.

"Life. Dangerous people sometimes, who want
to hurt him, or me." She thought of the previous
summer in Sardinia when she said it.

"I'm sure he can be dangerous too." Vladimir
had that quality about him, and Natasha seemed
so innocent that Theo wondered if she was aware
of it, but she wasn't as naïve as she looked. She had
seen and guessed a lot in seven years, although she
would never admit it to a stranger, out of loyalty
to Vladimir.

"I'm sure he can be dangerous," she said honestly. "But not to me. He would never let anyone
hurt me. I respect what he has built, from nothing. I admire him for that. He's a kind of genius,
in business."

"My father was too, as a painter," Theo volunteered. "They're never easy people. Don't you miss having your freedom, or are you freer than I think? Do you do whatever you want?" She laughed at the question, and he was curious about her life, if it was as it seemed or different.

"And what would I do with freedom? Go to school? Have friends? That would be nice. But who would protect me if I didn't have Vladimir?"

"Maybe you wouldn't need protection then," he said gently.

"We all need that," she said quietly, "even Vladimir. Life is dangerous. Being poor is dangerous. You can die from it. I almost did. So did he, like a dog in the streets when he was fourteen. We all need someone to watch over us." Theo could see why she was with him now—she had come from such a raw, barren, dangerous place that survival was all important to her, not furs and jewels and the expensive clothes she wore, or his yachts, which were important to him and not to her. She was focused on survival. She couldn't conceive of living in a safe world where she wasn't at risk every day, as she had been as a young girl. Vladimir had lifted her from that world into his own. It was all she knew. And even now she remembered the dangers too clearly. A life like Theo's growing up was utterly foreign to her. Or other people's lives, where there were few risks, if any, and you did ordinary things, met people, had friends, fell in love, had relationships, went to work or school. He sensed that she liked the idea of it, but it was all too unfamiliar to her. All she knew was a world of bodyguards and yachts, with a man at her side who was her savior and protector, in her eyes, no matter how dangerous he might be to others. It was all about that for her, safety from the demons and real dangers of her past. She cared about what he provided in an otherwise dangerous world.

"Russia is a hard place," she said quietly, "or it used to be. I think it still is for most people. The strong ones like Vladimir survive and climb out, and he pulled me out with him. The others don't make it, and many of them die. I might have been one of those."

"You gave up your freedom for all that," he said, still shocked by it, and sad for her. She seemed so fragile, but he suspected she was stronger than she looked. But her innocence was real.

She nodded, but didn't seem to mind sacrificing her freedom to Vladimir. "It's the price I paid for a peaceful life. We all give up something." She was philosophical about it.

"You never answered me when I asked if you love him." He knew he had no right to ask but wanted to know. It had tormented him for months, and he knew he might never get the chance to ask her again. He doubted that he'd be able to see her.

"I think I do. He is very good to me, in the ways he knows. He's not a soft man. He doesn't want children. I don't either. The world is a frightening place for a child. What if everything goes wrong for them? I couldn't do that to someone else and give them the life I had." It was hard for Theo to understand, his parents had adored him and doted on him, his entire life had been comfortable and safe. He had never been at risk in any way. How could he judge a life like hers? He knew he couldn't and didn't want to, and was willing to forgive her anything she had done to survive. And who knew what he would have done in her shoes, what he would have been willing to trade for his survival? She had known danger from the day she was born. And he suspected that she wasn't exempt from it with Vladimir now, but she didn't seem to see that, and believed herself safe with him. Theo couldn't assess it, it was just a feeling he had, a sixth sense, given who and what Vladimir was.

"And if it ends, then what happens?" he asked, looking concerned for her. They were all the questions he had had about her for months, and it was his only chance to ask them and get to know her better, in a single afternoon. The food had arrived by then, and they were eating, but the conversation was more important to both of them than the meal. She had wondered about him too, and men like Theo were a mystery to her, men close to her age, who had wholesome, normal lives. She never met men like him, and never would. Vladimir saw to it, and she was a willing partner in her own isolation.

"I don't know what would happen if it ends," she said honestly. "I don't think it will. He needs me. But one day there may be someone younger, or more exciting. He's a generous man. If I betray him, he will never forgive me. If I don't, I think he'll take care of me. And if not, I will have to find my way. I wouldn't go back to Russia then. I couldn't survive there, even now, without him. It's too hard." Theo knew there was another solution too, but didn't say it to her. As his mother had said, most women like her found another man like Vladimir if they were cast off. The mistresses of rich, powerful Russian men always seemed to find another one, perhaps not as important as the first, or sometimes more so, if they were lucky. But the life they had led made them unsuitable for ordinary men. There was no way they could adjust to a real life once they had existed in the rarefied atmosphere of men like him, and most of those women didn't want to. He wasn't sure about Natasha and what she would do. She seemed different to him, but maybe she wasn't, and perhaps she was addicted to all the benefits she reaped daily in Vladimir's world. How could you leave a life like his for a real one? Few women could, and most wouldn't want to. In a way, Vladimir had ruined her for everyone else if he ever left her, except a man just like him. Theo felt deep compassion for her, as they finished lunch and ordered coffee, and decided to share a dessert. They ordered the soft chocolate cake, which was delicious.

There was one last question he wanted to ask her, although neither of them knew the answer to it.

"What if you ever left him?" Admittedly, it was hard to imagine.

"Why would I? He's good to me, he's a kind man. I think he loves me in his own way."

"But if you did for some reason?" She thought about it for a minute and almost said "he would kill me," but she didn't want to shock Theo or frighten him.

"He would never forgive me." And they both suspected he could be dangerous then, but neither of them said it, they just thought it.

"When I first met you, I wondered if you were happy with him. He's so much older than you are, so hard, so tough. Men like that don't get softer when they go home at night."

"No, they don't," she agreed. "I'm happy enough. I would be more unhappy without him." And Theo knew now that it wasn't about the lifestyle or the perks he provided, but the safety she believed he afforded her. Theo hoped she was right. But whatever her reasons, he was sorry for her. He thought she was missing a lot, whether she knew it or not. But she seemed to have no regrets about her lost freedom. She seemed to think it was unimportant, as a trade for her allegedly protected life.

He felt astonishingly close to her as he walked her back to her building farther up Avenue Montaigne. It had gotten colder and there were snowflakes in the air, which caught on her lashes as they stood outside her address.

"Thank you for the painting." She smiled at him. "And lunch." She knew it was a special moment, for both of them. She and Theo had had some kind of connection from the first time they met. It was as though they had known each other for years. She didn't understand it. She could see it in his portrait of her, he knew her intimately, and she felt the same way about him. It had been just a chance meeting, but a nice one. And she felt a little sad, leaving him, knowing they wouldn't meet again. She couldn't. Vladimir wouldn't like it if they became friends. That didn't fit into her life, and Theo knew it.

"Thank you for having lunch with me, and answering my questions. I kept wondering about you, while I was doing the portrait." And he didn't say it to her, but now that he knew her better, he wanted to do another one, to capture a whole different side of her. She was a many-faceted woman, both wise and naïve, frightened and brave, and poignantly human. He wrote his phone number down on a piece of paper for her then, and handed it to her. "If you ever need me, or need a friend, or need help, or you just want to talk, call me. I'll be there." And she suspected he would. He seemed like a man you could trust and rely on.

"Don't worry about me." She smiled at him again. "I'm safe." She leaned toward him then and kissed him on the cheek and he held her for an instant, hoping that she was right and what she said was true, that she was safe. But how could she be with a man known to be ruthless, who had dangerous connections like Vladimir's? Theo found it hard to believe. Maybe she knew him better. But Theo wasn't sure.

She waved as she walked into the building, and used the code to let herself into the inner door, and then disappeared, and Theo walked back to his hotel on the Left Bank, lost in thought. He knew he wouldn't see her again, except by coincidence somewhere, and the time they had just spent together was a once-in-a-lifetime gift.

It was nearly five when he reached the hotel. They had sat at the table at L'Avenue for hours, and he took his time walking back to where he was staying when he left her, to digest what she had said. And as he let himself into his hotel room, he saw Inez packing her suitcase and looking enraged. Her eyes were blazing, and he realized he had never turned his phone back on after lunch, and had forgotten his promise to call her at lunchtime. He felt like a complete jerk, but once he had been with Natasha, everything else had gone out of his head.

"Where the hell were you, or should I guess? And why was your phone turned off?"

"I know. I'm sorry. I forgot to turn it back on after lunch. I had lunch with Jean, and we got engrossed in a conversation about the art world. I'm really sorry, I lost track of the time."

"I called him four times and you left him at noon," she said, looking irate. "Were you with the Russian girl in the portrait?" He thought of lying to her again and decided not to. There was no point.

"I took it to her. She should have it."

"And you stayed to go to bed with her?" she asked in a shaking voice as she closed her suitcase.

"No, we had lunch, and talked. That's when I turned off my phone, and I forgot that I'd promised to call you." In fact, he had stood Inez up for lunch, and he felt like a total heel, and didn't blame her for being angry.

"You're in love with her, Theo. I saw how you looked at her last night. And I don't care who she belongs to, or what Russian gangster is paying her bills. You're in love with her, regardless of how she feels about you. And for all I know, she's in love with you too."

"She isn't," he assured her. "She seems happy where she is."

"This is what I mean by drama. I don't need this in my life. I have a child, a job, I'm trying to make it all work. I don't need some guy who's in love with another woman, even one you can't have."

"She's given up all her freedom to be with him. We were talking about it." Inez looked even more furious as he said it.

"Oh, please, don't ask me to feel sorry for her. She's doing exactly what she wants. My heart is not bleeding for her. It's all about the money for women like that. There's nothing noble about it."

"Maybe not, but it's more complicated than you think."

"I don't care. Everyone's life is complicated. And I don't need you complicating mine more than it already is, while you chase some fantasy woman around, and paint portraits of a woman you can't have. I don't want to be part of your fantasy life. And if she turns out to be more than a fantasy, I'm not sticking around." She set her suitcase down on the floor then, and he looked worried, but not surprised.

"Where are you going?"

"To stay with my sister for a few days, and then I'm going home."

"Am I going to see you again?"

"I don't know. I'll let you know. I need some time to think about it. This is exactly what I told you I didn't want. I think you're in love with this girl. And I can't fight your illusions about her, and don't want to. My life is too real for that." And with that, she opened the door and walked out with her suitcase, and he didn't stop her. He knew he had no right to. And she was right. He could feel his obsession for Natasha fully alive again. She did that to him every time, and he didn't want to screw up Inez's life, or his own. He had to stay sane this time, and not let Natasha take over his life. He had a lot to think about.

He went for a walk in St. Germain after Inez left. It was freezing cold and snowing. All he could think about was Natasha and what she'd said to him over lunch about her relationship with Vladimir, and her past. He understood it all better now. And he doubted he'd ever see her again. He had lost two women that day, Natasha and Inez, and had never really had either one.

And in her bed on Avenue Montaigne, Natasha was staring at the portrait, and thinking of the artist who had painted it. And she wondered what Vladimir would say when he saw it. He would see it the moment he walked into their bedroom. She wasn't going to keep it a secret from him. It was too beautiful to hide. The only thing she wasn't going to tell him was about lunch. He didn't need to know that. She had put the slip of paper with Theo's number on it in her wallet. She couldn't imagine ever calling him, but it was good to have. And he was her only friend.

Chapter 9

When Vladimir came home from Moscow the night before they left for Courchevel, the portrait of her was the first thing he saw when he walked into their Paris bedroom.

"What's that?" he asked, looking startled and stopping to stare at it.

"A portrait of me." She smiled at him. She was happy to see him as she put her arms around him and he held her close. He had missed her while he was gone.

"I can see that. Is it a surprise for me?" He was touched and a little amazed that she had had herself painted for him, although he loved it and was curious who the artist was.

"It's a surprise for both of us. The artist saw us at Da Lorenzo, and painted it from memory."

"You never sat for it?" She shook her head. "It's remarkably good. Who's the artist?"

"Lorenzo Luca's son. Apparently he's an artist too. He was at the restaurant that night."

"Did you talk to him?" Vladimir pulled away and looked at her carefully when she answered. An alarm went off in his head, and he suddenly wondered if he had delivered the painting and had been the man she'd toured around the boat. Vladimir was no one's fool and had great instincts.

"Only briefly, when I looked at the paintings when you were on the phone. I thought he was a waiter. I didn't know he was Luca's son till now."

"Is that who brought the painting to the boat?" he asked her, and she nodded as he walked over to examine the painting again more closely. "He has talent. Did you buy it?"

"I saw it in an art show, and he gave it to us." She included Vladimir in the gift, and didn't mention lunch.

"How did you get it?" He looked at Natasha intently.

"He dropped it off."

"I should thank him. Do you know his name and how to reach him?" Vladimir seemed benevolent, but Natasha could sense tension in the air. Something unusual had occurred.

"I have his bio somewhere—it came with the painting. Theo Luca, I think. And I suppose you can reach him at the restaurant." She was casual about it to dispel the tension. Vladimir nodded, and she went to finish packing for their ski trip the next day. They were flying in to Geneva, and then driving to Courchevel, and spending a week there, and then going back to London for a month. They hadn't been in London for a while. He'd been in Moscow a lot recently, and in Italy about his new boat, and she'd been in Paris, finishing the apartment. It was almost done now, and they both loved it.

The maid had left them a cold dinner in the refrigerator, and they were eating in the kitchen that night, when Vladimir looked at her, and asked her a question he never had before.

"Is this enough for you, Tasha?"

"For dinner? Yes, I'm not very hungry." And he had said he only wanted a salad and some cold meat that night.

"That's not what I mean," he said thoughtfully, and she looked puzzled. "I mean us. The life we lead. I never promised more than this. But you were very young when we started. But not being married, not having babies, are you unhappy about that now? You could be married to some nice, normal man, with a regular job, who's around all the time, and having children with him. Sometimes I forget how young you are, and that this life may not suit you forever." As she looked at him, she felt panic rise in her throat and remembered Theo's questions at lunch two weeks before, about what she would do if her life with Vladimir ended. She hadn't wanted to say it to him, but she thought she would die. How would she live? Where would she go? Who would want her? What if she had to go back to Moscow? She had no skills—how would she find a job, except as a factory worker again? She was convinced she wouldn't survive it. She loved him, and this was her life now, one she was used to, and she had no idea how to exist in the real world. She knew she was desperately spoiled, thanks to him.

"Of course this is the life I want," she said in a choked voice. "I don't want children. I never did. They frighten me. I wouldn't know what to do with them, and it's too much responsibility to have for someone else's life. And we don't need to be married. I'm happy as we are." She had never asked for more, or pressed him about it, unlike some women, and he liked that about her. She wasn't greedy, which was so different from the women he had known before. "And I would probably be bored with a 'normal' man, as you put it. What would I say to someone like that? What would I do with a man like that?" She smiled at him. "Besides, he'd expect me to cook, and I don't know how." She didn't need to, they had cooks in all their homes, except Paris, and they usually went out when they were there, or ordered food in. He laughed at what she said and seemed relaxed again after the initial shock of seeing her portrait.

"I just wondered. I've been too busy lately.

Courchevel will do us good." Although he skied very little with her, he was too skilled and she was still learning and couldn't keep up with him. He was an excellent skier, despite the fact that he had only learned fifteen years before, and not as a boy.

But after he had said what he did, she felt uneasy. What if someone he knew had seen her having lunch with Theo and thought she was having an affair? The lunch hadn't been romantic, it had been friendly, although intense, but Vladimir had never asked her questions like that before. She vowed to herself to be especially careful from then on, and not encourage any friendships. Theo hadn't contacted her since their lunch, but if he did, she wouldn't respond. She couldn't take the risk, and suddenly she realized how easily it could all end, if Vladimir chose to banish her. It was a terrifying thought, and had happened to others before. The very idea of it horrified her. She would be lost without him and she knew it. It was a wake-up call to her. And she was even more attentive to him than usual when they went to Courchevel. She tended to his every need, kept him company, and saw to it that they had the meals he liked best, mostly Russian food. She found a Russian girl to cook for them while they were there, and Vladimir loved the meals she prepared. Everything went smoothly, and he enjoyed skiing every day. They spent their nights by the fire in the enormous living room of the chalet they had rented, and they made love more than usual in the holiday atmosphere. And she came in early to dress for him every night when he got back from the slopes. She wore the kind of clothes he liked to see her in, sexy and seductive.

And as he always did, he worked every morning before he went out skiing, and was in constant contact with his offices in Moscow and London. And he called the boat builder in Italy several times too. He said he had six weeks of hard work ahead, and in April they were flying to the boat waiting for them in the Caribbean, in St. Bart's. After that the boat would make the crossing back to the Mediterranean, so they would have her at their disposal in France in May. Their plans were well organized, and Vladimir seemed to have a lot going on with all his new deals. But by the time they left Courchevel, Natasha felt secure with him again. Vladimir had frightened her in Paris. His questions had reminded her of how much she had to lose. She could never take chances with that.

When Theo got back to St. Paul de Vence after his successful show in Paris, he started work on a new portrait of Natasha, but this one was different. It was much darker, tainted by everything she had told him over lunch about her early life in Moscow. It was the more painful side of her life experience, and her face was less recognizable in the new portrait. Marc saw it on his easel when he came to see him, and didn't realize who it was. And Theo worked on it less frenetically. The subject of the portrait was so soulful that he found he couldn't work on it as often or as intensely, or it depressed him, and he was working on two other paintings at the same time. And a part of him didn't want to paint her again. His head told him to release her, but another part of him didn't want to let her go. He was wrestling with the obsession this time, and not giving in to it as he had before. He knew he couldn't, for her sake, as well as his own.

He had been back for a week when he got a text from Inez. Predictably, she said she didn't want to see him again. She thought his life was too unstable, he was too steeped in his work. He had no plans for the future, other than for his career as an artist. He wasn't interested in marriage, and she said she needed someone more solid. She added that whether he admitted it to himself or not, she was convinced that he was in love with Natasha, a woman he couldn't have. She told him it was all too complicated for her, she thought their relationship was a dead end that would go nowhere, and she preferred to stop it before it went any further. He was sorry but not crushed. He liked her, but he didn't love her, and they both knew it. He sent her a text saying that he regretted her decision, but he understood. And in some ways, it was a relief. He had no room for her in his head or his heart, and she knew it.

Although he didn't fully agree with her about Natasha. He was intrigued by her, and fascinated by her, and had been obsessed with her at various times while he was working on her portrait, but how could he love a woman he barely knew? He would have liked to spend time with her and get to know her better, but he knew there was no possibility of that. But in quiet moments of introspection, he admitted to himself that he had never been in love. He had had infatuations and affairs and a number of wild flings, and dated a few women for extended periods of time, and even lived with one woman for a year, but he had never loved any of them passionately, nor been heartbroken when it was over. He wondered if there was something missing in him. The only woman who had seized him in her grip, to the point of distraction at times, was the one he didn't really know. He stopped working on the portrait for a while when he thought about it, to give his obsession with her time to cool again. He said something about it to his mother when she asked who he was dating. She'd had the feeling recently that he wasn't seeing anyone, and she was right. After Inez, he didn't go out with anyone for a while.

"So what are you up to?" she asked him over Sunday brunch when Gabriel was in Paris for a few weeks. His daughter had been complaining that he never came to the gallery anymore, so he was planning to spend some time in Paris for a while until she calmed down.

"Just painting," Theo said, looking peaceful. His work had been going well. It usually did when he had no distractions. He always found it hard to juggle women and work and be fair to both. And the women in his life never liked it.

"Are you seeing anyone?" He shook his head and didn't look bothered by it.

"No, I was seeing a girl from Cannes for a while. She hates artists, she says I have no stable plans for the future, other than for my work, I'm not interested in marriage, which is true, I don't want children for the moment, also true, or maybe ever, I haven't decided. And to be honest, I stood her up for another woman when we were in Paris for my opening. I just totally forgot she was there. It was very rude. She left, and then told me it was over. I don't blame her. I would have dumped me too." He smiled at his mother.

"Who did you stand her up for?" his mother asked with interest, and he hesitated before he answered. That was harder to explain.

"Actually, I did a portrait of Stanislas's mistress, from memory, and put it in the show in Paris. Gabriel was crazy about the painting, and so was Pasquier. She showed up at the opening by coincidence, and loved it. So I took it to her the next day, and we had lunch." He tried to make it sound as casual as it had been and not as intense as he had felt.

"Was Stanislas there too?" She narrowed her eyes as she looked at him.

"No, he wasn't. I think he was away, or out or something. I didn't see him."

"I'm surprised she had lunch with you. Men like him usually keep their women on a very short leash."

"We didn't have sex at the restaurant. Just conversation."

Maylis went straight to the point. She always did. "Are you in love with her?" Her eyes bored into his.

"Of course not. She seems happy where she is. And as you pointed out before, I can't afford her." He didn't want to get into it too deeply with his mother. And she knew him too well. She'd see through him if he didn't tell the truth.

"You're playing with fire if you are in love with her," she warned him again. "Unattainable women, or men for that matter, are dangerous. You can never win them, and they break your heart. Whatever the reason, and not just the money, you can't compete with Stanislas if she's happy where she is, if that's what she says and she's telling you the truth."

"I think she is happy, and seems totally willing to accept the limitations of her situation with him, in exchange for what she gets, in terms of security and protection. It seems like a sad life to me. He owns her."

"That's how it works. And in your case, wanting someone you can't have is very romantic, but it's an agony you don't need," she said wisely. "You need to forget about her, Theo. You need a real woman in your life, not a fantasy. She's lovely looking, but she'll destroy your life if you let her."

"Or I hers." And he didn't want that either.

"She won't let you," his mother assured him. "She has too much at stake. You have nothing to lose, except your sanity and your heart. Run away while you still can. Don't let her become an obsession." But she already was. And when he went back to his studio after lunch, he forced himself not to work on the new portrait of her. He needed to be free of her. And he knew his mother was right.

For the rest of the spring, Theo plunged into what he did best. He was working on several paintings, staying in his studio for as long as he wanted, without the distraction of a woman in his life after the brief affair ended with Inez. He didn't hear from her again, and he didn't miss her. He wanted to concentrate on his work. He stopped dating completely for a few months, and wasn't unhappy about it. He was enjoying his work. And he had managed to stay away from the dark portrait of Natasha. He had other paintings on his mind.

And in April his mother asked him if he would take her place at the restaurant for three weeks in May. She and Gabriel wanted to go on a driving trip through Tuscany, and as usual he agreed reluctantly, but he knew she had no one else to ask, and he thought the trip to Italy would do them both good. And at the end of the trip they were going to Villa d'Este in Lake Como, which would be like a honeymoon for them. Theo thought it was sweet, although three weeks at the restaurant wasn't going to be much fun for him. And on the first weekend in May, they left in high spirits, excited about the trip.

Everything went smoothly at the restaurant the first week, the weather was warm, the garden was filled every night. The waiters got along. And the reservation book was filled, but not with more than they could handle.

The second week was more difficult, tempers frayed, the chef got sick for a day, and halfway through the week, on a Thursday night, Vladimir and Natasha came in. And although it shouldn't have, seeing them together shocked him. Theo felt his stomach turn upside down the moment he saw them. He knew it was insane. She had a life with Vladimir and had lived with him for eight years. She was his mistress and claimed to love him, but when Theo saw them together, he felt physically sick. He stayed away from them all night, and assigned the headwaiter to them. And he finally had to face them when they left. Theo saw that Natasha averted her eyes and didn't talk to him, so he chatted with Vladimir for a few minutes, who looked at him intensely with an unspoken message to stay away. He never mentioned the portrait, nor thanked him. And then they sped off in the Ferrari. And the moment they left, Theo stood on the pavement looking after them, feeling abandoned. It made no sense even to him. And Natasha clearly felt no connection to him and didn't want one. She was taking no risks with Vladimir, and Theo had noticed that the Russian had watched them both closely for any telltale sign, but there had been none. Despite their friendly lunch in January, Natasha had been chilly and distant with him, as though they didn't know each other. It was a strong message to him to keep his distance.

He locked up the money that night, closed the restaurant when everyone had left, went home, and drank half a bottle of wine, thinking about her and wondering why Vladimir was so lucky. He didn't deserve her. Theo hoped they wouldn't come in again while he was there. He took the unfinished portrait out and stared at it again. He could feel the obsession intensifying, and he didn't want it to. But it had a life of its own and there was nothing he could do to stop it, except try to forget her. She was like a ghost who appeared in his life from time to time, and then vanished. But whether he saw her or not, she was always out of reach, and belonged to someone else. And he knew it did him no good thinking about her. His mother was right.

He was still asleep when the phone rang at seven the next morning, and when he opened his eyes, he realized that he had a hangover from the night before, and a nasty headache. He reached for the phone to answer it as he put his head back on the pillow and closed his eyes. It was his mother, and she was crying. He sat up in bed then, trying to figure out what she was saying. She was incoherent. All he could understand was that something had happened to Gabriel, and he was in a coma.

"What?" The connection from Italy was terrible. "Slow down, Maman. I can't understand you." He was shouting, and she only cried harder. "Did you have an accident? Are you hurt too?" He was panicked.

"No, he had a heart attack." Theo knew Gabriel had had heart problems before, and an angioplasty, but this sounded far more serious if he was in a coma.

"Not while he was driving, I hope." He was worried for his mother too, and concerned about Gabriel. It seemed bad from what she was saying.

"No, at the hotel. He thought it was indigestion,

but it wasn't. The hotel had to call an ambulance, and the fire department came. His heart stopped twice on the way to the hospital. I was with him. They used those awful electroshock machines, and thank God they got it started again. Oh God, Theo, and now he's in a coma." She sobbed for a full five minutes before she could go on again, or answer Theo's questions.

"What are the doctors saying? Are you near a big city?"

"We're in Florence. The doctors say it all depends on what happens in the next forty-eight hours. They said he might not survive it." She sounded devastated. Gabriel had been her tower of strength for twelve years, and now he had crumbled.

"Are the doctors any good?"

"I think so. They want to do another angioplasty, but they can't do it until he's stronger."

"Did you call Marie-Claude? Do you want me to?"

"I called her last night. She'll be here this morning."

"Do you want me to come, Maman?" Theo offered, wishing his head weren't pounding on top of everything that had happened.

"No, you can't leave the restaurant. Someone has to be in charge."

"They'll manage if they have to," he said firmly. "If you want me to, I'll come." It was a short flight from Nice to Florence. It struck him then how life could change in the blink of an eye. Ten days before, Gabriel had been fine, and in high spirits when they left on their trip, and now he was in a coma and might be dying. It was a powerful lesson about life.

"Let's see how it goes today, and Marie-Claude will be here." Although Theo wasn't sure how comforting she would be for his mother. The two women had never gotten along, and he knew Gabriel's daughter resented the time he spent with her, and complained about it often.

"Call me later and let me know how he's doing."

When Theo got up and showered, he was angry at himself for being upset when he saw Natasha the night before. She was the mistress of one of the richest and most powerful men in the world, and said she was happy with him. Mooning over her, and wanting a woman he could never have was doing no one any good. And what had just happened to Gabriel was a warning to them all. His mother had treated him as second best for all the years they'd been together, possibly never even realizing how much she loved him, and now she might lose him. And he had been infinitely more loving to her than Lorenzo, whom she worshipped. If Gabriel survived, Theo was going to give her a stern lecture. And he gave himself one about Natasha. She had the life she wanted, with a man who seemed to suit her. And there was no room for him in the story, except as some kind of voyeur or lovesick boy. As he waited to hear from his mother that morning, he promised himself that he wouldn't finish the second portrait of Natasha. He needed to get over her, not feed his obsession. Marc had said as much to him months before.

As he sat in his kitchen, drinking coffee, Maylis was talking to the doctors, and the news wasn't encouraging. Gabriel had had another cardiac episode that morning, and they weren't hopeful. She was sitting alone in the waiting room crying when Marie-Claude arrived from Paris. Maylis told her what was happening, and Marie-Claude hurried down the hall to see her father in cardiac ICU, where he was on a ventilator, and family could visit him only for a few minutes every hour. Maylis had said she was his wife, and Marie-Claude looked pale when she returned a few minutes later, sat down in a chair, and blew her nose.

"He looks awful," she said, and started to cry again, as Maylis went to comfort her, and was shocked when Gabriel's daughter pulled away from her. "I don't know what game you're playing," she said angrily. "All you've ever done is use my father. You never loved him." Maylis looked horrified at what she was saying.

"How can you say something like that? We've

been together for almost five years now, and we were close for years before that. Of course I love him."

"Really? All you do is talk about your husband, as though he was some kind of saint, instead of a narcissistic madman who drove everyone crazy, including my father, who did everything for him, while Lorenzo accused him of stealing." She had heard about it for years, and didn't have her father's patience with his artistic temperament, affection for him, or sense of humor. He had always thought it was funny when Lorenzo called him a crook. His daughter didn't. "It's my father who is the saint here. And if he dies, you'll have it on your conscience that he never knew if you really loved him. All he ever knew is how much you loved Lorenzo. You even made it clear to him that you could never love him as much as you did your husband, and he was willing to accept that from you. God knows why. He didn't deserve that." What she was saying left Maylis speechless, and it was like a powerful slap in the face. And she knew that everything Marie-Claude was saying was true. Every word of it. And all she could do was cry as she listened. And after Marie-Claude unburdened herself with a heartbroken look, she left the room to call her husband, and Maylis called Theo. She was crying even harder than the first time.

"Oh my God, did he die?" Theo couldn't understand her between the sobs. But he couldn't imagine anything else the way she sounded.

"No, he's still alive. It's Marie-Claude." She told him verbatim then what she had said, and when she finished, there was a long silence at Theo's end. He didn't know what to say to her. It was true, and she knew it. They all did. Gabriel had played second fiddle to an irascible, bad-tempered dead man for twelve years, four of them with Maylis as his mistress, but always pointing out to him that she had loved Lorenzo more. There were times when Theo wondered how he stood it. And he didn't blame Marie-Claude for being upset with his mother, especially now. She wouldn't even go to Paris to see him. She made him come to her in the South. Maylis had made very little effort. It was Gabriel who made the relationship work and was infinitely kind and loving to her. "What am I going to do? She hates me. And she's right. I was awful to him. How could I say all those things about Lorenzo, and that I loved him more?" She was suddenly consumed with guilt, and all she wanted now was for Gabriel to survive so she could tell him how much she loved him.

"He knows you love him, Maman. I think you thought you'd be unfaithful to Papa's memory if you admitted even to yourself how much you love Gabriel. I think he understood that. We just have to hope he gets better now. That's all that matters."

"It sounds like he's going to die." She sobbed as she said it.

"We don't know that. He's not that old." But he had just turned sixty-eight with a history of heart trouble. And several cardiac arrests in a short time was dangerous.

They talked for a few more minutes and then they hung up as Marie-Claude walked back into the room and looked like she'd been crying.

"I'm sorry," Maylis said softly, as Marie-Claude took a seat across from her again, not wanting to sit next to her. "What you said is true, and I was wrong. I've always loved him. I just didn't want to be untrue to Lorenzo."

"My father knew that," she said grudgingly, "but it was still a terrible thing to do to him. He loves you, and he was so lonely without you in Paris that he was in St. Paul de Vence all the time. My children and I never see him. You could at least have made the effort to come to Paris once in a while." Maylis nodded and realized that that was true too.

"I promise, I will in the future," Maylis said, deeply chastised, and hoping she'd have the chance.

"You may not have to," Marie-Claude said brusquely. She was irate for her father's sake, and she had never liked Maylis, and been jealous of her father's affection for her. She was letting her have it with both barrels now. And Maylis was honest enough to admit where she'd been wrong.

They sat in the waiting room in silence for two hours after that, hoping for news, until a doctor came in, and explained to both of them that Mr. Ferrand was not doing well. He was preparing them for the worst. Maylis nearly fainted when he told them, and Marie-Claude left the room to cry alone. Later they let them see him, still in the coma on the ventilator, which was breathing for him. He had had no more cardiac episodes, but his heart wasn't strong. He was hooked up to half a dozen monitors, and the ICU staff was watching closely.

It was a long night for both women, waiting for some improvement or change. They took turns going to see him for a few minutes each time, but he was still in the coma and unaware of their presence. And the two women hadn't spoken since Marie-Claude's outburst that morning. Maylis had been lost in thought ever since, consumed with guilt, remembering each instance when she must have hurt him. She was living the agonies of the damned, and Marie-Claude had no idea of the flood tides that had opened as a result of her words. Maylis looked ravaged by morning when one of the doctors came in to see them again, and asked if they wanted last rites administered. The two women sobbed openly after that, and this

time Marie-Claude allowed Maylis to take her in
her arms and hold her while they both cried.

The priest came, and gave Gabriel extreme unc-
tion, and afterward Marie-Claude and Maylis returned to their vigil in the waiting room. Neither
dared go back to their hotel for fear that he would
die while they were gone, or regain consciousness
for his last moments and they would miss them.
The nurses had brought them pillows and blan-
kets the night before, and there was a shower down
the hall which they used. And Maylis went to get
food from the cafeteria for both of them, but they
didn't touch it. They just drank coffee and waited
for the inevitable to happen. And during one of
Maylis's turns with him at lunchtime, she saw a
nurse react to one of the monitors and rush off to
get the doctor. She was sure the end had come.
And by the time the doctor came to check the
monitor, an alarm was sounding on another one.

"What's happening?" Maylis looked terrified as
they checked him, and the nurse turned to her.

"He's waking up," she whispered. And as she
said it, Gabriel opened his eyes and looked confused, and then closed them again and drifted
off. But he had been conscious for a few minutes.
And another doctor appeared to discuss whether
the ventilator should be removed, and their conclusion was to wait and see what happened next.

He woke up several times that afternoon, once
while his daughter was with him, the other time

with Maylis, and by eight o'clock that night, his eyes were fully open, and they took him off the ventilator to see how he would do breathing on his own. His voice was hoarse when he spoke to Maylis.

". . . too young to die . . ." he said and winked at her, and then croaked out the words "I love you."

"I love you too," she said and had never meant it more, as she stood next to him and held his hand. "Don't try to talk, just rest."

"I've been resting, but you look tired," he said, worried about her.

"I'm fine." But she looked nearly as bad as he did. It had been a hell of a scare and he wasn't out of the woods yet, and could have cardiac arrest again, the doctor explained. They wanted to do the angioplasty as soon as possible, but he wasn't strong enough. And after that, they let both women into the room at the same time. And they were so relieved that he was better that they got along with each other for the first time in years. And Maylis encouraged Marie-Claude to use her hotel room that night. Maylis wanted to stay with Gabriel, and Marie-Claude admitted that she'd be grateful for a decent night's sleep and left, while Maylis slept in the waiting room again, in case he took a turn for the worse. In an odd way, Marie-Claude's outburst had relieved the tension between them that had been building for years.

Gabriel was much better in the morning. He had color in his cheeks, his blood pressure was good, and he was responding to the heart medication they were giving him. Theo was encouraged by his mother's reports and even talked to Gabriel on the phone, who sounded pretty good.

"They're making a big fuss about nothing," he told Theo. "You know how Italians are." But Maylis said the doctors had been excellent and had saved his life. There was no question about that. And that night she went to the hotel herself, and she and Marie-Claude shared the room, since the hotel was full and they couldn't get another one for her.

"I'm sorry I was so angry at you at first. I just know how much my father loves you, and I never thought you loved him as much. I realize now that you do. You should tell him sometime," she said more gently, now that things had calmed down. Maylis had told him just that since he'd regained consciousness, and apologized profusely for how badly she had treated him, which he generously denied. And she promised to go to Paris with him when he was feeling better. She assured him that things were going to change from now on. She was infinitely grateful that he was alive.

They were able to do the angioplasty a week later, and it was successful clearing the blocked artery, and the next argument came over where he was going to convalesce. Marie-Claude wanted him to come home to Paris, and Maylis wanted to nurse him herself in St. Paul de Vence. In the end, it was Gabriel who made the decision. He wanted to go home with Maylis and stay with her, and he promised his daughter that as soon as he felt stronger, he would come to Paris and spend a few weeks there, hopefully with Maylis, and she promised to come. But first the doctor wanted Gabriel at the hotel in Florence for at least a week, so he'd be nearby if he had a problem, and he didn't want him to fly yet, nor take the long drive back to St. Paul de Vence. Maylis had made arrangements to have the car driven back.

Gabriel was chafing at the bit to go home, but both women convinced him not to rush, and Maylis reminded him that there were worse fates than spending a week in Florence at a five-star hotel. She was able to get a big suite on the top floor with a spectacular view, and by the time Gabriel left the hospital, he was stronger, walking on his own, and thrilled with the lovely suite. The three of them had dinner in the room that night, and the next day Marie-Claude went home, and she embraced Maylis warmly as she left, and Gabriel raised an eyebrow afterward.

"I never thought I'd see that day," he said, referring to his daughter, who had been vocal and strident against Maylis for years.

"We cleared the air while you were asleep," she said without explaining further, but knowing that Marie-Claude was now convinced that Maylis did in fact love her father, more than ever after their scare. Nearly losing Gabriel had been an eye-opener for them all.

Meanwhile, Theo had been running the restaurant for three weeks, and hadn't been in his studio for as long. He was monitoring the books, running the staff, coordinating with the chef about the menus, calling the florist, and getting almost hourly reports from his mother in Florence. And they weren't due home for another week. And when they got back, she would want to be with Gabriel at night. It was almost the end of May by then, and he could easily see himself running the restaurant for another month, and he wasn't happy about it, but there was nothing he could do. He didn't want to complain to her. She had her hands full with Gabriel, and had had a tough time herself.

And he groaned audibly when he saw Vladimir's name on the reservation book for a party of five that night. It was the last thing Theo needed now, but he felt ready to face Natasha, and was determined not to let seeing her rock him again as it had before. She belonged to Vladimir, and Theo was sure he had made his peace with it at last. There was no other choice, and he had too much on his plate to think about her at the moment. Real life had taken precedence over his fantasies about her. And knowing how she felt about

Vladimir, his obsession with her didn't even make sense to him anymore.

He was braced to see her when Vladimir walked in with a group of men at nine o'clock. They arrived in a van, and he left four bodyguards outside. And Theo realized as he greeted him that Natasha wasn't with him, which was almost a relief. The four men with him were Russian, and they looked like businessmen, although there was a rough quality to them. They were the kind of men Theo could easily imagine Vladimir doing business with, but he was noticeably much smoother and better dressed than the others. And Theo also knew that men like them were the power base of Russia now. For all he knew, they had the five richest men in Russia at the restaurant.

Vladimir gave him a pointed look when they walked in. Theo assigned the best waiters to their table, and sent over a round of complimentary drinks. All five men ordered vodka, including Vladimir, and they drank steadily through the evening. Vladimir ordered several bottles of two-thousand-dollar wine, and they finished it with abandon. And at the end of the meal they all lit cigars. Theo saw they were Partagás. And he sent brandy over for them. Vladimir looked pleased with the evening as they got up to leave. Da Lorenzo had become his new favorite restaurant. He stopped and said something to the others in Russian on the way out, and then took them into the house to see the paintings. Theo had no idea what he'd said, but it must have been favorable since all the men looked impressed when they came out. And Theo knew there were paintings Vladimir hadn't seen before, since his mother had recently rotated some of them, and put some of her favorite paintings from her private collection on the walls. There were some exceptionally fine ones on display, and Vladimir stopped and said something to Theo as the others headed toward the van. Their eyes met again. There was a message in Vladimir's that Theo pretended not to understand, like a warning of some kind.

"How much is the one of the woman with the little boy?" he asked Theo in a supercilious way. He had bought one of Lorenzo's paintings. Now he was sure he could buy more. It was one of a series that his father had painted of Maylis and him as a young child. It was a lovely painting, and one of his mother's favorites.

"There's no price on that, sir," he said politely. "It's part of Mrs. Luca's private collection, and very important to her. It's **really** not for sale." But since he had succeeded in getting what he wanted before, Vladimir was sure he would again, at the right price.

"We know it's for sale," he said to Theo conspiratorially. "The only question is the price." And he was not using an intermediary this time, since he knew who Theo was.

"I'm afraid not this time. She won't sell that one, or any from that series." The others in that series were at the studio, but there were at least half a dozen very important newer ones on the walls. And the one he wanted was the one she loved most. "It has sentimental value for her."

"She will sell it," he said, his eyes hard as he looked at Theo, holding the cigar close to his face. Theo remained courteous and professional but firm, while there was something slightly ominous in Vladimir's tone.

"It really isn't for sale," Theo said a little more strongly, "and I don't think she would be ready to sell another painting so soon after the last one."

"Call me tomorrow with the price," Vladimir said to him with flashing eyes.

"There is no price," Theo said, enunciating the words carefully, as rage sprang into Vladimir's eyes, like a lion about to strike, and for an instant Theo wondered if he was going to hit him. It made Theo wonder if he had ever looked at Natasha that way. Suddenly Theo had become an obstacle between Vladimir and what he wanted, and nothing was going to stop him. Theo took a step back to protect himself, and with a growl of anger, Vladimir stormed off to the van where the others were waiting for him. The bodyguards jumped in after him, and they left. It had been an unpleasant moment. And Vladimir hadn't been nearly as polite as usual, once he didn't get his way about the painting. After the vodka, wine, and brandy, Vladimir's temper was very thinly veiled. It accounted for how angry he had been at Theo about the painting, but there had been something more than alcohol in his eyes—there had been pure rage at Theo not agreeing to what he wanted and standing in his way. He had looked absolutely lethal, and Theo wouldn't have wanted to meet him on a dark street. He was an enemy one wouldn't want to have. And his previously personable exterior had instantly disappeared.

Theo was still thinking about it when he turned off the lights and locked up, and turned on the alarm, after all the employees left, and he drove home. He was relieved that he hadn't had to see Natasha that night. He thought he was ready for it, but he was in no rush to test his new indifference to her, and he was sorry that Vladimir had chosen to come to the restaurant with his cohorts. They were an unsavory-looking group, and would have looked like thugs if one didn't know who they were. Vladimir had covered his origins with a veneer of polish, but it had worn thin that night when he looked at Theo. They were an unpleasant lot, and he hoped they didn't come back soon. But all that really mattered, he thought as he let himself into his house, was that Gabriel had survived, and they would be home soon. The rest were all the usual aggravations of running a restaurant and dealing with unruly, arrogant clients. And for once, Mr. Stanislas didn't get his way. Theo smiled to himself. It was suitable revenge for Vladimir having the woman Theo wanted. The painting was not for sale.

Chapter 10

The phone rang the next morning just after seven o'clock, and Theo opened his eyes to a brilliantly sunny day. He'd been hoping to sleep in that morning, but now that he was running the restaurant, and had been for nearly a month, the staff called him with every detail and every question. He never understood how his mother managed all of it without going crazy. It was like running a school for badly behaved children, who argued about everything, couldn't get along, and couldn't make a decision on their own. He could see that the call was from the restaurant, and not from his mother in Florence, when he answered his cellphone. He was not pleased to have been woken up so early. He hadn't left the restaurant until nearly two A.M., after his brief confrontation with Vladimir, which had delayed him, and ended the night on an unpleasant note. And the kitchen staff had been slow cleaning up. He had promised his mother that he wouldn't leave before everyone else did, and he never had. He had kept his word. She wanted him to set the alarm.

The call was from one of the sous-chefs who had come in early. The chef had gone to the fish market at six A.M., and they'd been cleaning fish for half an hour, and had waited to call him at a slightly more reasonable time. The sous-chef sounded nervous as Theo made an effort to wake up and sound alert.

"What is it?" It was usually something ridiculous like they had noticed two chairs were broken and what should they do about it? Or one of the dishwashers wasn't coming in.

"Fatima says there's a problem," the sous-chef said cautiously.

"What kind of problem?" Theo frowned as he listened. The only thing he worried about seriously was leaks in the old house that could damage the paintings. They were heavily insured, but a damaged painting could not be replaced.

"She says you have to come in."

"Why? What happened?" Fatima was their cleaning woman. She was Portuguese, spoke very little French, and her two sons worked with her, and spoke none at all. "Can you at least tell me what's wrong?" If it was trivial, he wasn't moving.

The sous-chef nearly cried when he told him. "There are twelve paintings off the walls." He sounded strangled as he said it. "Fatima wants to know if you took them down."

"No, I didn't, and what do you mean 'off the walls'? Did they fall down? Are they damaged?" It sounded odd to him since they were bolted to the walls. Theo threw back the covers, and put his feet on the floor. It was obvious he had to go in. And what the sous-chef had told him made no sense.

"Not damaged. Gone. Someone undid all the bolts. The alarm was off when I came in, which I thought was strange, unless you forgot to set it last night, but you never have before." And Theo knew he didn't forget it. He was meticulous about it and remembered turning it on as he always did. "They're gone. Missing. Someone took them. I thought the lock on the door had been played with, but everything was in order. Just the twelve paintings."

"Oh my God." Theo felt dizzy as he stood up. Nothing like it had ever happened before. "Call the police. I'll be there in ten minutes." He didn't waste time asking which ones were gone. It wasn't possible. How could anyone rob them? They had a state-of-the-art alarm system, beams, video cameras, surveillance, and a direct line to the police. They had nearly three hundred million dollars' worth of art in the house, their alarm was infallible, or so they'd been told.

He pulled on a pair of jeans and a T-shirt, slipped

his feet into sandals, brushed his teeth and not his hair, and ran out the door with his cellphone and car keys and forgot his wallet on the kitchen table. He stopped at the house where his mother lived on the way, his father's old studio, where the bulk of her collection was, to see if she had been robbed too, but everything was intact there, the alarm was on, and nothing had been disturbed.

He jumped back in his car then and raced to the restaurant. He ran through the front door when he got there, and stood looking at the empty spaces that had been left. There had been no damage to the walls. The bolts hadn't been opened with force—they had been professionally disabled and the paintings removed. Theo thought to warn everyone not to touch anything, in case there were fingerprints the police could use. But there was no question in Theo's mind. They had been struck by highly trained art thieves who knew what they were doing. All the paintings his mother had recently put up, including the one Vladimir had tried to buy the night before, were gone. But this wasn't the work of thugs, it was entirely the work of pros.

He went into the office while waiting for the police to look at the security tapes from the night before, and all he saw was static. They had been able to cripple the cameras and disable them, so that they had recorded nothing of the robbery. The tapes were blank. They had stopped functioning an hour after he left, and were blank for nearly two hours. It had apparently taken them that long to remove all twelve paintings. He felt like he was in shock as two inspectors walked in, and he spoke to them in the office after they surveyed the scene. Theo was badly shaken. He hadn't called his mother yet, and didn't know what to say or how to tell her. And he wanted more information from the police before he said anything. Maybe there were known art thieves in the area, and they would have an idea who had done it.

The two inspectors had been dispatched from Nice, and were part of a high-end robbery detail that patrolled the entire coast where there were homes that were robbed most frequently, and jewels, art, and large amounts of money were stolen, and sometimes hostages were taken. One of the inspectors was older with gray hair, the other was in his late thirties, and both appeared to be experienced. They asked for the approximate value of what was missing, and if the paintings were by varied artists.

"No, only one. My father, Lorenzo Luca. All the paintings here are in my mother's private collection, and the value of the twelve that are gone is in the vicinity of a hundred million dollars." They didn't appear to be surprised, and were accustomed to robberies in those amounts from major villas along the coast in Cap-Ferrat, Cap d'Antibes, Cannes, and the other wealthier communities. St. Tropez was in a different district, in the Var, and Monaco was a separate country and had its own police force. "Have there been any other major art thefts recently? Could this have been done by a gang you know of?" Many of the truly dangerous professionals were Eastern European, and the police knew all of them, but they said none had been operative in the past few months, not since the previous winter. This was the first big robbery they'd had in a while.

The area was closed off, and police lines were set up. And a team of technicians and experts arrived half an hour later to take fingerprints, and examine the alarm system and cameras. Theo dispatched another of the sous-chefs to call everyone listed in the reservation book for that night, and cancel them, and say there had been an accident and the restaurant was closed.

It was noon before the two inspectors in charge had something to tell Theo. There were no prints. The alarm had been electronically disabled, possibly from another location by remote control, and the cameras along with it. All their high-tech devices had been crippled for the duration of the robbery and restored when it was over.

"The only good news," the older inspector said to him, "is that these people knew what they were doing, and they're not liable to damage the paintings or destroy them. We will contact all our informants. Someone is going to try to sell these paintings on the stolen-art market, or possibly sell them back to you at a higher price."

"Or sequester them," Theo said, looking as though he were about to cry. There was a market for stolen paintings sold to unscrupulous collectors who were anxious to acquire work at any price, knowing they could never show them, but simply have the thrill of owning them, and with his father's work so rarely on the market, they qualified for that kind of buyer. Some people would do anything to own them, even if they remained a secret forever. Some of the paintings stolen by the Nazis had disappeared that way.

"We'd like to bring Interpol into it. And I have a call in to the art detail in Paris. I'd like one of them to come down. I can assure you we're going to do everything we can to find your paintings for you, or as many as we can locate and reclaim. Time is of the essence, we have to move quickly, before they're shipped out of the country to Russia, South America, Asia. As long as they stay in Europe, we have a better chance of tracking them down. We'll need photographs of the work to put on the Internet throughout Europe." It was one of the most important art thefts of recent times. There had been a comparable one two years before. There were more jewel thefts, since they were simpler to break down into loose stones. Art was much harder to sell and transport, and was

too easily identified. "We'll stay on this, I can assure you. You need to put security guards on the
house." And Theo wanted them on his mother's
house too.

He still had to call their insurance company,
and his mother. The inspector gave him the case
number for the insurance company, and they
were still swarming all over the house when he
went into the office to call his mother, which he
dreaded, but it couldn't be avoided. And just as
he was about to, he thought of something. Vladimir the night before. He went back to find the
inspector, who confirmed that the back door
had been tampered with. And they were running
criminal checks on all the employees. They hadn't
ruled out the possibility that it was an inside job,
that one of their employees had tipped someone
off and sold the information about the security
system to them. Fatima was crying while her sons
were being interrogated. She was horrified to
think that someone could think they had com-
mitted a crime, and a police officer was trying to
explain to her that all the employees would be
investigated, not just her sons.

"This might sound crazy," Theo said to the senior inspector quietly. "Vladimir Stanislas was
here last night, with four Russian men. He wanted
to buy one of the paintings, and I told him it
wasn't for sale. He bought one from my mother

a year ago, at a very high price, which was also not for sale initially, and then she accepted his offer. But I knew she wouldn't sell the one he was inquiring about this time. He left in a rage. I just wanted to mention it, in case there is some sort of tie-in. You might want to talk to him. His yacht is usually off Antibes. It's probably there now. And possibly someone like him would be willing to buy a work that's not for sale normally."

The inspector smiled at what he said. "I think Stanislas could pay any price to get what he wants, legally."

"Not if it's not for sale," Theo persisted. "My mother wouldn't sell these. The one he wanted last night was among the twelve that were stolen."

"I think we can assume that's a coincidence," the inspector said in a patronizing tone. To him, Vladimir Stanislas might look like a rough customer, but he was no art thief.

"I don't think we can assume anything," Theo said doggedly.

"We'll keep it in mind," the senior inspector said, and then went back to the others, still conducting their investigation. They were taking the house apart, and examining all the other paintings for fingerprints, but there were none so far.

Theo called the insurance company then, and they said they would have their own inspectors there that night, including two from Lloyd's of

London, who had an umbrella policy for the paintings. And then he called his mother in Florence. She said they were having lunch on the balcony of the suite when she answered, and Gabriel was feeling much better.

"Maman, I have something awful to tell you." He plunged in quickly, not wanting to keep her in suspense. "We had an art theft here last night, by professionals who disarmed our system."

"Oh my God." She sounded as if she were about to faint. "Which ones did they take?" Her paintings were like children to her, and it was like telling her that her children had been kidnapped. He told her which ones and how many, and everything he knew from the police, and told her that there were inspectors coming down from Paris, and the insurance company, and that the men on the scene seemed to know what they were doing. He didn't tell her about Vladimir, because it was a long shot, and they didn't take it seriously, but Theo had put it out there just in case. She sounded heartbroken and agitated, and told Gabriel everything Theo was telling her, and then he spoke to Theo. He sounded much calmer than Maylis, and he reassured Theo.

"I only know of one stolen painting that wasn't recovered during my entire career. The police details that handle art thefts are very good at what they do. And your father's work is so distinctive and well known, they'll find them. It may take some time, but they will." Theo was slightly relieved to hear it, and it was good for his mother to hear too.

"I'll keep you posted about what's happening here," Theo promised. "I'm really sorry to burden you and Maman with this news."

"I'm sorry you have to deal with it," Gabriel said sympathetically. "You're going to be very busy. You should probably close the restaurant for a while," he said, and in the background, Maylis agreed.

"I canceled everyone for tonight. I just didn't know what was going to happen, but you may be right. I suppose we'll have the press on our backs any minute," Theo said, and an hour later, they were there, with news cameras and trucks, trying to get an interview with Theo, who said he had nothing to say at this point, except that it was a shocking and devastating event. And La Colombe d'Or sent over a note of sympathy. It hit close to home and could have happened to them too. They were just as vulnerable, and their art was just as valuable. It was the biggest crime that had ever hit St. Paul de Vence, it said later on the news. Inez called him that night and left a message on his voicemail, telling him how sorry she was. He was too busy to talk to her when she called. He was with the insurance inspectors at the restaurant until after midnight, and all the police details came back again the next day, along with the team from Paris to help them.

Theo felt as though his life had been taken over by aliens. He handled nothing but the art theft all week, with constant calls from his mother, asking questions. They closed the restaurant and canceled their reservations for the week, and had to figure out what to do after that. And on the fifth day the chief inspector of the art detail introduced him to two new officers who had joined their crew from the local art theft detail. They were younger than the others and seemed more aggressive. They wanted to speak to several of the employees again, and went over the crime scene with a fine-toothed comb, looking for clues. Athena Marceau seemed extremely bright and about Theo's age. Steve Tavernier, her male partner, was slightly younger, and they asked Theo a million questions and then said they'd get back to him. He knew he was being investigated too, to make sure it wasn't an insurance scam. And Theo had shared with the two new officers his concerns about Vladimir. Steve was not impressed, but Athena was intrigued.

The two detectives talked about it afterward on a break when they went to get coffee offsite and pick up some chemicals they needed for the investigation. The restaurant and main house were looking like a laboratory by then, and a high-tech junk shop with all their equipment.

"That's crazy," Steve said to her. "The guy's upset. He'd accuse anybody right now," he assessed, referring to Theo.

"Crazier things have happened. I worked on a detail in Cap-Ferrat a few years ago. Their neighbor stole ten million in art and had their dog killed, because his neighbor slept with his wife. Some of these people are nuts."

"Maybe Luca did it himself. That happens too. For the insurance money. And a hundred million is pretty sweet," Steve said cynically.

"I don't think so," she said seriously. "There's nothing to support that."

"Are you kidding? A hundred million in insurance? He should be our prime suspect."

"He doesn't need it. He's worth way more than that in his father's art, and he's got plenty in the bank. We checked. He just looks homeless. He looks like he hasn't combed his hair all week, but he's not our guy."

"You just think he's cute," Steve teased her.

"True." She grinned at her partner. "If he'd comb his hair and put decent clothes on, he'd be hot. I wonder what he's like when he's not running around like a lunatic after a robbery. Don't you want to go see that boat? We could go talk to Stanislas for the hell of it. You never know what will turn up." She smiled mischievously, and her partner laughed and shook his head at the idea.

"We need clearance, and the chief inspector would go out there himself. He wouldn't send us."

"Maybe he would. We can ask. Who knows? Maybe Luca is right. He thinks Stanislas could have had something to do with it. I'm sure he's no saint. Guys who've made that kind of money never are."

"I think Luca's nuts. Stanislas could buy the whole collection if he wants."

"Not if they won't sell it to him. Did you see all those 'Not for Sale' signs? They're not selling any of it. Who knows? It could have pissed him off, just like Luca says. Some of those Russian guys are tough customers and have nasty friends."

"Not Stanislas. Shit, he's probably the richest guy in the world."

"Then I'd like to meet him. Maybe he's hot," she said, teasing her partner again. "Don't you like boats?"

"No, I get seasick."

"You won't on his. It's bigger than a hotel. Let's go for it." Steve Tavernier rolled his eyes, but he was used to her. They had worked together for three years, and Athena Marceau followed every lead and ran them all to ground. She was tireless and clever, and often right. They had an amazing track record, which was why they had been assigned to the case. They were less seasoned, and zealous, Athena's style was that nothing was too small to pursue, and her arrest record was astounding. Steve liked working with her. She made him look good when she broke a case, and he would do damn near anything for her. As far as he was concerned, her instincts were infallible. She didn't have any about this case yet, but she was willing to check anything out. And a tour of Stanislas's boat sounded good to her, for a kick if nothing else. She asked their chief inspector for permission that afternoon, not to search the boat, but just to visit Vladimir, and he shrugged and told her she was crazy, but he agreed to let them do it, although he said he would have liked to see the boat himself, but didn't have time. He was following the serious leads, while they were planning to visit yachts.

"Just don't ruffle him, or accuse him of any-thing. I don't want a complaint on my desk to-morrow," their chief inspector warned.

"No, sir," she promised, which her partner knew was worth nothing. Athena always did what she wanted, and then played innocent with their superiors, and got away with it a lot of the time. She decided not to make an appointment and just show up. She managed to get hold of a police boat with a young officer to drive it, and two hours later they were on the way to **Princess Marina,** sitting at anchor off the Hôtel du Cap.

"What if they don't even let us on the boat?"
Steve asked nervously. Athena wasn't concerned
at all. She was looking forward to it.

"No problem—then we shoot them," she
teased him. "Watch, he's going to charm us to
death. He'll see us," she said confidently. "He'll
want to make a good impression on us, to prove
he's above it all."

They pulled up at the loading dock at the back
of the boat. She flashed her badge at the sailors,
and a broad smile, and got out of the police boat
in bare feet, with her high heels in her hand, and
a flash of great legs as she hiked her skirt up to
hop aboard. She explained that they were there to
see Mr. Stanislas, and needed his help with an investigation of an art theft. She was sure he could
guess which one, since it was all over the news by
then. Steve let her do the talking as he always did.
She looked like a sexy young girl and anything
but a policewoman, as the sailors grinned at her,
and one of them went to call upstairs while she
and Steve waited and chatted with them.

A moment later, the deckhand was back, and
said he would take them upstairs. She gave Steve
a knowing look, and followed the crew member
into an elevator that took them up five floors
to the outside bar, where Vladimir was having
a glass of champagne with Natasha. Steve and
Athena wandered onto the deck, and Athena held

out a hand, and thanked him profusely for seeing them. Vladimir gave Natasha a nod, and she
stood up. Her face was expressionless, as Steve
looked her over admiringly in her skin-tight pink
bodysuit that showed every inch of her body, and
her breasts. Athena saw her but concentrated on
Vladimir, as a stewardess offered them champagne. Natasha quietly went down the stairs to
a lower deck, which Athena found interesting
and Steve disappointing as she disappeared from
sight. Athena checked her watch before she took
the champagne.

"When we leave here, we'll be off duty, so yes,
thank you." She smiled at the stewardess and then
at Vladimir, and Steve accepted a glass too. Athena
then proceeded to charm him, and had Vladimir
laughing on a variety of subjects and then dragged
herself back to the art theft, as though it bored her
to do it, but she had to at least pretend to do her
job. She made it clear that they had only come for
the thrill of meeting him and seeing the boat, and
he was pleased. But he was nobody's fool either,
and they were both playing a game, and they were
good at it.

"The robbery is most unfortunate. I bought
one of Luca's works from them last year. A very
handsome piece. I saw one I liked the other night
when I was there for dinner." He knew that was
why they had come. "The Lucas are impossible to

deal with. They have successfully frozen the market for his work." He looked contemptuous as he said it.

"Why is that?" she asked innocently.

"To drive up his prices. One day they'll start selling. They're establishing the high-water mark now. The art theft won't hurt them either. It will only make the work more desirable. It could be a clever ploy on their part. People involved in the art world are capable of some very strange, desperate acts. You should explore all of it—the result may surprise you."

"You don't think the work was really stolen?"

"It's hard to say. I don't know. I just know there are some very odd stories, and characters, in that world, with twisted ideas and complicated motives."

"You could be right." She asked him about the boat then, and was fascinated by what he said, and that he was building a new one that would be even bigger, which he told them proudly. They chatted aimlessly for an hour, and then Athena set her glass down and stood up. "I'm sorry we stayed so long. Your hospitality was irresistible." She smiled at him, and saw him admiring her figure as she turned to Steve.

"Come back anytime," Vladimir said warmly, and put a hand on her shoulder. "I hope you find the paintings. I'm sure you will. Artwork never stays lost for long. A few paintings do, but not many. And it would be a shame to lose so many of Luca's works, although it only makes the one I have more valuable." He laughed as he said it, and Athena thanked him again, as the crew member escorted them back into the elevator, and down to where their boat was waiting. Athena gave them another flash of leg as they got in, and as the police boat pulled away and picked up speed, Vladimir waved to them from the upper deck. Athena waved back, smiling broadly. And then they saw Natasha reappear and stand at the rail with him, and then they both turned and disappeared.

"Holy shit, did you see that girl?" Steve said to her. "She was gorgeous. Who do you think that was? Hired talent or his girlfriend?"

"Better than that, bozo. Probably his mistress. That's a very special breed. A beautiful bird with clipped wings. Did you see him signal to her to leave? She's on a very, very short leash and does whatever he wants. There isn't enough money on the planet to pay me for that job."

"Well, that was a waste of time," Steve said, as he leaned back in his seat for the trip back to shore, "but the boat is amazing." It was like an enormous luxury hotel, or bigger, almost like an ocean liner.

"Not a waste of time," she said, looking pensive. The broad smile was gone. She was working. The champagne hadn't slowed her down, and she had only taken a few sips.

"Come on, don't tell me you think he did it."
Steve laughed at her. "If you think that, you're
crazy. Why would he bother? He can buy anything he wants. Why would he risk prison for an
art theft?"

"Because guys like him never get caught. They
let someone else do the heavy lifting. And I'm not
saying he did it. But he's got the balls to do it.
Whether he did or not remains to be seen. He
plays a good game."

"So do you. I thought you were putting the
make on him for a minute."

"So did he." She remembered the hand on
her shoulder when they left. "Not in a hundred million years. The homeless-looking artist,
however—now that's another story." She laughed
as they approached the dock. "Leave me alone in
a room with him for a minute, and I could teach
him a thing or two."

"You don't think Theo Luca did it, do you?"
Steve asked her seriously.

"No, that was just Stanislas's game, to create a
doubt in our minds. He didn't. Nice try, though."
One of her fellow officers helped her out of the
boat at the quai in Antibes, and she managed it
without flashing any leg this time, and a minute
later she and Steve were back in the car, heading
back to the restaurant.

"I thought you said we were going off duty. I
have a date tonight."

"Cancel it. We have work to do," she said, look-ing distracted.

"You're just hot for Luca."

"Maybe so," she said, smiling at him, as they headed back to St. Paul de Vence, not to talk to Theo, but to investigate the crime scene again. She had some new ideas she wanted to check out. Steve had already figured out it was going to be a long night. With Athena it always was.

As soon as the police boat pulled away and Na-tasha came back to the upper deck, she looked at Vladimir with surprise. "One of the boys said they were the police. What did they want?" Nor-mally she wouldn't have asked him, but it wasn't business, and she was curious. She had been read-ing about the art theft at Da Lorenzo, and knew Vladimir had been there that week with some of his associates from Moscow who had flown in to meet with him for a night.

"It was just a social visit. They wanted to see the boat," Vladimir said, looking unconcerned. "The robbery was a good excuse."

"Have they found anything out?" Natasha asked, intrigued by the expert art theft she'd read about. And it was an odd coincidence that the Lucas were the victims, since Vladimir had bought a painting from the widow and the son had done a portrait of Natasha. It made it seem more personal than if it had happened to people they'd never met.

"They probably don't know anything yet. It's too soon," he said, and changed the subject. He told her about a painting he was bidding on at auction that week, and showed it to her in the catalog. It was a Monet. "I'm buying it for the new boat." He smiled at her. "For our bedroom. What do you think?"

"I think you're incredible and the most brilliant man in the world." She smiled at him. He leaned over and kissed her then. He didn't tell her that he'd tried to buy another of Lorenzo's paintings the night before the art theft, nor that Theo had turned him down flat and refused to sell. Vladimir was tired of their games.

"And I intend to get the Monet," he added. "You know I never lose what I want." It was going to cost him a fortune, and he didn't care. They talked about it for a while, and then he whispered something to her, and she smiled at him. And a moment later she followed him down the stairs to their bedroom. They had better things to do than talk about an art theft or think about the police.

Chapter 11

The chief inspector asked Athena about their visit to the boat the next day, and she confirmed that nothing had come of it, which didn't surprise him. He knew nothing would. Vladimir Stanislas wasn't their man.

"I didn't think so," he said smugly. "You don't think he's a suspect, do you?" he asked her. She had a good reputation. She thought outside the box, to an extreme degree sometimes, and more often than not, it paid off.

"I haven't ruled that out yet. But probably not." She was honest with him. It would have been a nice tidy way to wrap up the case, but even if he had a hand in it somehow, she knew it would be damn hard to tie him to the crime. Not impossible, but difficult, and it would take time, more than a brief visit to the boat.

"And the son? Theo Luca?"

"He's not it either." But she and Steve went back to see him anyway, and she told him they'd paid Vladimir a visit on the boat, to follow his suggestion that they talk to him.

"What did you think?" Theo asked her intently.

"He's a tough customer, but probably not our guy. What about the woman who's with him? Do you know anything about her?"

"She's his mistress. She's Russian. She's been with him for eight years."

"You know her?" Athena looked interested in that.

"I've seen her a few times. I talked to her twice when I delivered paintings to them. One of my father's, and one of mine."

"Do you have images of the paintings?" she asked him, not even sure why. It wasn't even a hunch. Just curiosity on her part. He hesitated when she asked him, and then went to look for them on his computer. And brought up both. Athena looked startled when she saw the portrait of Natasha and recognized her immediately. "Did she sit for you, or did you do that from a photograph?" She was on to something, but not sure what.

"Neither. I did it from memory after seeing her at the restaurant. She has a haunting face." Athena nodded. She thought so too, and a sensational body. And something about the way she had just vanished on command had unnerved her. She asked Theo some other questions then, and a little while later she and Steve left. He hadn't been paying attention and asked her about it in the car.

"Get anything?" he inquired as he lit a cigarette and she made a face.

"You're disgusting to work with, by the way." She pointed to the cigarette. "And the plot thickens."

"How's that?"

"I don't know how it happened or how he pulled it off, or if she even knows about it. But he's in love with the girl."

"What girl?" Steve looked confused.

"The one on the boat. Stanislas's mistress." Steve whistled.

"Well, that's interesting. I wonder if Stanislas knows."

"My guess is he does."

"How did you figure that out?"

"Luca painted a portrait of her, and she has it. Guys like Stanislas always know. And then they strike. She could be in deep shit. Guys like him are never good sports about what they consider 'betrayals.' They have very simplistic rules."

"I'd say sleeping with another man could be called a betrayal."

"I didn't say she slept with him. I said Luca is in love with her. That's different. But it could be bad news for her."

"Did he tell you he's in love with her?"

"Of course not."

"Jesus, these people are complicated. You have to be as twisted as they are to figure it out."

"That's what they pay us for," she said, smiling at him.

Gabriel and Maylis came back from Florence a week after the robbery, and things started to settle down. The art theft details in several cities were working on it, but no leads had turned up, and no sign of the paintings. And on Gabriel's advice, Theo opened the restaurant again, in order to maintain an air of normalcy, although they had security guards in the house now, and two at night.

Maylis settled Gabriel at the studio with her, and Theo was relieved to see him looking as well as he did. He shared his theories about Vladimir's involvement in the art theft with him, because he wouldn't sell him the painting he wanted, and Gabriel confirmed that it would be hard to pin it on him, even impossible. But nothing could convince Theo he wasn't part of it in some way. And he wondered if the paintings were on the boat. It would be the perfect place to conceal them. But the police had told Theo point-blank that there was no justification to get a search warrant on Stanislas, and even Athena thought it was unlikely that he was actually responsible for it. He didn't have an adequate motive for it, except for a temper tantrum that Theo wouldn't sell him the painting he wanted. And she didn't think Vladimir was crazy enough to steal it along with eleven others. Only a madman would do that. Or a major criminal. Theo thought he was both and had said so to the police.

The only thing that consoled Maylis from the tragedy of losing twelve of Lorenzo's paintings was worrying about Gabriel and taking care of him. Theo was still running the restaurant for her, because she didn't want to leave Gabriel alone at night, and he didn't need a nurse. He was recovering well, and she was lavishing affection on him, and deeply grateful that he had survived. Their relationship had blossomed since his heart attack, and nearly losing him, and Marie-Claude's harsh speech to her, which even Theo thought had been warranted. Gabriel's heart attack was a turning point for them all.

Theo was working with the insurance company and their investigators every day. But they had discovered no more than the police. And even Athena and Steve had hit a slump. While they pondered the little information they had, and continued interrogating the employees, **Princess Marina** sailed away. Athena was slightly bothered by it, but Vladimir wasn't a suspect and there wasn't a shred of evidence to tie him to the crime.

Vladimir had suggested a trip to Croatia to Natasha, and she liked the idea, and a few days in

Venice on the way back. They were planning to be gone for the rest of June. They had no reason to stick around Antibes, and Vladimir got restless if they stayed at any anchorage for too long.

The cruise to Croatia was peaceful and relaxing, but once there, their trips ashore were boring and less interesting than Natasha was used to, and she found the people unfriendly. There was something sad about it, the scars of the war were still evident in some places, and Natasha was anxious to get to Venice. They decided to head back earlier than planned, and cut farther out to sea than usual. They passed a small battered freighter one day that hailed them and showed signs of distress. It was flying under the Turkish flag, which didn't seem unusual, and the yacht crew was about to put a tender in the water to help them, when the security guards came to tell Vladimir that they were sure the freighter was manned by pirates, and they were at risk to be boarded. They had been watching closely with binoculars and had seen that the crew members on the freighter's deck were armed. When the guards warned Vladimir, Natasha was standing nearby and heard what they'd said. She looked frightened as Vladimir turned to her with a stern expression. Nothing like it had ever happened while Natasha was onboard, and she was terrified.

"Go down to the safe room immediately," he said to her, and he spoke to the bodyguards, and

told them to distribute the guns they had onboard. They raised the tender back up. Natasha
hurried down the stairs, and she heard gunshots
outside, as she ran past the room where the security guards were handing out automatic weapons
to the crew.

The door to the gun room was standing wide
open, as they handed out the weapons. She
glanced in as she ran past, and suddenly she saw
them, a dozen wrapped paintings standing in the
corner of the room. She didn't have time to look
carefully, but she suspected instantly what they
were, especially since there were twelve of them.
She was sure Lorenzo Luca's paintings were onboard. Vladimir had stolen them, or had someone do it. Natasha's eyes flew open wider as she
realized what she'd seen, and then she ran to the
safe room, as Vladimir had told her to do, and
locked herself in. There was food and water, a
small refrigerator, a communications system, and
a toilet and a sink in a separate room. The door to
the safe room was armored and bulletproof, and
there were no portholes or windows. It had been
designed to keep them safe in the event of an attack or a kidnapping attempt, or an act of piracy
like the one they suspected was about to occur.

There was a narrow bed, and she lay down on
it, with her heart pounding as she thought of the
twelve carefully wrapped paintings in the gun
room. Vladimir called her on the radio system

in the safe room a little while later, and told her everything was all right. The incident had been avoided. They had left the freighter far behind them, and were moving at full speed. They hadn't been boarded, but he said he wanted her to stay in the safe room for a while. He didn't sound concerned, and said he'd come for her soon. All she could think of was what she knew was in the gun room. She was certain they were the missing paintings, otherwise what were twelve wrapped paintings doing concealed in a locked room? She couldn't believe he would do a thing like that, but he had. And she had no idea why. To own them? To sell them? To possess them? To punish the Lucas in some way? To get even with Theo for doing the portrait of her? It made no sense to her, and she wondered if she was responsible for it by accepting the portrait from Theo, if that had angered Vladimir so he was seeking revenge. But that wasn't adequate justification for Vladimir to steal twelve paintings of enormous value. He had eventually told her that he had tried to buy one the night he went to dinner there without her, and he was angry that they had insisted the one he wanted wasn't for sale. But to steal twelve of them as vengeance for their not selling him a painting he wanted was insane. It made her wonder what he was capable of. She felt sorry for Theo and his mother, but there was nothing she could do about it. She couldn't tell anyone, or

Vladimir might go to prison. And if she did tell someone, he would know that she had given him away. It would be the ultimate betrayal, and there was no telling what he would do to her then. But she didn't want the Lucas to lose their paintings either. She felt as though her whole existence were at stake, and she wasn't willing to risk everything for twelve paintings. But if she didn't speak up, she was as guilty as he was for the theft, if they were indeed the Lucas' paintings. Her head was spinning when Vladimir came for her two hours later. She was pale and shaken, which could have been her reaction to the danger they'd been in. It was her visceral response to what she'd seen and what it told her about him.

"What happened?" she asked him, worried.

"They were pirates. They're around here and there. Fortunately our men caught on to it quickly, before they had a chance to board us. And we were too fast for them. They're far behind us now. We reported it to the authorities. They'll keep an eye out for them. They weren't Turks. They looked more like Romanians, or a motley crew of some kind. It was bold of them to try and board us." She nodded, frightened by the incident, and even more so by what she'd seen in the gun room. Her life was unraveling, or could be. And she was well aware that the pirates could have killed them.

"I heard shooting," she said, still looking nervous.

"Just warning shots, so we'd cut our engines. No one was hurt," he reassured her. Vladimir seemed calm about it, although he had acted quickly the minute he'd been warned of what was about to happen.

"Did we shoot anyone?" Natasha asked in a whisper as she followed him upstairs.

"No," he laughed. "Do you want me to go back and shoot them?" he asked as he put his arms around her, and held her for a moment to calm her, but he was thinking about what the head security guard had just told him, that he had seen Natasha look into the gun room as she ran by, and he was certain she'd seen the paintings wrapped up in the corner. He thought Vladimir should know. But Vladimir wasn't convinced that she knew what they were, in the panic of the moment, about to be boarded by pirates. And if she had seen them, Vladimir felt sure she would ask him about it. She had an innocent, unsuspicious nature, and she hadn't said a word. He trusted her. But she was intelligent and might wonder about it later, whether she mentioned it or not. She had changed everything by looking into the room, and she now represented an important risk. There was no telling when or if she'd figure out what she'd seen.

They were sailing closer to shore by then, in touch with the local coast guard, heading toward Venice at considerable speed. And as he looked at

her asleep in their bed that night, he told himself
that she would never suspect him of anything, or
even whose paintings they were. It would never
dawn on her to accuse him of an art theft. He was
sure that she would never imagine that he had
done it to punish the Lucas for not selling him
the painting he wanted. It was time they learned
a lesson. He hadn't decided what to do with the
paintings yet. But he liked knowing that now
they were his. It was an extraordinary feeling of
power, taking what he wanted. No one could tell
him they weren't for sale, or that he couldn't have
them. He allowed no one to make the rules for
him, or to control him. He paid handsomely for
what he wanted. Or took it, if denied.

They reached Venice two days later, after a vigilant trip. They had doubled the men on watch
and stayed alert, and all the officers, security
guards, and deckhands remained armed, just in
case the freighter had been in collusion with another boat that would cross their path, but none
appeared. And those who were armed remained
in full view on deck. They didn't put the weapons
away until just before they reached Venice, and
then they locked them in the gun room again.
Natasha was on deck with Vladimir, admiring
Venice when they did. She was nowhere near the
gun room that time.

Natasha was relieved to be in a civilized place
again. Their close encounter with the pirates

had unnerved her. To calm her, Vladimir went
shopping with her in Venice. They visited several
churches and the local sights, and had dinner at
Harry's Bar, and he took her on a gondola ride
and kissed her under the Bridge of Sighs. And
then they got back on their boat and headed back
to France.

Natasha was quiet on the trip, trying to decide
what she should do. There was no doubt in her
mind what was in the gun room, and who it belonged to. The only thing she didn't know was
how it had gotten there. And she didn't know
who to tell or if she should. She never questioned
Vladimir about it. She didn't dare. And he was
more loving to her than ever, which made her decision harder.

She still had Theo's number on a piece of paper
in her wallet, but she knew that if she called him,
it could be traced to her phone or whatever phone
she used, and somehow Vladimir might find out.
She didn't want anything bad to happen to him,
but she wanted Theo and his mother to get their
paintings back. They didn't deserve to have this
happen. What Vladimir had done was wrong.
She was sure he had done it. And she hated knowing, and the burden it put on her now. There was
no denying what she had seen. She had much to
think about. And she didn't notice Vladimir observing her.

"Are you all right?" Vladimir asked her when

they reached the Mediterranean again. She seemed troubled and he wasn't sure why.

"I didn't like what happened," she said about the pirates, looking worried. "What if they had come onboard? They would have killed us," she said. She made it clear that they had frightened her badly. It had happened to others before, though mostly in more troubled countries and dangerous waters. It had startled him too, and had been an unexpected, inconvenient episode. And he was upset that the gun room had been left open, and that Natasha had happened by at the wrong time, with the paintings hidden there in plain sight. They were wrapped but clearly didn't belong there. But she still hadn't mentioned them to him. The pirates concerned her more. He wondered if she'd seen the paintings at all in her terror, but the head of security was sure she had, and said she had paused for an instant once she saw them. Vladimir wasn't convinced. It wasn't like her to be secretive with him, and she hadn't said a word.

"That's why we have guns onboard," he said in a soothing tone, "in case of incidents like that." But he could see that she was still distressed. She didn't seem to relax again until they were back at anchor off Antibes. They had been gone for three weeks. Even telling her he'd gotten the Monet at auction didn't distract her, or even seem to please her.

* * *

Maylis was working alternate nights with Theo at the restaurant by then, to give him some relief, and Gabriel was feeling well again and going for long walks every day. It had been such a stressful time for Theo that his mother tried to give him a break.

And one of Athena's fellow officers told her when the boat was back. She mentioned it to Steve the next day.

"We don't have any reason to go and see him again," Steve reminded her. "None of the evidence points to him." It didn't point to anyone yet. And there was no sign of the twelve missing paintings. All their informants had come up dry, which Athena thought was strange. And all the employees of the restaurant had been thoroughly investigated. No one on the task force, or even at the insurance company, thought it was an inside job. But clearly whoever had done it were professionals, and had high-tech methods.

"I wouldn't mind talking to his lady friend," she said, thoughtfully. "If he'll let me." She had a feeling that he wouldn't want her to, which explained why he'd sent Natasha away last time.

"I don't know what that's going to get you. She didn't steal them. Why would she?" Steve said, thinking that for once Athena was looking in the wrong direction.

"Maybe she knows something." But even Athena knew she was clutching at straws. She saw the boat the next day when she drove through Antibes, and noticed a helicopter taking off from the aft helipad, and wondered if Vladimir was on it. It was worth a shot. If she could get her alone, maybe they'd connect. She looked at Steve and sprang to life. "Get us a boat. We're going visiting."

"Now?" He was tired, they'd had a long day, and they were shooting blanks.

"Yes, now!"

Half an hour later they were in a police boat and back at the loading dock of **Princess Marina,** as Athena flashed her most winning smile at the crew and asked for Vladimir again. She wanted to hear what they'd say. One of the deckhands told her that he'd just left. Athena looked disappointed and then asked if Natasha was there. Theo had mentioned her name to her. They said they weren't sure and went to ask. And a moment later Steve and Athena were on their way upstairs again. Natasha looked nervous when she saw them, and didn't know what Vladimir would say about her talking to them. But she couldn't refuse to speak to the police either, or thought she couldn't. She was frightened by their visit and what it might mean. What if they knew something, and accused her of being an accomplice, since the paintings were on the boat and so was she? What if they arrested her and she went to prison? The thought of it was horrifying. She hadn't decided yet what to do about what she had seen in the gun room, whom she should tell, or if she owed it to Vladimir to stay silent. And what it could mean for her if she didn't. She didn't dare contact Theo, but she could imagine how distressed he was, with twelve of his father's paintings gone.

Athena moved into the conversation gently, as she sat with Natasha on the upper deck, and asked her about the portrait Theo had done of her and if she liked it.

"It's very pretty," she said, smiling. "He's a very good artist." Athena nodded agreement, hoping she'd relax. She could see how nervous Natasha was, and she wasn't sure why. Maybe she wasn't allowed to talk to anyone without Vladimir present. He seemed to keep her in seclusion. Athena asked her then how well she knew Theo. "Not at all," she said quickly. "I've only seen him a few times, at the restaurant the first time we went, when he delivered a painting here, and when he brought me the portrait, and I ran into him once at an art fair in London. I didn't know he was Lorenzo Luca's son until I saw the portrait and his bio at an art opening I went to in Paris." She didn't mention their one lunch in Paris and didn't want Vladimir to find out.

"You're not friends, then?" Natasha shook her head and then looked worried.

"Did he say we are?" She looked surprised.

"No, he didn't," Athena said honestly. She didn't want to lie to her and scare her off totally. She didn't know why, but she had the feeling Natasha knew something, but she couldn't figure out what. She would have given a week's pay to read her mind. "He seems like a nice guy, though. He's very upset about his father's paintings, as you can imagine. It's pretty shocking to lose twelve of them at once." Especially to the tune of a hundred million dollars.

"It must be terrible," Natasha said softly, looking upset and sympathetic. And then she glanced at Athena. "Do you think they'll find them?" She hoped they would, she just didn't want Vladimir to go to prison for it. She felt torn in both directions.

"I don't know," Athena said quietly. "Art thefts are strange. Sometimes people keep them and hide them, just to know they own them. Or they get frightened and destroy them, or they disappear to other countries. It depends on why they were stolen. By a frustrated art lover who couldn't buy them, or as some kind of revenge. Or to sell them. We don't know why they were stolen, which makes them harder to find." It had been a month since they were taken, and there were no clues. Natasha nodded thoughtfully as she listened. "Do you have any ideas about it?" she asked her innocently, and Natasha shook her head with an unhappy look, as though she didn't want to discuss it.

"No, I don't." She wished that Athena would stop looking at her as though she knew something. She had eyes that seared right into Natasha's brain and tore at her conscience. She kept thinking of what she'd seen and wished she hadn't, and she knew what he'd done was wrong. But she didn't want to betray him. He had always been good to her. But he had stolen a hundred million dollars' worth of art, and perhaps if they found out, they would blame her too, and think she had known about it. Why were they talking to her now? Maybe they suspected her. "We were almost boarded by pirates off Croatia," she said to change the subject, and Athena looked shocked.

"How awful. That must have been terrifying."

"It was. But we got away, and no one was hurt." But she still looked troubled as she said it. She was thinking of the gun room again. And Athena could tell something was upsetting her, more than just the pirates.

"That could have been very dangerous if you were boarded," Athena said sympathetically. She was startled by how young Natasha seemed. She had the feeling that Natasha didn't speak to strangers often, and led a totally sequestered life.

"I know," Natasha almost whispered, remembering the pirates, and the paintings. And then feeling swept away by a wave of compassion for Theo, Natasha knew she had to tell her. It was too wrong, and she didn't want to be part of it. She wanted Theo to get his father's paintings back. And Vladimir hadn't stolen one, he'd stolen twelve. "The crew got out the guns. We keep them in a locked room for emergencies." She looked straight at Athena as she said it. She stood up then, as though she had to go somewhere, and Athena understood that the visit was over. They had come up dry again. She was discouraged by her gut feeling that whatever this girl knew— and she thought there was something—she obviously wasn't going to tell her. Natasha walked her downstairs herself from the upper deck, and halfway between two levels, she turned to Athena and spoke in a whisper.

"I think they're in the gun room. I saw them." And then she continued down the stairs, expressionless, as though she had said nothing. Athena was shocked for an instant, but didn't react, and looked casual and relaxed as they continued down to the loading dock, and thanked her for letting her come onboard. She knew that Natasha had just endangered herself by giving her the information, and didn't want to increase the risk she had just taken. It was incredibly brave of her. They shook hands formally, and Athena looked disinterested as she and Steve got in the police boat. He had stayed downstairs to talk to the crew and shoot the breeze. Athena had wanted to be alone with her, in case she was shy, and they connected better without a man present. She was still struck by Natasha's seeming innocence, and bowled over by what she'd told her, but it didn't show.

They were halfway to shore when Steve asked her the question he already knew the answer to. He could see it from the expression on Athena's face. "Blanks again, right?" She waited until they were out of the speedboat before she answered in a low voice.

"They're on the boat. Now all we need to do is get a warrant. I'm not going to tell them who told me. I'm just going to tell them I know. I don't want to put her at risk. He could hurt her, or worse." She was deeply concerned for Natasha and sensitive to the position she was in. If Vladimir knew Natasha had betrayed him, there was no telling what he would do to her. Athena felt honor bound to protect her, and somehow Natasha had felt that, which had allowed her to speak.

Steve looked shocked. "Wait a minute! She told you they're on the boat?" Athena nodded. "You **have** to tell them how you know. They're not going to give you a warrant for a guy like him on a hunch. He's never been in trouble before. You'll have to reveal your source," Steve said with a determined look, stunned that Athena had a lead and had gotten it from Natasha.

"He's just never been caught. We'd probably be horrified if we knew what he's done in his own country. If I reveal my source, he'll kill her. I'm not taking that chance. I don't care how much the damn paintings are worth. I'm not trading her life for them, at any price. And God knows what he's capable of. He'll chain her to a wall for the rest of her life, or throw her overboard. He won't take it lightly if he finds out." She was dead serious as she said it, and Steve knew she could be right about Natasha, and what Stanislas might do to her.

"He'll be in prison," Steve said calmly, if what his partner had said was true, and they found them on the boat. "That would protect her."

"Maybe not. Or maybe he'll have someone else kill her. It's my way or no way, and that goes for you too. She's my source! If you put her life on the line, I'll kill you." And Athena looked as though she meant it.

"Okay, okay. Relax. But you're not going to get a warrant out of anyone with hocus-pocus like that. And he'll get away with it if you don't get a warrant."

"Watch me," she said with a determined look in her eye.

She went straight to her chief inspector later

that afternoon, and he told her there was no way
he was going to get a warrant on flimsy information from an informant she wouldn't identify. He didn't believe her, and was afraid she was
just guessing, since she had refused to reveal her
source. "You're going to have to get me more than
that," he said.

"I can't. This is the best I've got. But it's solid,
I can swear that to you. Are you going to let him
get away with it, because everyone is too chicken
to give me a warrant?"

"That's how it is," he said stubbornly. "Get me
more. No judge is going to give us a warrant with
what you've got."

She argued with him for three days and got
nowhere. And by then, Vladimir was back from
London, and the chief purser had told him about
Athena's visit, and Vladimir asked Natasha about
it at dinner the night he got back. He had told
Natasha he'd seen their new Monet in London
and it was spectacular.

"What did she want to know?" he questioned
her about Athena. He watched Natasha carefully
as he asked her.

"She wanted to know about the portrait and the
painting you bought and if we know the Lucas,
and I said we didn't, we just saw them at the restaurant. I told her about the pirates off Croatia,
and she said it could have been very dangerous for
us. And she said they don't have any clues about

the art theft yet. She said sometimes paintings like that just disappear." He nodded, and seemed satisfied with her answer. Natasha looked as innocent as ever, and far more concerned about the pirates than the art.

"Did she ask anything else?"

"Not really. She seems smart. Maybe she'll find the paintings and who took them."

"She is smart," he confirmed. He didn't like that she had visited Natasha while he was away. "You don't have to see her if she shows up again."

Natasha nodded obediently. "She asked to see you. She only asked to see me because you weren't here. And I thought I had to, because she's the police." She sounded childlike as she said it.

"You don't," he informed her. "We don't know anything about it. She's been here twice. That's enough. We have nothing to tell her. She's just fishing, and she wants to say she's been to the boat. You know how people are." Natasha nodded again, and played with her food. She wasn't hungry. It had been three days since Athena's visit, and nothing had happened. She wondered what they were going to do. She had been a nervous wreck since then. She said she had a headache that night and went to bed, but she couldn't sleep. Vladimir was in his office, working, and she heard one of the tenders leave after midnight, which was unusual. She wondered who was going ashore, probably some of the crew, although it was late for them too, or maybe they were picking some of them up from shore. But she never heard the tender come back, and she was asleep when Vladimir came to bed. He didn't wake her to make love to her. He just kissed her, and she smiled in her sleep.

Chapter 12

Theo was asleep when the police called him at seven A.M. He was used to being woken up now. There was always something, some problem, some crisis, some question. He hadn't had a decent night's sleep in a month, and hadn't set foot in his studio for as long. He ran a restaurant now, he didn't paint.

The call was from the chief inspector, who asked him to come to the restaurant immediately and wouldn't say more. Theo was panicked that there had been another robbery, and they'd lost more paintings. He drove to Da Lorenzo as fast as the **deux chevaux** would go.

The chief inspector was waiting for him outside the restaurant and got right to the point. He told Theo that both security guards had been shot with tranquilizer guns and tasered the night before, and had been unconscious for several hours but were unharmed. They had called the police when they woke up and were being tended to by paramedics in an ambulance parked outside. Theo braced himself for what he was going to hear next, that the rest of the paintings were gone. He followed the inspector inside, and stared at the walls in disbelief. The stolen paintings were back, in their right places, bolted to the wall. Everything was immaculate. None of them were damaged when he examined them. It was as though they had never left.

"Do they look like forgeries or the real deal?" the inspector asked him, and Theo looked at them closely. He hadn't even thought of that. They could have been stolen to be replaced by forgeries, but they weren't. He was sure of it.

"They're my father's," he said quietly. "What does this mean?"

"Technically, it makes the whole art theft a prank. As far as the police are concerned, it's over. What really happened and why, we'll never know. No one's talking. One of our inspectors got a tip that Stanislas had them onboard, but we couldn't get a warrant based on that, and we can't prove it. I think it was a bogus tip. Whoever took them may have figured the whole thing was too hot and got scared, so they put them back. I think you got lucky, Mr. Luca," he said seriously.

"So do I," Theo said, smiling broadly, shook the inspector's hand, and thanked him for their hard work. An army of people had been working on it. And now the paintings had been returned. It seemed like a miracle to him, and he knew it would to his mother.

He called her and told her the good news, and an hour later Athena got a call too.

"You don't need a warrant," the inspector told her.

"The hell I don't. They're on the boat."

"Not anymore, if they ever were. All twelve of them are in their right places at the restaurant. Someone tasered and drugged the two guards, and put everything back sometime last night. Same MO—they disabled the alarm and the cameras. But all's well that ends well. We're done. Good work." She couldn't tell if he meant it or was making fun of her, and she was shocked. What the hell did it mean? She wondered if Stanislas suspected Natasha had talked, or decided that prison wasn't worth it, if he got caught. She hoped that Natasha hadn't said anything, and confessed, and put herself at risk. But Athena had no way of contacting her safely, and knew better than to try.

It was all over the news by that afternoon, and Natasha saw it too on TV on the boat. It was totally strange. She wondered if that was the tender she heard leaving the night before. Or if someone had warned him. But at least the Lucas had their paintings back. She was happy for them, and wondered why Vladimir had returned them. She had no idea what had changed his mind. Or had he intended to return them all along?

Vladimir made love to her that afternoon, and then told her they were going out to dinner at eight o'clock. He didn't tell her where and said it was a surprise. She put on a new dress that he had bought her at Dior in January—and she hadn't worn it yet since it had arrived only a few weeks before. She looked exquisite as she stepped into the tender, and he smiled at her and told her she had never looked more beautiful and he loved the dress.

He got out of the tender first and stood watching her as they handed her out of the boat, and she put on her shoes on the quai. The Rolls was waiting for them, and as they walked toward it, he stopped and looked down at her with an expression she'd never seen before. His eyes were like ice, but his face was a mask of regret.

"It's over, Natasha. I know what you saw. I don't know if you told that woman, but I can't take the chance. I'm not going to prison for you, or anyone. He should have sold me the painting—it would have been simpler for everyone. But I can't trust you anymore. I have the feeling that you said something, but it's just a guess. I'll never know for sure. You have a month in the apartment in Paris. I'll send your clothes from the boat there." She was staring at him in disbelief as he said it. It was over, just like that, after eight years, without a look back. "You can have all your clothes and jewelry. You'll get a good price for them if you sell them. And you can have whatever is in your bank account. Be out of the apartment by the end of July. I'm going to sell it. You're a beautiful girl, Natasha. You'll be fine." And then he added softly, "I'm going to miss you. The plane is waiting for you at the airport." And with that he walked back to the tender with his head down, as she stood watching him go. She wanted to run after him, to stop him, and tell him she loved him, but she didn't know if she did anymore. She couldn't respect him after what he'd done.

He had saved her before, and now he had thrown her away, to survive on her own. Without even knowing for certain if she'd betrayed him, he was severing all ties with her to protect himself. He was taking no risks. She wasn't worth it to him. She watched the tender pull away from the dock and go back to the boat with him on it. He never looked back at her. And she didn't make a sound. She got into the Rolls with tears running down her cheeks and sat staring out the window as they drove to the airport. She was alone in the world, with no one to protect her or take care of her, for the first time in years, and as terrifying as it was, she knew he was right. She would be fine.

And as Vladimir stood on the deck, thinking about her, he had no regrets. He couldn't risk everything he'd built for a woman, or for anyone.

He still wondered if she had some kind of tie to Theo Luca, or if she had betrayed him to the police. He'd never know now. It didn't matter. The problem was solved. He had taught Luca a lesson. And he would miss Natasha. But not for long. And by the time he went to his cabin after dinner, her belongings had been packed, and all signs of her were gone.

Chapter 13

Natasha wondered, as Vladimir's plane flew her to Paris, if the crew onboard knew that they were serving her for the last time. Had someone told them? Had they been warned? Did they know why she was going? She had on a dress to wear out to dinner when he told her, and she looked like she was going to a party as they landed at Le Bourget airport in Paris. She thanked them, although she hadn't said a word on the flight, and had sat staring out the window, wondering what would happen now, how she would manage, where she would go. She didn't know what she had in her bank account or how long it would last. She had to look into all of it, and she would have to get a job. She hadn't had one since the last factory she worked in, and she knew she wouldn't go back to Russia. Maybe she could find something at a gallery in Paris. And her heart snagged for a minute when she walked into the apartment on Avenue Montaigne. She had loved putting it together for them nine months before. She had chosen each item and fabric so carefully to make it feel like a home to both of them, and it had. But no more. All she could allow herself to think of now was what she was taking and what she was leaving. Vladimir had been very clear. Only her clothes and her jewelry belonged to her, and none of the art. Except Theo Luca's portrait of her, which Theo had given her as a gift. Vladimir had never given her art, since he considered it an investment. And she wouldn't have dreamed of taking anything he didn't want her to. She knew she was fortunate that he had left her what he had.

She never went to bed that night. She kept walking around trying to absorb what had happened. He had said he could no longer trust her after betraying him, if she had, since he said he wasn't sure. But she could never have trusted him again either, once she discovered he was a thief and had stolen a hundred million dollars' worth of art. She wondered what he had been planning to do with it before he changed his mind and returned it. She would never know now. All she did know for certain was that he had had it stolen and concealed it on the boat. It was shocking and a revelation of who he was, in a way she had never understood before.

She kept opening cupboards and closets in the apartment all night and realized that his suggestion to sell what she had had been right. There was no point keeping all the fabulous couture, furs, and evening gowns, the alligator Birkin bags with the diamond clasps. She had nowhere to wear them, and couldn't imagine herself in that kind of life again. It was the only one she had known for eight years, but she wanted a simple life now, a life where she depended on no one but herself. And she could use the money to live on, after whatever she had in her bank account ran out. She had to call the bank and look into that in the morning.

She was still up when the maid came in at eight, and she asked her to get boxes when the stores opened. She asked no questions, so Natasha knew that someone had warned her that Natasha was moving out. Ludmilla was very quiet as she made a cup of tea and set it down in the bedroom while Natasha went through drawers. And she asked her to set up racks in the long hallway to her dressing room so she could divide things up between what to keep and what to sell. She knew there would be a lot more of the latter. It was like being deported from the life she had known, and becoming a refugee overnight. Ludmilla said nothing to her as Natasha began dragging clothes out of her closets and putting them on the racks. She tried to think in an organized way, but every few minutes she had to stop just to catch her breath, or sit down. She was trying hard not to panic, and not to remember his face and his words when he banished her, standing on the dock in Antibes.

The golden life was gone forever, and she didn't know if she'd miss it or not. She was about to have the freedom she had longed for occasionally to do what she wanted, that she had given up when she accepted being his mistress. She could get to know people as someone other than the woman who lived by his schedule and waited for his commands. But in many ways, she thought it had been a good life, and a safe one. Or maybe she'd been wrong. She wondered now. She thought of the two women who had been murdered the year before while they were in Sardinia, women like her, whose only crime was that they lived in servitude to the men who kept them and paid their bills. Just being his woman had its risks. She saw that now, but she couldn't allow herself to dwell on it as she made order in her life, or tried to.

She hung all the gowns on a rack and divided them by designer. They were all haute couture, and she realized quickly that there were far too many for one rack. She filled six racks with them, all with their numbered tags to identify them as haute couture, and she had the presentation drawings to go with them, which she had kept as souvenirs, and the photographs from the fashion shows they were in, with famous models wearing them, before they were handmade for her. She had gone through only the evening gowns by noon, and took a break to lie on her bed for a few minutes and then got distracted by what was in the drawers in her bedroom, mostly papers, and costume jewelry, and some nightgowns, which were all satin and very sexy, the way Vladimir liked them. As she looked at them, she saw them for what they were for the first time, the costumes of a sex object, who wore them to arouse and entice the man who paid her bills. In the end, she had not been so different from her mother, just luckier and better dressed. Now she wanted that to change. She was no longer going to trade sex for protection and a lifestyle. She could see now why Theo Luca had asked her the questions he did, and realized what he must have thought of her. But it hadn't stopped him from wanting to paint her, and talk to her. She had liked him when they met and would have liked to be friends with him. She thought about calling him at the restaurant to tell him she was glad they had gotten the paintings back, but it didn't feel right. She had no part in it really. She had informed the police, but Vladimir had had them returned himself, by the same people who had taken them in the first place, without ever being caught by the police. It had been brilliantly done, without a hitch. As revenge for the painting he couldn't buy, or the one of Natasha. He had proven his point, that he could do whatever he wanted.

She went back to her sorting then, and took out jumpsuits and winter suits, pantsuits and dresses, and the things she wore out to dinner in London and Paris. There was a rainbow of colors on the racks, in myriad fabrics, each outfit exquisite and wonderfully made. It took her all day to get all the clothes on the racks, and she remembered to call the bank in the late afternoon. She needed to know what she had in the account. It sounded like a large sum of money to her, and then she realized it wouldn't have been enough to pay for one of her evening gowns, but if she was careful she could live on it for a while. She had never paid rent in Paris, or anywhere, or for a hotel. He had taken care of everything with his staff, and she could only guess what a small apartment would cost to rent, maybe somewhere on the Left Bank on a quiet street. She hoped what she had in her bank account would carry her for several months, and once she sold the clothes and jewels, she would have more, possibly a great deal more. But she had to get busy selling things. She continued sorting and hanging until late at night, and finally collapsed on her bed still wearing her jeans and T-shirt, and fell asleep.

When she got up in the morning, she called the real estate agent she had liked best, and told her she had a cousin arriving from Russia who needed a small, inexpensive apartment in a safe neighborhood, preferably in the sixth or seventh arrondissement, where many of the art galleries were, or a less expensive neighborhood if necessary. She asked who to call for a rental, and the woman offered to help her—they had been great clients and Vladimir had paid a staggering price for the apartment. Natasha hoped he wouldn't lose money on it now, which was more than most women would have thought in her situation, being banished overnight. The realtor told her how sorry she was to hear that they were already selling, and that she had heard that Natasha had done a beautiful job decorating. So Natasha knew they had already called her to put it on the market. Vladimir had thought of everything and lost no time. The realtor said they were going to begin showing it as soon as she moved out. Vladimir was selling it with the furniture. He wanted no souvenir of their lost life either, which hurt her for a moment, and she forced herself not to think about it. She couldn't afford to or she knew she would fall apart. She couldn't allow herself to get sentimental now, or frightened. She just had to keep going until it was over and she had found safe haven somewhere. She told Ludmilla to pile the boxes she had gotten in the living room. Natasha didn't ask her to help otherwise, and she didn't offer. She stayed in the kitchen and was about to

be out of a job too. Vladimir's office had notified
her that she could stay until the apartment sold,
and then they would give her a month's pay when
she left. It was proper but not overly generous.
He was a businessman above all.

The real estate agent promised to call when she
had researched some rental listings. The charade
of looking for an apartment for a mythical cousin
was no longer necessary since the woman knew
so much. And Natasha reminded her to keep the
prospective apartments small and not too expensive, since she didn't need much and had a modest
budget. The woman assured her that she understood, probably better than Natasha wanted her
to, which was embarrassing. She realized that she
had countless humiliations ahead now, selling her
belongings, moving out, looking for work with
no job experience. She wondered if anyone would
even hire her. Maybe she'd have to work as a maid
in a hotel, she thought to herself in bad moments,
but if so, she would have to do it. Or she could
take a job as a maid in a private home, when her
money ran out and she needed a place to live. She
realized that anything was possible now, but she
would do whatever she had to. It never dawned
on her to try and meet another man like Vladimir, or that another one would come along to
save her, and pay for her beauty and her body and
company. That was the last thing she wanted, and
she was prepared to starve first. She was on her

way to freedom now, and nothing would make her turn back. With all the doors closing behind her, there were others opening. She just didn't see them yet, but hoped they were there.

It took her four days to empty her closets in an orderly fashion and figure out what to keep and what to sell. She had decided to keep the two plainest evening gowns, and then increased it to four in case she ever got invited somewhere formally again. Three were black and very simple but beautifully made, and the fourth one was red, and she had loved it when she bought it. It was one of the few she had picked herself. There were dozens of others, and she felt guilty when she saw how many she had, but Vladimir had ordered them all. She realized now that she had been an accessory to him, and not a person in her own right in his eyes.

She kept a few wool suits, and a number of skirts and pants, all her sweaters and blouses, even though the blouses were haute couture, but she might need them for a gallery job. She kept half a dozen of her heavy wool coats, and some light ones, and had three racks of furs to sell. They were magnificent, and then she hesitated again and kept a black fox jacket, two sporty ones, and she retrieved the sable coat he had bought her at Dior the previous winter. It was so beautiful, she didn't want to give it up. And she weeded through her shoes too, and kept only those she thought she'd wear, and none of the fanciful ones that she had worn to parties, or lolling on the boat or at home. She kept the ones she'd need for work, and some sober, dressier ones, and her boots. All her fur hats went except the one that matched the sable coat she was keeping. She was going to sell all the Birkins, most of them alligator, and all with diamond clasps, which she had never liked, but Vladimir had insisted on them, as part of the role he cast her in. He had paid over two hundred thousand dollars for each of the Hermès alligator bags with the diamond clasps, and their price at Hermès had gone up since, and she wondered what she could get for them for resale or at auction. She was selling a dozen of them, and she had always heard they sold for high prices to Hermès customers desperate for them on the resale market, so they didn't have to wait three years to order new ones in the colors they wanted, since Hermès was slow to deliver. It worked in her favor now.

And she had all the jewelry neatly stacked in the boxes it had come in. Vladimir had been more inclined to highly styled design pieces than large stones, but she was sure there would be a market for them. She just didn't know where yet. Undoing a life to this extent was entirely new to her, but she was organized and methodical about it.

And the real estate agent called about three rental listings after a few days. She said they were very small and not too expensive, and she asked if Natasha would have any furniture since the apartments didn't, and Natasha suddenly realized she hadn't thought of it. But the realtor suggested she go to IKEA, where they had everything for the home, and it was dirt cheap. She could even buy it online, which would be a new experience for her too. She was going to be living a real life now, not that of a rich man's mistress. But it was a long way from the dormitory and factory in Moscow. She had been banished from her luxurious life, but she would not drown. And once she sold almost everything, she would have enough to live on for a long time. She no longer had Vladimir's protection, but she had her own. Her life of luxury had been on loan, and she was returning it in exchange for her freedom and independence, which were even more valuable to her now. The suddenness of her change in circumstances was shocking, but it felt right.

The realtor described the three apartments to her, and said she hadn't seen any of them. She suggested they go that afternoon, and she had the keys to two of them, and could get keys to the third if Natasha was free. She had been in the apartment, working feverishly, for five days by then, and thought it might be good to get out, and she needed to start researching where to sell her clothes. And she had no idea where to go with the jewelry, except maybe to put it up for auction at Sotheby's or Christie's, but she thought she might want the money sooner, and they might not have room in an auction for many months. She agreed to see the apartments that afternoon, and braced herself for what they would look like. The prices sounded reasonable to her, and the real estate woman warned her that they were very small, and not what she was used to. Natasha assured her that she wouldn't mind.

She took a cab to the first address on the rue du Cherche-Midi and met the realtor outside. Natasha was dressed simply in jeans again, but had put on heels and a decent blouse and was wearing one of the Birkins she decided to keep, a "So Black" with black hardware that she had pulled out of the "sell" pile before she boxed them up. And she had pulled out a black leather Kelly bag too. And whatever she kept she could sell later, if she needed more money.

The apartment was a third-floor walkup, with no elevator, that looked out on a back courtyard, and was dark and seriously depressing. And they both knew that it was too awful, even at a decent price. The bedroom was barely big enough for a bed, and the living room was small too, and the kitchen and bathroom were grim.

"I don't think so," Natasha said politely, and the realtor agreed. They walked to the next one on the rue St. Dominique. There was a string of restaurants up and down the street, and they both thought it would be noisy, and it was more expensive than the others. It was nice enough, although the elevator was rickety and the size of a phone booth, and it was on the fifth floor and lighter than the previous one, but Natasha said she would prefer something cheaper. So they went on to the last one on the rue du Bac around the corner from a gallery and a small bistro, and there were a pharmacy and a small grocery store nearby, which seemed practical. It was the least expensive of the three options, so neither of them expected much, and Natasha was shocked by how small it was, but it was on the second floor with no elevator in a pretty little building that seemed well kept and clean.

"The woman who owns the apartment owns the building, and her daughter lived in the apartment but is married and just had a baby, so they moved upstairs to a bigger apartment. And I think the owner may live in the building herself."

Natasha didn't see how a couple could have lived there, let alone with a baby, but it was immaculate and sunny. It had a tiny bedroom like the last one, but there were flower boxes outside the windows, which gave it a cheerful look, and high ceilings since it was an old building, and the living room was a decent size with a fireplace. The closet space wasn't great, but she wasn't keeping many clothes. And they had put in new kitchen appliances when her daughter got married, and there was a funny old-fashioned bathroom. It was a far cry from Avenue Montaigne, but Natasha could see herself living there, and the area was safe, and the building well tended. There was a door code and an intercom, so no one could get in who didn't belong there. And the price seemed about right for what she guessed her budget might be eventually. She was being very cautious, to make whatever money she got last longer. And she had enough money to pay rent now from what was left in her bank account, which wasn't a lot. And she wouldn't need a lot of furniture, just the basics—a couch, chairs, table, a bed and a dresser, some lamps, a carpet.

"I'll take it," she said gratefully. It was available on the last day of July. It seemed meant to be. She felt lucky that she had an apartment and would have some money left to furnish it and live until she found a job. The money from the clothes and jewelry would be her nest egg to use over time as she needed it.

"I hope you'll be happy here," the realtor said with a sympathetic look. Natasha had been quiet and polite, and the woman felt sorry for her. It was obvious she was leaving a grand lifestyle and was obliged to live simply now. She had already guessed what had occurred, and she liked Natasha and wanted to help. She normally never did rentals and referred them to someone else, but she had sensed that something bad had happened, and felt concerned for her. The realtor wrote down the name IKEA on a piece of paper and handed it to her.

"You'll find everything you need there, furniture, linens, plates, rugs, lamps." Natasha hadn't thought of all that, but she had only her clothes. She didn't want to ask Vladimir for anything from the apartment, and she was sure he wouldn't give it to her. She was lucky he was letting her have her clothes to sell, since he thought she had betrayed him. She wondered how he knew, or if he had sensed it. She knew he could have thrown her into the street with nothing, so she didn't want to ask for more, and was just grateful for what he was allowing her to take. What shocked her was how willingly and suddenly he had given her up, like an object he no longer wanted, with no emotion. It was still hard to understand. She had wanted to believe they loved each other, which was clearly not the case. And she wasn't heartbroken either. Just scared and sad, which was normal after eight years with him, and having everything change overnight. "Someone will have to help you put the furniture together," the real estate agent explained about IKEA, and Natasha looked puzzled. "It all comes taken apart, in pieces, but I'm sure you can find someone to put it together for you. My son and I have bought a lot of it for his apartment, and he's a whiz at assembling. It's a nuisance, but it's not hard. I have a great Russian handyman, if you want his name." Natasha's face lit up when she said it.

"That would be wonderful. I'm not so good at putting things together," she admitted, and they both laughed.

"Neither am I, but I've learned." Natasha knew from their earlier conversations that she was divorced and had two grown children.

The realtor promised to get her the lease in the next few days. It was a standard French lease, for three years, with two three-year renewals at a minimal increase each time, and she could leave anytime with sixty days' notice. The realtor explained that French rentals favored the tenant more than the owner. And if Natasha wanted to, she could stay in the tiny apartment for nine years. She'd be thirty-six then, and had just turned twenty-seven, so if her situation never improved, she would have a home for a long time. It was comforting to know that now, and she felt sure she could manage the rent with a decent gallery job. She didn't want anyone else helping to pay her rent ever again. She wanted something she could afford on her own.

Thinking about her tiny new apartment, it was a shock when she went back to the apartment on Avenue Montaigne with all its grandeur, boiseries, and high ceilings, and the antiques she had bought, but she couldn't allow herself to think of it. She had a place to go, and there was no point looking back or comparing her old life to her new one. And she had so much left to do, she couldn't falter now. She looked up auction houses in the phone book that night, and found some she recognized, and wrote down their phone numbers. It was time to let go of her possessions and her old life. And knowing where she was going now, she had a better sense of how much she could keep. She put more of her wardrobe on the racks to sell that night, and told herself she didn't need it. But she couldn't afford to buy new clothes either, so she kept anything practical, and a few things she felt pretty in, and she liked what she kept. The rest had all been advertising for Vladimir, and she didn't have to do that anymore. There was some comfort in that.

Her conversations with the auction houses in the next few days were educational. She called the two most important ones she remembered, and they asked her if it was an estate, and she said it wasn't. They wanted to know how old the clothes were, and she said they were all fairly recent, and some from this year's collections and not yet worn. They told her the items would be sold for approximately half of what the seller had paid for them, or less, with a reserve if she liked, and she would have to pay the auction house a twenty percent commission of the hammer price of everything that sold. So she would receive eighty percent of half of whatever Vladimir had paid for any of it, which seemed acceptable. Unless, of course, people went crazy and bid the prices high, in which case, she'd get more, but some of it might not sell at all. And both houses had auctions in September, when the Hôtel Drouot opened for the fall, where they rented auction rooms. One of the houses had a big Hermès auction coming up, and they were anxious to see her Birkins and photograph them for the catalog if she agreed to sell through them. She made an appointment with their expert to come and see them the following week. Natasha explained that there were too many for her to take to their office. And she sat down with a pad and paper that night, to figure out the original cost of her things, and what she might derive from a sale. It was an impressive sum and would keep her going for quite some time. She felt relieved when she saw the numbers, and at ten o'clock, she decided to walk up to L'Avenue, where she had had lunch with Theo, and get something to take home. Ludmilla was off for the weekend, and there was nothing in the house. She didn't want much, but she needed to keep her energy up.

She ordered a salad to go, and some smoked salmon and mixed berries, and sat at a table on the terrace waiting for them to give it to her. It was a busy Saturday night, and she heard someone call her name as she sat staring into space, thinking about her conversations with the auction houses. It was the undoing of a life, and exhausting to organize, but thank God she had something to sell. Without that, she'd be penniless and destitute, and might be on the street. Those things happened to people, and she never forgot that, just as Vladimir didn't, although he had nothing to worry about, and was dependent on no one but himself, unlike her, who had been entirely dependent on him. She heard her name called again and looked around, and then she saw a tall, good-looking older man in black jeans and a white shirt, with gold chains around his neck and a heavy gold and diamond Rolex on his wrist. He was twenty years older than Vladimir, but still attractive. He and Vladimir knew each other from Moscow. They'd had him on the boat several times for dinner, always with very young Russian girls who appeared to be interchangeable and giggled a lot. He liked them very young. His name was Yuri, and his face lit up the moment he saw her.

"I'm so happy to see you!" he said, looking genuinely pleased. "Will you join me for dinner?" There was nothing she wanted to do less. He talked a lot, and was very jovial, and she wasn't in the mood. She wasn't ready to see anyone yet, and he wouldn't have been high on her list, or on it at all, as someone to have dinner with.

"No, thank you." She smiled at him, trying not to look as exhausted as she felt. It had been an endless week of stress, fear for the future, mental adjustment, and hard work lugging boxes and suitcases around and emptying closets, and making decisions and trying not to think of Vladimir. He hadn't called her at all. "I just ordered dinner to take back to the apartment."

"You **must** eat with me," he insisted, as he sat down across from her at the small table, without invitation. "Champagne?" he offered, and she shook her head, but he ordered it anyway, and had the waitress pour her a glass when it came, and she didn't have the energy to resist, so she accepted. "I saw Vladimir two days ago, in Monte Carlo, at the casino, with . . . friends . . ." He hesitated just a beat, and from the way he looked at her, she understood instantly that Vladimir had already been with another woman and was trying to impress her at the casino, and that Yuri knew that Natasha was no longer part of the picture. Vladimir hadn't lost any time. She knew he wasn't a gambler, but only went to the casino in Monte Carlo when he wanted to show off to guests. Otherwise he wasn't interested, although he played high-stakes roulette and blackjack when he was there.

"What are you doing for the rest of the summer?" Yuri asked her, with a wide smile. She was sure he was a nice person, but he got on her nerves.

He was a little crass, definitely a rough diamond, and was always in competition with Vladimir. He had always had a weak spot for her, and said he wished he could meet a woman like her. Vladimir liked to tease him at her expense and told him to look on the streets of Moscow in the dead of winter and find a poor one with pneumonia. They both liked the joke, although it embarrassed her.

She almost laughed before she answered him about her summer. She was moving to a tiny apartment, going to buy cheap furniture, selling her clothes, and eventually looking for a job in the fall. And cleaning her apartment herself. If she had told him the truth, he would have been horrified and felt sorry for her. She was definitely not going to the casino in Monte Carlo, or doing anything that would interest Yuri.

"I haven't figured it out yet. I'm busy in Paris this month. Maybe I'll go somewhere in August," she said vaguely, wishing her dinner would come quickly, but the restaurant was crowded, and the service slower than usual.

"Why don't you come on the boat?" he said as his face lit up again. He had a two-hundred-foot yacht that was dwarfed by Vladimir's, but a truly lovely boat. "I'm going to Ibiza. We'd have fun." She wasn't sure if he was inviting her as a guest or a date, but either way, she had no desire to go anywhere with him, and certainly not on vacation. She thanked him but said she thought she'd be staying with friends in Normandy, which wasn't true, but she wanted to decline the invitation. It would have been wonderful to be back on a boat for the rest of the summer, just not his.

It had shocked her to hear him imply he had met Vladimir out with "friends," obviously a woman, but he would need to show everyone that he hadn't "lost" her, he had replaced her, to protect his ego. He wouldn't want anyone to think she had left him, which she hadn't. And he'd make sure they knew. He had probably already told Yuri, which was humiliating, but there was nothing she could do about it. If he had thought she was still with Vladimir, he would never have invited her on his boat. He knew it was open season. Otherwise he wouldn't have wanted to make Vladimir angry by flirting with her. Clearly, he knew now that Vladimir wouldn't care. It hardly supported her theory that they had loved each other. Apparently he didn't, since it was over in an instant, as soon as he even remotely suspected she might have betrayed him. He didn't wait to be sure. As always, he trusted his instincts, and he was right.

"Normandy is boring. Come to Ibiza," Yuri said, as he gently placed a hand on hers on the table, and she discreetly withdrew hers. "I've been thinking about you since I saw Vladimir. I wanted to call you. He said you were here. I'm so glad I ran into you." She wasn't, but she smiled and nodded, she had gotten trapped at the small table with him, waiting for her food.

With that, the waitress made a mistake and brought her dinner plated and not to go, and said she thought Natasha might like to have dinner with her friend, and she brought his at the same time. There was no way Natasha could leave now, without seeming openly rude, so she smiled and nodded at his conversation, as they began eating. Yuri was delighted by the girl's mistake and smiled at her. Like all the waitresses at the restaurant, she was scantily dressed in a tiny miniskirt and a halter top, and was young and very pretty. "I want to talk to you," Yuri said, as Natasha ate her dinner as quickly as she decently could. All she wanted was to go home. It depressed her to be sitting there with him. "Vladimir told me what happened," he said, lowering his voice, as she looked at him curiously.

"And what did he say happened?" She was interested to hear what story he was telling, surely not that he suspected her of informing the police he was an art thief and had stolen a hundred million dollars' worth of paintings.

"He said you'd been hounding him for the last year to have children, at least in the next few years. And he doesn't want them, so he thought it only fair that you part company and he leave you free to find a man who will give you babies.

It's very decent of him, actually. He said it was very painful for him to make the decision, but he wants you to be happy. He said he gave you the apartment here."

"Really?" Her eyebrows shot up at that. "Actually, he didn't." Not that it mattered. It was all lies anyway, to soothe his ego, and make him look like a hero, instead of a bastard.

Yuri looked suddenly serious, squeezing her hand in his until it hurt. He was holding it too tightly for her to pull away, as she stared at his perfectly capped teeth, gold necklace, and hair transplants that had been impeccably done, but he still looked his age. He was handsome, but in a showy, artificial way. "Natasha, I want to speak frankly. I've always liked you. I have two children who are older than you are, and I would love to have a baby with you. We could marry if that's important to you, I don't really care. I'm willing to settle a large amount of money on you to begin the arrangement. Deposited into a Swiss account in your name. Perhaps twenty million to start, or thirty if you feel that's necessary, and the same amount again when the child is born. All your bills paid, houses wherever you want. I think we'd have a very good time together," he said, with a glint in his eye, and looking as though he was sure he'd convinced her, and for some girls he might have. It was a remarkable offer, and actually more than Vladimir had ever given her. Twenty or thirty

million dollars in a Swiss account was serious security, and the same again when she delivered his
child. It was the kind of offer that every girl like
her prayed for, and she and Vladimir had only
been apart for a week. She was stunned. "I could
buy the apartment here from Vladimir if you
want, if he's not giving it to you. That way you
wouldn't have to move. I stay at the George V."
She knew he had a flat in London too. He didn't
have the flotilla of huge yachts that Vladimir did,
or the houses. He didn't own entire industries in
Russia, and the president wasn't in his pocket. But
he was a very, very rich man, worth several billion
dollars, according to Vladimir, who knew about
such things. And he had no trouble surrounding
himself with beautiful women. But not her.

"I don't know what to say," she said, realizing
what he was offering her, security for life, a child
if she wanted, and marriage, so she would be allegedly respectable, although not in her own eyes,
and the apartment she loved so she wouldn't have
to move. She could keep her clothes and jewels,
and she knew he was a generous man. She had
seen what he gave the girls he went out with.

He was offering her the kind of security she was
used to, even more than Vladimir ever had. Yuri
had waited years to make her the offer, hoping
that at some point she and Vladimir would part
ways. "It's extremely generous of you, Yuri. But
I don't want to settle down with anyone. It's too

soon." She tried to look demure, and what could she say? That he disgusted her and made her skin crawl? That she wanted to live in a tiny apartment smaller than one of her current closets? And get a job that she could barely survive on? That she was selling everything she owned and when she ran out of money, she had no idea what she'd do? What she wanted now was her freedom, not to trade her life and body to a rich man for security. Maybe the women who did so were smarter than she was, she told herself. But she didn't want to sell herself into slavery again, at any price. She wasn't for sale, but Yuri would never understand it if she said it to him any more than Vladimir would have. In their minds, she was a commodity they could buy. The only question was for how much. He was offering her a business deal and a good one, and she wondered if others would too. The competition between men like him and Vladimir was fierce, and they all thought that acquiring what he had, even his cast-off women, would somehow make them more like him. But there was only one Vladimir, and she had had him. She didn't want another one, neither a worse nor a better one. She would rather try to make it on her own now, even if she drowned. She hadn't realized it, but she had wanted this for years, and Vladimir had handed her her independence on a silver platter. She wasn't willing to give it up again. "I'm not ready," she said kindly, and he looked disappointed, but said he understood.

"Well, when you are, I'll be waiting. And know that the deal stands. I won't take it off the table. If you feel you need more, we can talk about it." He was used to women who negotiated hard. Natasha never had. She had asked Vladimir for nothing, and received much, but she had left it up to him.

She finished her dinner sitting with Yuri, and tried to pay for her own, but he wouldn't let her. He kissed her lightly on the lips when she left him at the restaurant, and he asked to stay in touch, which she knew she wouldn't do. She ran back to the apartment and wanted to shower when she got there. She had passed up a major business deal, and the idea of it made her feel sick. It made her realize what she had done for the past eight years. She had sold her body and soul to one of the richest men in the world. And no matter what happened now, she knew she would never do it again. No one would ever control her, and she wasn't selling her body, her life, or her freedom at any price. Not to Vladimir or Yuri, and to no one else. She was free at last, and no longer for sale.

Chapter 14

Natasha's clothes arrived from the boat the week after she had left, and she sorted through them too. She kept very few of them except the white jeans and bathing suits and a white Birkin she could wear in the summer. She couldn't imagine having a boat life again, and she shuddered every time she thought of Yuri's proposal. He meant well perhaps, but she felt dizzy when she thought of selling herself again. Another woman, and many she had met with the men Vladimir knew, or even most, wouldn't have cared how old Yuri was, what he looked like, or whether they were attracted to him or not. It was all about what he had and what they could get. In a way, she thought they were high-priced prostitutes, and she wondered if she had been too. She had dignified her relationship with Vladimir by believing that she loved him and that he needed her, but as it turned out he didn't love or need her. She had been a possession, and maybe what she had felt for him wasn't love, but gratitude and respect. And now she didn't even respect him. And the only feeling she had for Yuri was revulsion, although he had certainly made her a good offer, and he would never have understood why she turned him down.

Her final meetings with the auction houses were efficient and depressing. It occurred to her that they had been right to ask her if it was an estate. The person she had been when she wore those clothes no longer existed and had died. She was selling a dead person's clothes, from a dead life. She would get decent money out of what she sold, to live on, not to show off. But she would only get big money if she sold her body again, and took an offer like Yuri's. But she didn't need big money now or want the life offered, or the one she'd had.

She stood to make the most money on the Birkins with the diamond clasps, which usually sold at auction for more than what they went for at Hermès, which was good for her. And she still had the jewels to sell. She took them to a jeweler and sold them for a fraction of what Vladimir had paid for them and put the money in the bank.

She signed the papers with the larger of two auction houses she'd spoken to, to include her clothes in an haute couture sale in September at the beginning of the auction season. And she consigned her bags to an Hermès auction later that month. They were picking everything up the day before she moved. And she felt strangely free and unencumbered after signing the papers. The symbols of her slavery were slowly disappearing, like chains that were falling away. She wanted to be rid of the trappings of her old life and everything she didn't need. She didn't want the reminders of a past she was ashamed of.

She had signed the lease for her apartment by then, and rented a van and went to IKEA after measuring the spaces in the apartment so she knew what would fit. She bought all the basics she needed, including plates and cooking pots, and went to a slightly nicer place for linens and towels. They were nothing like what she was used to buying, but she was willing to give that up too. There would be no fancy lace-trimmed Porthault sheets in her new life.

She called the Russian handyman, and he promised to assemble all the furniture for her, the day she moved in. She could hardly wait, and she was ready to leave the apartment on Avenue Montaigne. It had felt like their home for a few months, but she realized now that it never was. It had just been another showplace, and none of it had been hers. Her tiny new apartment was far more real, and that was all she wanted now: a real life of her own.

When she was going through her papers, she found Theo's number on the scrap of paper in her wallet and remembered what he had said when they had lunch, about calling him if she ever needed him, wanted help, or was in danger. But she wasn't, and she was managing surprisingly well. She was just glad he had his paintings back. She was happy knowing it, and whatever small part she'd played, even if all it had done was cause Vladimir to sense danger and return the paintings himself. She didn't need to talk to Theo again. She didn't want his pity, or to have to explain what had happened, or what knowing the truth about his paintings had cost her. He owed her nothing. She loved the portrait he had painted of her, and was taking it with her. It was the only piece of art that belonged to her. But she and Theo were strangers. He had his life as an artist, and she had to make her own way now, with no one's help. She had to do this herself, and she was. She doubted she would ever see Theo Luca again.

By mid-July, Maylis was back at the restaurant full-time, Gabriel was feeling well and going for long walks every day, and Theo had been released from his duties and was back in his studio. They had heightened security at the restaurant, and

Maylis was still shaken by what had happened. The return of the paintings, and the way it had been accomplished, seemed like a miracle to all of them.

When Theo asked her, Maylis said that Vladimir and Natasha hadn't been back to the restaurant. He was still convinced that he had been involved in the art theft, because they wouldn't sell him the painting he wanted, and as some kind of sick revenge. But at least whoever had taken them had given them back, after giving everyone a hell of a scare, and the police details involved had done a lot of work for nothing. Neither their informants nor their police work had turned up who the culprits were.

Maylis said she'd heard from one of their other Russian clients that Vladimir had taken his boat to Greece for the rest of the summer. Theo was relieved and didn't want to run into him again, although he thought of Natasha at times. He was looking at his unfinished portrait of her one day, and knew what he had to do with it. He put it back on the easel, and painted over it, so it became a blank canvas again. He had painted one portrait of her, and that was enough. His obsession with her was over, and he was free at last. She had chosen the life that suited her, and he was no part of it and never would be. She was a rich man's dolly, which worked for her, and Theo had his own life to lead and needed to get on with it. He had been thinking of calling Inez again, although he wasn't sure it was the right thing to do, their life goals really weren't the same. She wanted a husband and more children, and he couldn't see himself getting there for a long time, if ever. For now, his art was more important to him, so he didn't call her, which seemed the cleaner thing to do. And with the art theft, he had missed going to the fair in London, so he hadn't seen Emma again. He still laughed when he thought of her, and the good time they'd had, although a strong dose of her on a regular basis would have been too much for him. And for now, there was no one else, and he didn't mind.

Marc came by the day he painted over Natasha's portrait, and he told him what he'd done. Marc was impressed and silent about it for a moment, as Theo explained that it was a kind of liberation, and he opened a bottle of wine for them. They spent the afternoon drinking and talking about the strangeness of women, and the ones that had gotten away. Marc was relieved to hear that he was over his obsession, although neither of them had a woman in his life at the moment. Theo said he was happier that way for now, and concentrating on his work. He was thrilled not to be working at the restaurant.

"What about the girl who works at the gallery

in Cannes? She was good looking, though a little square," Marc commented.

"More than a little," Theo said, on his second glass of wine, referring to Inez. "She's not for me, and I'm not the kind of man she wants."

"Maybe we'll be lonely bachelor artists forever," Marc said mournfully. He had just broken up with another girlfriend who had taken the little money he had. They always did. "Maybe you can't have a love life if you're a serious artist," he said pensively, and Theo laughed.

"My father had four major mistresses and two wives, and eight kids. I'd say you can have women in your life, **and** art. You just need the right one."

"That's the problem. They're so damn hard to find," Marc said mournfully. Theo nodded in agreement, and they continued to drink until they finished the wine. It was the first day he had taken off in weeks, and it was nice to spend time with his friend. They admitted to being drunk by the end of the afternoon, and decided to go to the beach in Antibes and go swimming instead of working for a change. And they took the bus because they'd been drinking. By the time they left the beach, Marc had picked up a girl, and he went home with her. Theo went home alone. He was thinking about Natasha and wished her well, and then he went to bed and slept off the wine. He was glad that he no longer dreamed of her, and hadn't in a while. He hoped he wouldn't again. He needed to let Natasha go, into the mists of memory, where she belonged.

Once the paintings were returned, Athena and Steve were assigned to another case immediately, a major burglary in St. Jean Cap-Ferrat, where all the servants had been tied up and held hostage while the family was away. They had been released unharmed, but ten million dollars' worth of jewels had disappeared, and a million in cash from the safe. Athena was sure it was an inside job, and she was right. They solved the case quickly, and the butler and cook were taken into custody and charged with the crime. It was another notch on her belt in her long history of successful arrests.

It had been three weeks since the paintings had been returned by then, and she told Steve one afternoon that she was going to St. Paul de Vence to see Theo. She wanted to have one last conversation with him and had never got the chance because of the burglary in Cap-Ferrat.

"You're going without me?" She nodded, and he laughed. "I know what that's about. Some fun and games with a local artist?"

"Don't be such an idiot. This is work."

"Tell that to someone else." He knew her better.

"What do you think I'm going to do? Rape him at gunpoint?" She grinned, and he laughed.

"Probably. Don't leave any marks."

"You're disgusting."

"Coming from you, I take that as a compliment," Steve teased her.

She drove to St. Paul de Vence, and Steve did paperwork at his desk for the rest of the afternoon. They had a mountain of work to catch up on. And Athena had called Theo and asked if she could come by.

He was pleased to see her when she got to his house. She wore a plain white skirt and a blouse, nothing too sexy or alluring. She was actually there on business, to tie up the loose ends. There were some things he didn't know that she wanted to tell him. It made no difference now, but in all fairness she thought she should.

He offered her wine when she arrived, but she declined. Contrary to what her partner believed, she wasn't there to put the make on him, although she wouldn't have minded if he did, now that the case was closed, but she hadn't gotten that kind of vibe from him. He was a straightforward guy, and their dealings had been strictly police business. And she still felt in her fairly reliable gut that he was in love with Natasha. The portrait he had painted of her gave him away.

They sat at his kitchen table over coffee, and she looked at him seriously for a minute.

"It doesn't change anything now, but we had an informant in the end." He looked surprised by what she said, and waited to hear the rest. "I went out to see Stanislas's girlfriend, Natasha, on the pretext of seeing him. I wanted to get a feeling for if she knew anything. I had a sixth sense that she did. We talked for a while, and she seemed very uncomfortable and a little off. Apparently, they were almost boarded by pirates off Croatia. And Stanislas ordered them to take out the guns. They keep AK-47s on the boat, and the crew know how to use them. That's a very self-sufficient little ship," she said wryly. "She was telling me about that, and we were getting nowhere, so we got up to leave, and I followed her downstairs. We didn't take the elevator, and I realized afterward that there are surveillance cameras in it, and she didn't want anyone to see what she did. She turned to me halfway down the stairs and whispered that the paintings were in the gun room, and she'd seen them. That was all she said. I tried like hell to get a warrant to search the boat, but my superiors said I didn't have enough to go on. I wouldn't identify my source, which made it tougher. I was afraid of what Stanislas would do to her if he found out. I don't trust the guy, and if he went to prison because of her, God knows what he would do. I wasn't willing to take the chance with her life. I've made that mistake with informants when

I was younger. It doesn't turn out well. I always protect my sources now."

"She'd seen them?" He looked shocked, referring to the paintings.

"If they were in the gun room, which they keep locked, maybe she was around when they were handing out the weapons to defend themselves against pirates. Anyway, I never got the warrant, and they told me to forget it. And then the paintings came back mysteriously. I don't know if he knew she had told me, if someone saw her, or he suspected she had talked after I'd been there. If he knew she saw the paintings, that might have done it for him. We'll never know, and we can't pin the theft on him. Anyway, you got them back, possibly because she told me. I just don't know. But I thought you should be aware that she had the guts to tell me. That was a very brave thing for her to do. She could have been risking her life."

"Is she all right?" Theo looked worried. "Has anyone seen her since then?" What if he had killed her, or was holding her prisoner on the boat, or was torturing her? Theo's imagination was running rampant after what Athena had said.

"I don't know much. The boat's not here, and rumor has it that he took it to Greece for the rest of the summer, which is plausible. I can check if you want, but I don't think it matters. My partner had drinks with a couple of the deckhands from **Princess Marina** before they left, and they said it's very hush-hush, but Stanislas dumped her the day after you got your paintings back. The same day technically. They came back to you between two and four in the morning, and he dumped her at dinnertime right on the quai. He was supposedly taking her out to dinner, and he just told her it was over, and sent her back to Paris to pack up her stuff. If he did suspect her, she's lucky he let her go, and didn't do something worse to her. The boat pulled out a few days later, so he's not with her. I don't know where she is now, or where she'd go. Maybe back to Russia."

"I doubt it," Theo said, looking pensive and remembering what Natasha had said about her life there when they had lunch. He was a million miles away as he thought about her. He knew the address of the Paris apartment, but had no phone number for her. She had never given it to him, and she hadn't contacted him.

"You really think he dumped her?"

"So they say. The crew was pretty shocked. They'd been together for eight years and they said she's a nice woman. He just told her it was over, left her on the quai, got in the tender, went back to the boat, and never looked back. Those guys are cold. They'd just as soon kill you as look at you. I don't like the type."

"Neither do I," he agreed. "Thank you for telling me."

"Maybe he knew about it and it scared him, or woke him up. I don't think he's anxious to go to prison. And if he even thought she said something to me, he knew he couldn't trust her anymore. And girls like her see a lot of what happens around those guys. He can't afford a woman who talks to the police." Theo nodded agreement again, and a little while later Athena stood up, wished him luck, and left. She stopped in at the office on her way home, and Steve was still there. He was surprised to see her.

"That was quick. No fun and games?" He had assumed she'd be there for hours if Theo went for her, or if she made a move on him.

"No fun and games. I sacrificed myself to young love." That was why she had gone to see him. If he was in love with Natasha, as she suspected, he had a right to know what she had done for him, and the price she might have paid for doing it. Athena had told him all she knew. The rest was up to him. The information she had shared was a gift.

Theo sat thinking about Natasha for a long time that night, wondering what he should do about what he had learned: that Natasha had informed on Vladimir, and that she was no longer on the boat and was possibly in Paris, and that Vladimir had ended his relationship with her. He hoped she was all right.

He tossed and turned in bed, wondering if he should go to Paris and try to see her. But if she wanted contact with him, she would have called, and she hadn't. Or maybe she was too embarrassed, or in need. He barely slept all night, and had almost decided to go to Paris when his mother called him in the morning. She had slipped on the last step on the staircase in the studio, and sprained her ankle. She had just been to the emergency room, and asked him if he could cover for her for a week. She was truly sorry and apologetic, but she was in pain and couldn't get around. The doctor had given her crutches.

"Sure, Maman." He could always go to Paris in a week, and he was used to running the restaurant now, after her long stay in Italy with Gabriel. And he didn't mind it as much as he used to. "Do you need anything?"

"No, Gabriel is waiting on me hand and foot."

And Theo had made a decision by then. As soon as his mother was back at the restaurant, he was going to fly to Paris to see Natasha, and thank her for what she'd done. He had no delusions that something would start between them now, even if she and Vladimir were no longer together. He understood more about her life now, and how unsuited she was to be with "regular" people. Whether it was Vladimir or someone else, she lived in a rarefied world, and Theo was sure she would find another man like him, or perhaps already had. But hopefully a kinder one this time, and a less dangerous man than Vladimir. He hoped so for her sake. And he just wanted a chance to thank her for having the guts to speak up to the police. It was the most generous and courageous thing anyone had ever done for him. And there was no way of knowing if her informing on Vladimir had forced his hand and made him bring the paintings back. Either way, Theo wanted to thank her. He owed her that at least.

Chapter 15

Natasha's last week in the apartment on Avenue Montaigne was a whirlwind of activity, and left little room for emotion. She packed up what she was taking with her. She had bags of new linens scattered among the boxes, and had Ludmilla wash them before she left, so she wouldn't have to do it in a washing machine shared with the entire building, since there was none in the new apartment.

She had all the furniture from IKEA she needed, and she and Dimitri were going to put it together. The auction houses picked up everything she was selling as promised, the day before she left. She had so much that they took it out on racks, and it filled an entire truck. She wasn't sorry to see almost her entire wardrobe go. The Birkins were in their original Hermès boxes, and there were stacks of them in the truck, and cartons of un-worn designer shoes.

And on the day she moved, she rented a van again to move her suitcases, a few boxes, and her portrait. Dimitri, her new handyman, came to help her carry it and load it in the van. She thanked Ludmilla and shook her hand, and gave her a handsome tip for her help in the past few weeks. She was pleased with the amount Natasha gave her. And Natasha saw the concierge as she was leaving and thanked her too. She left no for-warding address. She wasn't expecting any mail. She never got any. She had no relatives or friends, and the limited communication she had was by email. She knew her credit card tied to Vladimir's account had been canceled. She got a new one from her bank with a small limit on it, unlike the unlimited credit cards Vladimir had given her.

And when she got to the new apartment, Dimi-tri got to work putting all her IKEA furniture to-gether: the bed, a chest of drawers, some closets where she could hang clothes, a desk. She had bought bright, fun, contemporary furniture, and the apartment looked cheerful, as she hung her portrait over the fireplace herself.

She and Dimitri conversed in Russian, and they worked late into the night until everything was done. And when it was, she thought it looked ter-rific. She had bought flowers and gotten a couple of vases, and she set a vase of bright flowers on the coffee table. The apartment was warm and inviting, and she had even bought rugs she liked. Lamps, two big comfortable chairs, and a very good-looking leather couch. It would be a nice apartment to come home to at night. He charged her a ridiculously small amount to put it all together, and she thanked him and gave him a big tip.

It had taken her a month to get everything organized, but she had done it, and she felt as though she had severed all ties with her past. She hadn't heard from Vladimir and didn't expect to. She had never contacted Yuri again and had no intention of doing so. She had a home and enough money in the bank to live on for a while, and when her things sold in the fall, she would have more. She still needed to look for a job, but she knew she couldn't until the fall. Everyone was on vacation in the summer, in either July or August, and most of the galleries were closed. And she was thinking of signing up for an art history course at the École du Louvre. She felt as though she had been reborn as a new person. All vestiges of her past life were gone, except a few clothes.

And as she looked around her new apartment on her first night in it, she felt like she was home. She didn't need to live on Avenue Montaigne, or on a five-hundred-foot yacht, or in a legendary villa in St. Jean Cap-Ferrat, or a house in London. She had all she needed, and everything in it was hers. Every now and then she'd feel anxious for a few minutes, but then she'd remind herself that she could take care of herself, and that what she didn't know how to do yet, she would learn.

It took Maylis a week longer than she'd hoped to get back on her feet again with her sprained ankle. And as soon as she did, and was back at the restaurant, Theo booked a flight the next day to Paris. The story was almost over for him, but he still wanted to thank Natasha. And he wanted to do it in person. It was the first week in August by then, and Paris was dead. Shops and restaurants were closed, there was almost no one on the streets. There was no traffic. The weather was hot, and it looked like a ghost town, as he walked down Avenue Montaigne to number fifteen. He hadn't told his mother where he was going. And he hadn't told her about Natasha informing on Vladimir, he thought the fewer people who knew, the better for her. He didn't want to do anything to put her at risk any further, just to thank her.

The building looked deserted when he got there. He rang her bell, and no one answered. And then he rang at the concierge's lodge. She came to the door and looked at him suspiciously when he asked for Natasha.

"Why do you want to know?" she asked him.

"I'm a friend of hers," he said, stretching the truth a little.

"She doesn't live here anymore. She moved a week ago."

"Do you have a new address for her?" he asked, looking sorely disappointed. He had missed her.

"No, I don't. And if you were a friend of hers, you would know it. I don't know where she went. She didn't tell me. She doesn't get mail here anyway. It's all for him." He nodded, not surprised to hear it. "She sent everything away the day before she left. She just had a few suitcases with her the day she moved. And there was a Russian man with her." Dimitri had come to help her with her heavier suitcases.

"Mr. Stanislas?" he asked, worried, and the concierge in the house dress and slippers shook her head.

"No. Another one." That didn't surprise Theo either. It was what his mother had said when they first talked about her. Women like Natasha had to move on to another man like the last one. It was the only way they knew to survive. And he didn't condemn her for it. He just hoped that this one was a better man than Vladimir. It hadn't taken her long to replace him. "He just sold the apartment," the concierge volunteered then. "The maid left yesterday. She said she wouldn't be coming back here." He nodded, sad to have missed

Natasha. He would have liked to say goodbye to her and to wish her well. But all roads from her past life were dead ends now. He had no idea where to find her, and no one to ask. He thanked the concierge and she closed the door soundly, and he walked back out to Avenue Montaigne, and wandered slowly toward the restaurant where he had had lunch with her. It felt like a thousand years ago, and had only been January. A lot had happened in seven months, and her life had completely changed.

He walked past the restaurant and smiled at the memory of her there, and wondered where she was now, and with whom.

He caught a flight back to Nice that night, with all the families leaving on vacation. People were wearing beach clothes on the plane. They all looked happy to be on holiday. And as soon as they landed in Nice, he got his car out of the garage and drove home.

Theo spent the rest of the summer painting furiously, and whenever his mother spoke to him, he said it was going well. She was back in full swing running the restaurant again. It was their best summer ever, and Gabriel spent many evenings with her there. In mid-August, she decided to close the restaurant for the rest of August and September, and possibly longer. She and Gabriel wanted to travel, but first she wanted to spend part of September with him in Paris, at his apartment. It was the first time she had ever done that. And the first time in more than thirty years she had gone back to Paris. Gabriel was thrilled. They had acted like honeymooners ever since they'd come back from Florence, and Theo was happy for them. He promised her he'd check on the restaurant and the house every day, and there were still two security guards there every night, and Maylis planned to keep them there. And before she left, she shared a new plan with Theo that she and Gabriel had been talking about for a while. She was thinking about closing the restaurant entirely by the end of the year, and turning the building into a small museum of Lorenzo's work, which was what it really was anyway. And Gabriel was going to help her set it up.

"We'll need someone to run it on a day-to-day basis. I don't want to be tied down here all the time. We want to spend time in Paris, and be free to move around." She sounded like a new woman, and was much happier than the old one who had mourned Lorenzo for so many years. And although she still honored him, Gabriel was her main focus now. She fussed over him like a mother hen, and he was thriving. And Marie-Claude was thrilled they would be in Paris together in September.

They left St. Paul de Vence at the end of August, and Maylis was excited about all the things she and Gabriel wanted to do in Paris, the exhibits she wanted to see, the museums she hadn't been to in years, the restaurants Gabriel promised to take her to. And the day after they arrived and settled into his apartment, which suddenly seemed small for both of them but very cozy, they had dinner with Marie-Claude and her husband and children on Sunday night at Marie-Claude's apartment. There was lots of laughter, and jokes, and good food and the children interrupting, and one of them brought a friend to dinner. Maylis made a hachis Parmentier for all of them that everyone said was delicious. She had learned to make it from the chef at the restaurant. They felt like a real family, sharing Sunday-night dinner together.

It was exactly what Marie-Claude had hoped for her father for all these years, while Maylis had been worshipping at Lorenzo's altar, and forgetting who was beside her. Maylis was fully cognizant now of how important Gabriel was to her and always had been, and how much they loved each other.

"Thank you," Marie-Claude whispered to her when they kissed each other goodbye and Maylis thanked her for dinner.

"For what? I'm a very, very lucky woman," she said, glancing over at Gabriel, who was talking to his son-in-law and his grandson. "Thank you for putting up with me for all these years. I was blind."

"We all are sometimes," Marie-Claude said, and hugged her again before they left.

The month of September was busy for them, with exhibits to see, places to go, and antique fairs they loved prowling, and they stopped at his gallery on Avenue Matignon often. His health had never been better, and they were both happy. They had plans to go to Venice in October, and Maylis told Gabriel she hated to leave Paris, and he laughed at her.

"Well, that's a new song for you." She was so relaxed and happy these days that he hardly recognized her. For years there had been an underlying sadness about her as she continued to mourn Lorenzo, now she had finally laid him to rest. She still cherished the memories and talked about him, and was dedicated to the body of his work, but he was no longer a saint, and her memories of him were more accurate and still deeply affectionate. But she was fully present in Gabriel's life now, and had allowed him wholly into hers.

"Now, there's something that might be fun for you," Gabriel said one morning in mid-September, when he opened his mail and handed her a catalog. It was a sale of vintage and new Hermès bags, and the one on the cover was a gorgeous red. And when Maylis flipped through, there were Birkins and Kelly bags in every color, both alligator and leather. The sale was taking place at the Hôtel Drouot, the city's most illustrious auction house, where they had fifteen auction rooms and forty-five auctions a week. Gabriel loved to poke around the exhibits where people could see the auction items before the actual sales. "Why don't we stop by and check it out?"

"The prices are crazy," she said wistfully, looking at the estimates. "They're as expensive as they are new at Hermès."

"Most of the bags at auction are new too," he commented. He was familiar with the sales at Drouot and went often. "The only difference is that you don't have to wait three years to get them." Maylis was sorely tempted to take a look.

She left the catalog on his desk, and the following week, on a Friday, he reminded her that it was the day of the exhibition and asked her if she would like to go.

"I'm ashamed to say I would," she said, looking sheepish.

"Don't look so guilty," he teased her. "You can afford it. If you find one you love, buy it." She was interested in a beautiful black alligator Birkin, the red leather one on the cover, and a deep navy blue one. They were the size she liked and incredibly chic for her new Paris life with him. She hadn't bought new clothes in several years, and didn't need much in St. Paul de Vence, but he had been shopping with her and enjoying it since she got to Paris.

They went to the Hôtel Drouot that afternoon, amid the hustle-bustle of antique dealers running in and out and to look at the exhibitions, take notes, and decide what they would bid on at the auctions the next day. And it wasn't all antiques. It was everything from vintage clothes to gardening equipment, military uniforms and insignia, contemporary furniture, Persian rugs, wine, old books, taxidermy, and anything one could imagine. If there was something you wanted to buy, you could find it at Drouot, and the auctions were exciting. Sometimes Gabriel bid on the phone, especially in art auctions, but he liked the thrill of the treasure hunt and introduced Maylis to its delights, as they went from room to room, through the exhibits for all fifteen auctions, until they reached the one with the Hermès bags. They were a feast for the eye, with beautiful handbags on display. She looked at several intently. Maylis said she didn't like the ones with the diamond clasps, and they were ridiculously expensive anyway.

"Well, that's fortunate," he teased her about the bags with diamond clasps, "since they're five times the price of the others."

"That's absurd," she said dismissively, but she found the three bags she wanted to bid on, and they agreed to come back the next day and at-

tend the auction. The exhibition room would
be dismantled then, folding chairs set up with
a podium for the auctioneer, a long table with
several phones for phone bids, and the auction
would take place in the same room. And the day
after, the same fifteen rooms would be flooded
with new treasures on exhibit, and every other
day, there were fifteen auctions. It was one of Gabriel's favorite things to do, and he was proud of
the spoils of war he had gotten there. He warned
Maylis that it became an addiction, and she could
easily believe it, and was excited about bidding
on the three bags the next day. She was only planning to buy one, and they weren't cheap. But all
three were in perfect condition, looked like they
hadn't been worn, and were in their original or-
ange Hermès boxes. And only the black alligator
was liable to be truly expensive.

They arrived right after the auction began the
next day. The items she was interested in were due
to come up a little later, and they settled into their
seats to watch the bidding, which was lively. They
had started with some smaller items, and older,
less exciting handbags. The alligator Birkins were
the pièces de résistance of the auction, so they
saved them for later to keep people in the room.

The navy blue leather bag came up first, half
an hour later. It was very chic, and the bidding
went higher than Maylis had expected. She raised
her hand timidly at first, and then got braver as

Gabriel watched her, smiling, and she was the un-
derbidder, and didn't get it. She whispered to him
that she was saving herself for the red leather or
black alligator, which she thought she'd use more,
and he nodded approval. And as she spoke to
him, she noticed a familiar face across the aisle. It
was a young woman in a peacoat with her hair in
a braid. She was simply dressed but looked chic,
and Maylis couldn't place her at first as she stared
at her. She didn't bid on anything while Maylis
watched her, but was observing the sale intently.
And then a few minutes later, Maylis realized who
she was, and she whispered to Gabriel and nodded in her direction.

"That's Stanislas's mistress. I'm surprised she
buys her bags here. He'd buy her anything she
wanted."

"Everybody loves a bargain," he whispered,
although the prices in the sale they were watching were anything but cheap. And several times
when the prices went sky high, particularly the
bags with diamond clasps, she saw Natasha smile
and look pleased. But she never bid on any of
them, and she wrote down the hammer price of
every item in the catalog she was holding. Maylis
commented on it to Gabriel, and he glanced at
her too. Natasha didn't notice them, she was too
intent on the sale.

"She's not buying," Gabriel whispered to her
then. "I think she's selling."

"Really?" Maylis looked surprised. "How amazing."

"You'd be surprised how often you see people you know here, doing both."

"She certainly doesn't need to sell anything," Maylis commented.

"Maybe he doesn't give her enough pocket money," Gabriel whispered back. "I've heard that a lot of the Russian girls sell the gifts that they get. They get a fortune for them. Some man they scarcely know gives them an alligator Birkin, and they turn around and sell it. It's found money for them."

"But she's not a hooker, for heaven's sake, she's his mistress. And the way I've seen her dressed, he must be very generous with her. She wears couture from head to foot." Gabriel glanced over at her, and she looked like any schoolgirl in jeans to him. She looked about sixteen. "Maybe not today," Maylis commented, "but her clothes were the latest haute couture when she came to the restaurant. She must be incognito today, and trying to be discreet."

The next item in the auction was one of the big guns, another alligator Birkin with a diamond clasp, and it went for twice what the others had, as two women battled over it, and when the hammer came down at a shocking price, Natasha was smiling from ear to ear. It confirmed Gabriel's guess about why she was there, and Maylis agreed. She was definitely selling. And then the red bag Maylis wanted came up, and she got it, and looked at Gabriel, delighted. It had been a good deal.

"I told you you'd get hooked!" he chuckled as he watched her.

And when the black alligator bag came up, she bid timidly and dropped out early. The hammer was about to go down at a much higher price, when Gabriel stunned her and put up his hand. The black alligator bag went to him, as Maylis stared at him with her mouth open. He had paid a fortune for it.

"What did you just do?"

"It'll look great on you when you're here with me," he told her, and after the auction, they lined up to pay for what they got and collected both bags in their original boxes. And as they waited, Maylis noticed Natasha again. She looked different than she had before, at the restaurant. She was wearing no makeup, and she blended into the crowd. Maylis glanced around for Vladimir but didn't see him, and she wondered if he knew Natasha was there selling her Birkins. It seemed odd to her. And after the auction, Natasha didn't collect any purchases. Instead she put her catalog in the plain black leather Birkin she was carrying, with discreet black hardware, pulled up the collar of her peacoat, and scurried away looking pleased.

"I wonder what that's about," she commented to Gabriel, and then thanked him profusely again for his extravagance. And then she had a thought about Natasha. "I don't think we should tell Theo we saw her," Maylis said quietly. "He was torturing himself about her for a while, that whole thing about being obsessed by unattainable women. He seems to have gotten over it, but I don't want to get him started again," she told Gabriel, and he nodded.

"I won't say anything. Promise. She's a beautiful girl, though."

"Of course she is. She's a billionaire's mistress, and that's what she'll always be. That's how it works. She has no use for a boy like Theo." He was no longer a boy—he was a thirty-one-year-old man. "And obsessions are a strange thing. He painted a beautiful portrait of her, and I think he gave it to her."

"I remember it. I told him to put it in the show. It was one of his finest pieces. For an artist, obsession can be a good thing."

"But not in life." She wanted her son to be happy, not tormented over a woman he couldn't have. And she had no intention of telling him she'd seen her, for fear it would cause him to obsess about her again. And whatever she was doing there, buying or selling, had nothing to do with them anyway.

Maylis left the Hôtel Drouot looking very

pleased. The bag Gabriel had bought her was a beauty, and had never been used.

"I like Drouot," she said happily to him in the cab on the way home. And he promised her they'd come back again. Paris was turning out to be a lot of fun after all.

And on the Metro on the way back to the seventh arrondissement, Natasha was looking at the catalog and smiling too. She could live for a long time on what she'd just made at the sale that day, and little by little she was feeling more secure. Her new life was going well.

Chapter 16

As she had done with the apartment on Avenue Montaigne, Natasha kept adding to her tiny apartment on the rue du Bac, just on a smaller scale. She found some unusual items at Drouot, some jades to put in her bookcase for an absurdly minimal price, a terrific Italian table and chairs for her kitchen, even a painting or two. None of it was expensive, but it had a good look, and she applied her own sense of style now to cheap things the way she once had to expensive ones, and she had created an atmosphere that she loved.

The sale of her haute couture clothes at Drouot had gone well. It had exceeded all their expectations, and between the Hermès sale and the haute couture sale, she had enough money in the bank not to worry for quite a while and to support herself. And she intended to work. She was going to look seriously after the first of the year. She had made enough on what she'd sold to coast for a few more months, while she adjusted to her new life.

She loved her course on twentieth-century modernism. It had just started that week and was exactly what she'd wanted. Everything was going well for her, and she felt more like her own person every day. She was still ashamed of what she'd done for the past years—it suddenly felt like prostitution to her, but it hadn't seemed that way at the time. She had to learn to forgive herself and move on, but at least she was proud of her life now. She was starting all over again. And the truth was that she would never have been able to get out of Moscow without Vladimir, and might have died of illness or despair.

She didn't miss the clothes or jewelry she had sold, or her life with Vladimir. She had never heard from him again since he left her on the quai. And she was relieved that she had never run into Yuri again. He had no idea how to contact her, so he couldn't repeat his offer. She had gotten a new cellphone with an unlisted number. She never used it, she had no one to call, but she had it in case she ever needed it. And even without Vladimir, she still lived in a totally isolated world. She had no friends yet, but she had been busy building her nest for the past four months. The rest would come in time.

* * *

Theo painted as frantically through the fall as he had during the summer, and Jean Pasquier asked him to come to Paris in October, to talk about a new show. He asked if Theo felt he had enough new work, and he said he did. Jean was thinking about February. They had done so well with the last show that he didn't want to lose momentum and was anxious to exhibit his new work.

They spent the day together and had dinner, and set the date for the show. Seeing the gallery again reminded him of the portrait of Natasha, and he wondered how she was, and if she was happy with her new Russian that the concierge had mentioned. It seemed a sad life to him. She would forever be a bird in a gilded cage, but it was the only life she knew. It was light-years from his world, which centered only on his work these days. He realized that it had taken him a long time to get Natasha out of his system. She had haunted him so intensely. For a while, he had felt ill every time he saw her with Vladimir, and completely disoriented every time he ran into her. He felt foolish for it now. She had been a phantom in his life, a kind of mirage, his dream woman who appeared to him on canvas, but not in his real life. His mother had been right, she had nearly cost him his sanity and his heart. But he had salvaged both, and he felt strong now and focused

on his work. And he hadn't had a date or relationship with a woman since Inez nine months before. He had seen her at an art event in Cannes in
September, and she said she was dating someone
who had two children of his own, and she seemed
happy.

Theo spent the next day in Paris, after his meeting with Jean Pasquier on Friday night, and on
Saturday it was raining and he had nothing to
do before his flight to Nice. His mother and Gabriel were in Venice for the trip they'd planned,
and then were coming back to Paris for another
month before going back to St. Paul de Vence.
The restaurant was still closed, and she was planning to open briefly for Christmas, and then
close forever when she turned it into a museum.
The holidays would be their farewell to Da Lorenzo and all their devoted clients who had been
faithful to them. It was going to be a bittersweet
final chapter of an adventure that had served her
well, but she was ready to move on, before it became more of a burden than a joy. She and Gabriel wanted their freedom now, to spend time
together while they could still enjoy it, and do
whatever they wanted. Theo had had a call from
her in Venice, and she sounded like a young girl.

She had told him how much she and Gabriel
enjoyed their forages at Drouot, and with nothing else to do, he decided to stop in there and

have a look around that afternoon before he left. She made it sound like a treasure hunt.

He wandered through a room of somber Gothic paintings, and another one of pop art, and then one of truly awful paintings, and a room full of what looked like what they'd found in someone's grandmother's attic, complete with lace doilies and ancient fur coats and tiny old-fashioned shoes. There was a room of exquisite china, including a service for forty-eight with a royal crest on it, another of photographs, which he found more interesting, and then one of statues and taxidermy, and some paintings he liked. The estimates were low, and he was following the labyrinthine flow of traffic, came around a bend, and almost bumped into a young woman, and was about to apologize, and then he gasped when he saw who it was.

"Oh my God . . . Natasha . . . are you all right?" They were both talking at once, and she laughed.

"I wasn't looking where I was going," she confessed, stunned to see him there.

"Neither was I." She looked young and fresh-faced and happy. Her new life must have been going well. She wasn't wearing makeup, and her hair was wet from the rain.

"What are you doing here?" she asked, curious.

"I'm killing time before my flight tonight. I came to see my art dealer. He's doing another show for me in February. No portrait of you this time, though," he teased her, and she laughed.

"It looks spectacular in my new apartment. It's over the fireplace in my living room." She didn't tell him it was the size of her whole apartment, and he imagined her in some palatial hotel particulier that her new boyfriend had provided for her, like the last one on Avenue Montaigne.

"Where are you living?" He was curious about her too.

"In the seventh."

And then he looked serious. "I tried to find you this summer, to thank you. But I was helping my mother at the restaurant, and I got here too late. You had already moved. Athena, the policewoman, told me what you did. That was incredibly brave of you. I'm glad nothing bad happened to you as a result." She smiled as he said it, not entirely sure that that was true, but the bad things had turned out to be good ones. **"Un mal pour un bien,"** as the French said. "You're not with Vladimir anymore?" It was more a statement than a question, since he knew that, and she shook her head.

"No, I'm not." He didn't want to tell her that the concierge in her old building had told him about her new Russian man. It made him sound as gossipy as she was, that they had talked about it. But she looked different and better and younger, and happy. Lighter somehow. He didn't question her about her new man and didn't really want to know. It was enough to see that she was all right and that no harm had come to her. And he had thanked her now, which was what he had wanted to do three months before and hadn't managed, arriving too late on the scene.

"Do you travel a lot?" he asked her, not wanting to let her go. But he didn't feel dizzy this time, or sick when he looked at her. He wasn't aching with longing for what he couldn't have. He accepted it now.

"Not anymore."

"Do you still come to the South?"

"No," she said simply, happy to see him too.

"No boat this time?" The way he said it sounded odd to her, and she looked at him quizzically.

"What do you mean 'this time'?" She looked him in the eye when she asked.

"I mean . . . you know . . . well . . . if there's someone new since Vladimir."

"There isn't," she said quietly. "Why would there be?"

"I thought . . ." But he was in it up to his neck by then. "Your concierge on Avenue Montaigne said you left with a Russian man, when I tried to find you to thank you." She laughed out loud at what he said.

"I think she meant my handyman, Dimitri. He helped me move out. I live alone, in an apart-ment the size of a postage stamp. Your portrait of me is the biggest thing in it." She looked proud as she said it.

"No yacht?" He was stunned.

"No yacht," she confirmed, and they both smiled.

"I'm sorry for my assumption. I just thought . . ."

"You thought I moved on to the next one, just like Vladimir. I had an offer like that," she said honestly. "I decided I'm out of the business of selling my soul for a lifestyle. I didn't do that with Vladimir. It was all kind of a coincidence, who he was and the life he gave me. I don't want that anymore. Besides," she said with a twinkle in her eye, "the other guy's yacht was too small. Only two hundred feet. But it was a great offer. Thirty million in a Swiss bank account, and another thirty if I had his baby. I could have been right back where I was a month after Vladimir kicked me out and left me on the dock in Antibes. I'm not doing that anymore."

"He kicked you out?" Theo looked horrified at what she'd said.

"Not literally. Escorted me off the boat, and walked away. I'm fine," she said, smiling at Theo. "I really am. I've figured it all out. And no one makes the rules for me anymore, or tells me what to do, or dresses me, or tells me when to come and when to go away, who I can talk to, or when to leave the room." The realization of the extent to which he had controlled her had been shocking to her once she admitted it to herself. She knew she could never let that happen to her again.

"Why didn't you call me? Did he do that because of me?"

"Maybe—who knows? He thought I betrayed him, and he was right. I did. I had to. What he did was so wrong, I couldn't let it happen to you. And he probably would have done that to me eventually anyway. That's who he is." Theo had seen the level of his fury the night he had refused to sell the painting to him. And the art theft was his revenge. "And I didn't call you because I needed to figure it all out for myself, what I want to do, who I want to be, how I want to live, and what I've been doing for the past eight years. It was a lot to think about, and I didn't want anyone to help me, not even you. Except for my handyman, Dimitri." She grinned at Theo. "He's terrific. He put all my IKEA furniture together for me."

"You have IKEA furniture? This I want to see." Theo looked amused.

"You can come to dinner next time you come to Paris, after I learn to cook."

He was smiling at her. His mother had been wrong about her, and so had he. She wasn't with another Russian billionaire. She was with herself. "Do you want to have a cup of coffee somewhere before I leave for the airport?"

She hesitated and then nodded, and they left Drouot together. It was pouring, and they found a cab a block away, and he gave the address of the bistro where he went with Gabriel sometimes. And when they got there, they ran in to get out of the rain, sat down at a back table, and ordered coffee, and he ordered a sandwich and asked her if she wanted anything to eat, but she said she didn't. They talked for two hours about his painting, his mother planning to close the restaurant and turn it into a permanent museum, and her being in Paris with Gabriel now, and her epiphany about it. Theo said it was sweet to watch.

"Some people wake up very late. At least she woke up," he said, and Natasha nodded.

"He sounds like a nice man," she said gently.

"He is. And he's always been good to her. Much nicer than my father was. He was a genius and impossible at times. Gabriel is the way everyone wishes their father was. He's a kind person. And he puts up with my mother," Theo laughed. "So what are you going to do now?" he asked her, and she thought about it for a minute.

"I'm still figuring it out. I found an apartment. I'm taking a class at the Louvre. I've been selling everything Vladimir gave me, so I have something to live on, and some savings. Now I want to find a job. I want to finish the class at the Louvre first. That's all I know for now."

"You want to stay in Paris?"

"Maybe . . . probably . . . yes . . . I think so."

She smiled at him, looking like a young girl again, and he smiled at her.

"My mother is going to be looking for someone to run the museum for her. She doesn't want to be tied down the way she was with the restaurant. It was fun for a long time, but now she wants to be free to be with Gabriel."

"Me too. Free, I mean. I was a robot for eight years, a slave. A doll he dressed and showed off to enhance his image. I could never do that again. It's scary sometimes now, when I don't know what I'm doing or where I'm going. But then I remind myself I can figure it out. I think I can. It's not as bad as it would have been at nineteen when he found me. And I had nothing then. I'm twenty-seven now. I can work it out."

"I'm thirty-one," he said, smiling at her, "and I ask myself the same question sometimes. Everyone always looks like they're doing it better. Maybe no one knows what they're doing."

"I'm trying to decide what I want. Not what someone else tells me to do." It was a big change, making decisions on her own. It was all new to her.

"Will you call me if you need help, Natasha?" he asked her seriously. He knew how alone she was, and that she had no family or friends. She had told him that at lunch long ago.

"Maybe. I don't know. I kept your number, just

in case. But I didn't want to use it." He could only imagine how scary the last four months had been after Vladimir threw her out, after protecting and controlling her so completely. But she seemed to have done well, and he admired her for it. "At first, I didn't want to talk to anybody, and I didn't want anyone to help me. I had to do it for myself. And I think I've done okay. Some things I haven't figured out yet, like a job, but I have time."

"Think about coming to work at the museum. It might be interesting, if you want to live in the South." And that reminded him of something else. "The house is empty now. There are six bedrooms upstairs. She used to rent them out occasionally. If you want a place to stay, or need one, or just want to be there for a while to think, you can stay for as long as you like. Those rooms won't be used anymore this winter, except for art storage or maybe an office or two. Come whenever you want. You don't even have to talk to me. And I live in my own house a few miles away. I won't bother you, and my mother lives at the old studio, or here now. You'd have the house to yourself, with two bodyguards to protect you."

"It's nice of you to offer." But he could sense that she wasn't going to take him up on it. She wanted to be independent.

"Do you have a number where I can call you?" he asked cautiously. "Just in case." She hadn't offered, and he didn't want to leave without knowing where she lived or how to reach her. She jotted it down on a piece of paper and handed it to him solemnly.

"You're the only person who has that number."

"I'll text you if I come to Paris. I hope you come to my show." It was four months away, and he hoped he'd see her before that, but he wasn't sure he would. "And remember the offer to stay at the house anytime you want. You can use it as an escape."

"Thank you," she said, and followed him out of the restaurant after he paid. He hailed a cab to take him to the airport, and she ran toward the subway, and he waved at her as they drove past. He laid his head back against the seat in the taxi, reeling again with the sight and sound of her. He couldn't believe it. He was falling in love with her all over again. And this time it was worse. She was real. And just as unattainable as before, only differently. She had vowed never to let anyone clip her wings again. She was always somewhere out of reach. Before, she'd been a prisoner and belonged to someone else. Now she was free. But either way, she wasn't his.

Chapter 17

Theo attacked his work with renewed energy after he'd been to Paris. He was excited about his upcoming show, and wanted to finish a fresh body of work for it. And seeing her had fueled him too. She was still the same, so magical and ethereal and bewitching, and yet she had a real life now, or wanted one, and was trying to forge one for herself. He didn't use the number she had given him. If she wanted to talk to him, she'd call, he told himself. But she didn't. He didn't hear a word from her all through November.

Marc dropped by from time to time, to take a break from his own work. He had taken on a big commission for a local museum, and he was doing well. He promised to come to Paris this time for Theo's show.

And Theo's mother was in Paris. They were having fun and enjoying the city. She kept saying she'd be home soon, but they were making up for lost time, and even making noises about getting married in the spring, which their children thought was sweet.

At the end of November there was a terrible cold spell in the South, with frost on the ground every morning, and a light snow on the last day of the month. He would have thought it was pretty, but there was no heat in his studio, and his hands were always freezing, which made it hard to paint.

He was coming back from checking the deserted restaurant on his bicycle just after dusk, when he turned into his driveway and saw her, just standing there, with snow on her hair, freezing too. He knew she couldn't have been waiting long, since he had left half an hour before. And she had a car in the driveway, but she had been standing in the falling snow, and smiled when she saw him. He got off his bike and walked it to the front door where she stood. He didn't want to ask why she had come, but she saw the question in his eyes. She was wearing heavy boots and a warm coat.

"I came to ask you if you meant it," she said softly.

"Meant what?" He was almost holding his breath, afraid to frighten her away, like a bird about to take flight, perched on his finger.

"That I could stay at the restaurant for a little while."

"Of course." He couldn't believe his good fortune. It had been six weeks since he'd seen her in Paris and hadn't heard a word since, and now here she was. She had suddenly appeared.

"I finished my class at the Louvre. I want to look for a job." But she was scared, and didn't want to say it. She felt like she had nothing to sell and no experience. Who was going to hire her at her age, never having worked anywhere except a factory eight years before? And what would she say? "I should have called before I came," she said, looking apologetic. "I could stay at a hotel."

"We've got six empty rooms." He wanted to tell her that she could stay with him too, but he didn't dare. She had to get there on her own. "I'll take you over now if you want. There's no food, but we can get something to eat after you drop off your bag. Can I ride with you?" She smiled, and they got in the car she had rented. She had driven down from Paris to clear her head. It had taken ten hours, but she liked the drive. And they were at the deserted restaurant a few minutes later. He opened the door with his keys and turned off the alarm, and then he turned the heat on for her. The house was cold, and the two security guards were posted outside. They greeted him pleasantly when he walked in, and he told them Natasha would be staying there.

He turned the lights on in the living room, and she wandered past the paintings she had seen before. They were more beautiful than she remembered. And it felt odd being there with him. She had been with Vladimir before, even if Theo had been there too. And then she laughed as she stopped in front of one of the paintings and looked at him.

"I should be wearing one of those 'Not for Sale' signs now."

"Then someone might steal you," he said softly. "I wouldn't want that to happen."

"Neither would I." Her eyes looked huge in her face.

He took her bag upstairs then and let her pick the bedroom she liked best, and he turned the heat on upstairs so it would be warm when they got back. And she smiled as she followed him downstairs, and they went back to her car, and went to a local place that served **socca,** which she had never had before. And they talked over dinner, remembering the past and savoring the present.

"I remember all the questions you asked me when we had lunch together," she said quietly. It seemed a thousand years ago.

"I was trying to understand the choices you had made. But you don't owe anyone any explanations."

"I told you I loved him, and I thought he loved me. It turns out that neither of us knew what that was." A chapter of her life had closed, but it had had merit in the beginning, just not at the end.

Without Vladimir, she would never have survived in Russia. And finally, she had risked everything, maybe even her life, to help Theo. He couldn't forget that as he looked at her, and he knew he never would. And he could see that in her months alone, she had made peace with her history. And Theo respected the choices she had made in her early life, and since. They made sense at the time, and so did the decisions she was making now. No one could truly know what she'd gone through in Moscow, and how terrifying it had been for her, and how it had influenced the path she chose. He didn't judge her. How could he? And now it was all different anyway. She was no longer anyone's mistress. She was free to make her own choices, and the mistakes she made would also be her own. The past no longer felt like a heavy burden to her, as she looked at him. She liked taking responsibility for herself, she had longed for that, and a normal life. She had given it all up with Vladimir. And now she had years ahead of her to do what she wanted, make good choices, meet new friends, and fall in love with the right man.

And Theo was no longer obsessed by a woman who belonged to someone else and he could never have. It was all human scale now, the good and the bad. She didn't need or want what Vladimir had given her. It came at too high a price. She was no longer willing to sell her soul or deny who she was.

Theo was smiling at her as they finished dinner. "What are you looking at?" she asked him.

"You're not a portrait anymore. You're real." She had lived in his studio for months, and in his head, and now he could reach out and touch her.

They went for a walk after dinner. It was a cold November night, but the air felt good on their faces. They could do anything they wanted now, and no one could stop them, or frighten them, or shame them. He stopped while they were walking, and put his arms around her, and kissed her. She smiled at him after they kissed, and then they walked back to the car, holding hands. The past was history, and the future lay ahead full of promise and hope. They had come a long way to find each other. And the woman who had haunted him since he'd met her was finally within reach, as he kissed her again.

About the Author

DANIELLE STEEL has been hailed as one of the world's most popular authors, with over 650 million copies of her novels sold. Her many international best sellers include **The Award, Rushing Waters, Magic, The Apartment, Property of a Noblewoman, Blue, Precious Gifts, Undercover, Country,** and other highly acclaimed novels. She is also the author of **His Bright Light,** the story of her son Nick Traina's life and death; **A Gift of Hope,** a memoir of her work with the homeless; **Pure Joy,** a tribute to the many dogs her family has loved; and the children's books **Pretty Minnie in Paris** and **Pretty Minnie in Hollywood.**

daniellesteel.com
Facebook.com/DanielleSteelOfficial
@daniellesteel

LIKE WHAT YOU'VE READ?

If you enjoyed this large print edition of
THE MISTRESS,
here are a few of Danielle Steel's latest
bestsellers also available in large print.

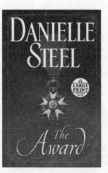
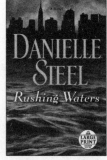
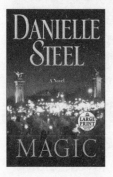

Large print books are available wherever books
are sold and at many local libraries.

All prices are subject to change. Check with your
local retailer for current pricing and availability.
For more information on these and other large print titles,
visit <u>www.randomhouse.com/largeprint.</u>